A ... NOVEL

SAMANTHA WHISKEY

Copyright © 2020 by Samantha Whiskey, LLC All rights reserved. This book or any portion thereof may not be reproduced or used in any manner whatsoever without the express written permission of the publisher except for the use of brief quotations in a book review. This is a work of fiction. Names, characters, businesses, places, events and incidents are either the products of the author's imagination or used in a fictitious manner. Any resemblance to actual persons, living or dead, or actual events is purely coincidental. This book is licensed for your personal enjoyment only. This book may not be re-sold or given away to other people. If you would like to share this book with another person, please purchase an additional copy for each person you'd like to share it with. Thank you for respecting the author's work.

ALSO BY SAMANTHA WHISKEY

The Seattle Sharks Series:

Grinder

Enforcer

Winger

Rookie

Blocker

Skater

Bruiser

Wheeler

Defender

The Carolina Reapers Series:

Axel

Sawyer

Connell

Logan

Cannon

A Modern-Day Fairytale Romance:

The Crown

The Throne

NOW AVAILABLE IN AUDIO!

Grinder
Enforcer
Winger
Rookie

Let the Seattle Sharks spice up your morning commute!

To those who fall at first glance

1

CANNON

Sunlight streamed through the massive windows of the hotel suite, revealing the Vegas skyline in all its morning-after glory. I blinked, but the motion felt slow, heavy even, and nothing about me was ever slow. I'd made myself a damn good career out of being fast. My entire body felt sluggish, as though I'd had way too much to drink last night, which didn't make sense. Vegas meant I was here for a game, and a game meant there was no way I'd been drinking.

Something about that didn't quite fit the situation, but I couldn't pin my groggy little finger on it.

What the hell had I done last night?

I rolled over, turning my back on the window and the morning it promised and found the most exquisite woman I'd ever seen lying beside me.

Persephone VanDoren.

I was dreaming.

That explained…everything. The corners of my lips tugged upward, and I relaxed into the buttery soft sheets. I propped myself up on my elbow and almost congratulated myself on having the perfect fucking dream, but I was too busy studying her in a way I never could in real life.

The woman was gorgeous with a flawless, oval face, thick lashes that rested in crescent moons on her porcelain skin, and the most kissable, bow-shaped mouth on the entire fucking planet. The covers rested just above her breasts, and she slept with her left hand cradled under her pillow and her right only a few inches away from mine. Her long, blonde hair fanned out around her like a luminous halo, and I rubbed a few strands of the silk between my thumb and forefinger, savoring just how soft it felt. Funny, I'd always thought it was all that same pale, color, but it wasn't. Various shades of blonde, from nearly white to honey-gold ran across my skin. The contrast against the heavy, colorful tattoos of my forearm nearly made me groan.

I was covered in tattoos from the nape of my neck to my toes, and her skin was as virgin as the day she'd come into the world—at least what I'd seen of it.

My blood heated, pulsing through my veins in an all-too-familiar rush that swelled my cock. I knew exactly how this dream would end—it wasn't like it was the first time I'd had it, and yet I couldn't keep myself from reaching for the covers.

I drew them down her frame and growled in appreciation. Of course, she wasn't naked—she never was. My imagination would never let me fill in that particular blank. Instead, this time she was covered with a white, spaghetti-strapped silk slip that dipped low at her neckline, then hugged every fucking curve the woman had until it ended high on her thighs. Damn, those thighs looked so creamy and soft, and while they would never part for me in real life, well, this was a dream. Who the fuck cared about the real world?

I slid one arm beneath her, cradling her light frame, and

rolled her to her back as I rose above her. Her lips parted, and she murmured as she shifted underneath me.

Her. Thighs. Fucking. Parted.

I put one of my own between them. God, she was so small, so delicate. So breakable next to my six-foot-five bulk. How far would this dream go?

Keeping her cradled beneath me, I filled my free hand with the curve of her hip and squeezed lightly, then moaned my appreciation for that curve against the soft skin of her neck. She smelled like apple blossoms, sunshine, and everything good and right in the world—everything I'd never have. Fuck, she'd never felt this real before. My cock pulsed against her thigh in agreement.

She shifted again, letting loose a small, breathy sigh as she arched her neck, giving me full access. I kissed her gently just beneath her jawline like I'd fantasized every time she stuck that chin of hers in the air at me. She was such a contradiction in the real world. Easy-going and stubborn as hell, kind and sweet, then salty and harsh, delicate in one breath and a force of nature in the next—she was all of it.

The one thing she never was? Mine.

The only place I'd be good enough for Persephone and the only place she'd be safe with me was *here*—in my dreams.

She whimpered, as if coming awake, but when I moved to lift my head, she tangled her fingers in my hair and kept me right where I was.

I took the hint and put my mouth against her throat in an open-mouthed kiss. How could she taste so fucking good? I groaned and swept my tongue over her skin, then sucked lightly at the patch.

She shifted her thigh, lifting her knee so she rubbed against my hip.

"Cannon," she moaned, her fingers tightening in my hair.

Fuck. Need, hot and insistent, raced down my spine. I

pressed against her center with my thigh, and the heat I found there set every cell in my body on fire.

She gasped, then rocked against me.

Keeping my weight on my elbow, I lifted my head and found her lashes fluttering slowly as she opened her eyes.

God, her eyes were beautiful, just like the rest of her—crystal blue, like Caribbean pools I wanted to dive into. I wanted to dive into *her*. She looked up at me with wonder, like I was her fantasy too, and my heart jumped to a fast, skittering rhythm

"Cannon," she said again, her voice husky as if she'd truly been asleep.

"Persephone," I answered.

Her hands slid to my face, and she ran her thumbs over my cheekbones with a sleepy grin. "You're so beautiful."

Speechless. Even in my dreams, I couldn't come up with a response to that one.

She rocked against my thigh again, then bit her lip and groaned. It wasn't just heat warming my skin. She was wet. I felt it even through the material of her panties. *Of course, she's wet. This is your dream.*

Her fingers traced the line of my face, and I sucked the tips of two of them into my mouth as she ran them over my lips. She gasped as I flicked my tongue across the digits, tasting the salt of her skin. Her gaze flickered from my eyes to her fingers and back again, widening.

"Cannon..." Her voice shook slightly.

I raked my teeth over the pads of her finger before letting them go free. "Persephone." Wasn't that always my reply? I couldn't hear one name without saying the other.

"Cannon." She pulled her hand away, staring at her fingers with alarm. "Oh my God. Cannon!"

That was not the way I'd fantasized her saying that particular phrase. I sat back on my knees, and she scooted herself to sit against the headboard. The change in positions started a vicious throbbing in my head, and I lifted my hand to my temple to help assuage the ache. *Wait. Why would I have a headache in my dream?*

"Oh my God. Oh my God!" she chanted, staring at her hand.

Oh shit. I bit my tongue lightly and felt the sharp sting of pain at the same moment my stomach sank.

This was *not* a dream.

This was real.

I ran my hands down my face, trying to clear my head.

Persephone was actually in my bed, in Vegas, currently losing her shit—

"Holy shit! You have one, too!" she shrieked, then gripped my wrist.

"What are you talking about? And what the fuck are you doing in my bed?" I growled, pulling out of her grasp. Never mind that I'd had my fucking tongue on her sixty seconds ago; I never touched her if I could help it. Not because I didn't want to—of course I wanted to. I'd have to be dead not to want to. But I didn't exactly have willpower when it came to the woodland fairy princess Barbie that was currently staring at me like I had two heads.

She thrust her hand in front of my face.

A giant fucking diamond winked at me from the fourth finger. Her ring finger. Holy shit, that was her left hand, and there was a narrow band of gold just behind it. Complete, utter rage turned my blood to ice.

"Who the fuck did you marry?" I ground out. Whoever it was—he wasn't good enough for her. I didn't care how much breeding or money he had, a *saint* wouldn't be good enough for Persephone, and God knew that she needed someone stronger than a saint to remove the giant stick she kept up her ass.

She scoffed and picked up my wrist again, replacing her hand in front of my face with my own.

"Apparently, you!"

Words failed me as I looked at the thick band on my left ring finger. It was black, inlaid with a textured sort of silver that might have been attractive if it wasn't mocking me so loudly.

Someone pounded on our door three times. "Let's go, newlyweds. Breakfast is here. And put some clothes on before you come out of there." That voice...Nathan Noble, one of the defensemen on my NHL team—the Carolina Reapers.

My gaze jerked down to my boxer briefs. Not naked. Had I seriously had Persephone under me and not remembered?

"They know. Oh God, they know." Persephone whispered, still staring at my ring. "What did we do?"

"I have no fucking clue," I muttered, then got the hell off the bed.

"I don't remember last night at all. Do you?" Her hair fell all around her, making her look all the more angelic as she looked up at me with eyes that begged for an answer.

I thought back. We'd all boarded the plane in Charleston. Nathan and his fiancée, Harper, Sterling—one of last year's rookies—Nixon Noble and his charity auction date, and us. "We came for the charity auction thing," I said as I stared down at a pile of clothes on my side of the bed. Persephone had demanded I participate in the Reaper Charity Auction to help raise funds for the public library. When I made my own demand that she not sell me to someone I wouldn't consider fucking, she bought me herself, which I guess fulfilled that part of our bargain since I'd never willingly take her to my bed.

And yet I'd married her?

"Right, but I don't remember anything past mid-flight," she said, scooting off the bed.

"Maybe this is a prank. I highly doubt we'd do something stupid like get married in Vegas." I heard a rustle of fabric and turned to see Persephone holding up a wedding dress on her side of the bed.

"The evidence suggests otherwise." She dropped the dress in a puddle of lace and silk and wrapped her arms around her waist. "What are we going to do?"

It took everything I had not to replace her arms with mine, to tuck her against me and tell her that everything would be fine.

"We're going to get dressed and find out just how stupid we were last night." I picked up my clothes—yep, it was a fucking tux—and headed for our suitcases, which sat next to each other against the wall.

"Right. That sounds like a good plan." She took her suitcase and marched right past me, shutting the bathroom door behind her.

Don't panic. Whatever this is, it's fixable.

I dressed quickly, putting on athletic pants and a Reaper T-shirt. Then I stood in front of our window and looked out over the strip while I waited for her, refusing to let the reality of what was happening sink in. Why the hell couldn't I remember anything past the flight? Why couldn't Persephone?

I turned my head as I heard the door open, and Persephone stepped out of the bathroom with a slightly surprised look on her face. "You waited for me?"

"I figured we should probably question everyone together." I took in her tiny white shorts, blue silk blouse, and simple braid that started just beneath her ear and ended nearly at her waist. Good. She looked more like *her*, except she'd never wear those shorts to the office, thank God, or I

7

would have walked around with a permanent erection because holy *shit* her legs were incredible. Toned and supple and long, especially for someone as petite as she was.

"Thank you. That was really…considerate." Her thumb toyed with her ring.

"I'm not a complete asshole, you know."

Her eyes slid shut. "That is *so* not what I meant."

"Let's go." I held the door open for her, and she muttered her thanks as we walked into the vast suite. We'd rented out the biggest one the casino had, boasting five bedrooms throughout two stories.

I followed Persephone down the stairs and found our friends sitting at the dining room table. Nathan sat near the center with Harper on his right, and his twin, Nixon, to his left. The NFL star had brought his own charity auction date…Liberty—that was the pretty brunette's name—and she took the seat at the end of the table.

Great, I could remember her name, but not how I'd wound up in bed with Persephone.

Sterling held down the opposite end of the table, raking his hand through his short, black hair. His eyes widened as he saw us.

"Well, if it isn't Mr. and Mrs. Price!" Harper said with a grin. "We ordered a smorgasbord, so hopefully there's something that you like." She gestured to the buffet of food laid out on the various room service carts.

"Could someone please tell us what the hell kind of prank this is?" I pointed to my left hand. "Not that it's not a good one, but if this is Connell's doing, you can tell that practical-joke-loving asshole—"

"Prank?" Nathan interrupted, slowly shaking his head.

"Surely there has to be some explanation about how any of this happened," Persephone said with that sweet southern drawl.

"You said you wanted to get married, and then got married." Sterling shoved in a mouthful of waffles and started to chew.

"We *what?*" Persephone shrieked, going for Sterling.

I caught her around the waist. "Maybe we should sit down."

She nodded, and I let go, ushering her into a chair. I took the one next to hers and reached for the carafe of coffee.

"Yes, please," she said when I nodded toward her cup.

I filled hers then mine, noting that she dumped a heap of sugar and cream into hers as I started to sip mine as black as it had come.

The entire table stared at us in between bites of their breakfast.

"Okay, so Persephone and I don't remember anything from about halfway through the plane ride," I stated, then sat back, waiting for the holes to be filled in.

"I told you!" Harper jabbed her fork toward her fiancé.

"Fuck," Nathan muttered.

"Are you going to tell them?" Nixon prodded his twin.

When no one spoke up, Liberty sighed. "Well, since I'll never see any of you again, I don't have much to lose by filling you in. You both complained of headaches, right?"

We both nodded.

"Right." The woman grimaced but forged ahead. "The flight attendant said she had some pain relievers, and gave them to you from the bottle of ibuprofen."

"Sounds harmless enough." Persephone's hand shook slightly as she put down her coffee.

"Right, except about ten minutes later, she told her coworker what she'd done, and then that woman freaked out. I mean majorly lost it because she'd taken the bottle from *her* bag, and she'd stashed her sleeping pills in there."

My gaze narrowed. "Okay?"

Liberty's eyebrows shot up. "And you'd both already had a couple of drinks, and then you had a couple *more...*"

"And it basically turned into *The Hangover* from there," Nathan finished for the girl. "You two were fucking insane, and the rest of us just tried to keep you from skydiving and shit."

"Could you skip to the part where the rings appeared on our hands?" I growled, my patience already razor-thin and disintegrating at a rapid rate.

"I caught that on film, actually." Sterling slid his phone across the polished cherry wood, and I caught it, putting it between Persephone and me.

She pressed play.

"Bigger," I said, pointing to a ring case. "She has to have the best one you've got."

"I like that one!" Persephone pointed to a spot on the glass.

"This one is going to set you back a pretty penny," the attendant warned as he brought the ring out.

"I don't care what it costs as long as she's happy."

"I love it!" Persephone slid it onto her finger. "And it fits! See? We're meant to be, Cannon." She smiled up at me adoringly. "But you need one too!"

The camera turned around, the frame filling with Sterling's face. "Just for posterity's sake, we've told you guys this is a bad idea at least two dozen times, but you're pretty insistent."

"Sterling! We need to get the license! Let's go!" I shouted.

The video ended, and Persephone and I stared at each other.

"No way," she said, turning toward Harper. "There's zero way you guys let us get married when we were drunk and drugged out of our minds! This is all some really sick joke, right?"

"It's not a joke," Harper said softly. "I went with you to pick out your dress."

Persephone blanched.

"But we're not actually married, right?" she insisted.

"You are," Liberty said gently. "It was the cutest ceremony by this little, old, singing Elvis, and you guys looked so happy—"

"There is *no* way I got married by a singing Elvis!" Persephone shouted.

Damn, I'd never heard the woman get that loud before. If this wasn't Connell, I was going to have to give it to whoever had seen this prank through. It was some pretty realistic shit.

"Okay, if that really happened, then where's the video of *that*?" I challenged, sliding the phone back at Sterling.

"They said we couldn't record," he answered with a shrug as he caught it. "But you bought their recording, and he said it would be mailed to you on disc within two weeks." He thumbed through his phone. "Here, I have this one, though."

He slid it back, and we repeated the earlier pattern.

"It looks so good on you," Persephone said as her thumb stroked over my ring finger.

"What's the silver part?" I asked.

"It's meteorite. I figured it fit since you're out of this world. Get it?" She giggled.

"You are incredible, Mrs. Price." I hoisted her into my arms, fluffy white dress and all, and carried her into our hotel.

Suddenly it didn't feel like a prank. My stomach twisted at the very real implications of what we'd done last night.

"I knew you were going to regret it," Nathan muttered, shaking his head.

"Then why the fuck didn't you stop us?" I snapped.

"Man, have you ever seen...you?" Nixon asked, gesturing to my torso. "You were really fucking goal-oriented, and we all have million-dollar contracts. You look like you could easily rip off my arms."

I *could* easily rip his arms off, but I kept that fact to myself.

"And he's a quarterback," Liberty nodded slowly. "He kind of needs his arm."

"True story," he said to her with a grin.

"Okay." Persephone sat up even straighter. "Let me get this straight. We decided that we should get married. How?"

They all exchanged looks. "None of us saw that part. You guys were sitting next to each other on the plane, and by the time it landed, you were on a mission," Harper supplied.

"And you're telling me that this isn't a prank? That we actually bought rings, bought a dress and a tux, purchased a wedding license, and then got married by a singing Elvis?" Persephone restated what we'd already heard, keeping her voice miraculously calm.

"Pretty much," Nathan agreed.

"Okay," she sat back and folded her arms across her chest with a Cheshire cat grin. "If this is real and you're not pulling our legs, where is the marriage license?"

They all exchanged knowing looks, and Nathan nodded toward Sterling.

The kid turned in his seat and grabbed a folder from the buffet table behind him. Then he slid it straight at me.

I caught the white and gold folder emblazoned with the name of a wedding chapel on the front and opened it slowly.

My stomach twisted into a hellacious knot.

"Oh God," Persephone whispered next to me.

It was a perfectly executed copy of a marriage license, signed by both of us. A certified copy, to be specific.

"Where's the original?" I questioned. This was fixable. It had to be.

"You guys were married at four p.m. and made it to the clerk and recorder by four-thirty," Harper answered. "For being out of your minds, you were ridiculously thorough.

The county took your original for recording and gave you the certified copy."

"Let me guess, we'll get that in the mail too?" I quipped sarcastically.

"Pretty much," the scientist answered, then sipped her orange juice.

I stared down at the license, letting the reality of it sink in.

"Holy. Shit." Persephone's words were a breath of a whisper. "We did it."

Three facts hit me simultaneously.

The first was that I was actually, really, completely married to Persephone.

The second was the way she'd signed, officially taking my name.

And the third—the most ridiculous out of all of this—somehow, I'd managed to kiss the very woman I'd fantasized about for the last two fucking years, and I couldn't remember a single second of it.

Married. Bound. Chained to a woman I'd never be worthy of, a woman I'd destroy with my temper or my reputation. She'd never survive it unscathed, not in the debutante circles she ran. Her family had more blue blood than freaking aliens. She represented everything I hated about class warfare, and I was everything she turned her nose up at.

"Cannon, I think we're really married," Persephone whispered.

My reply came without hesitation. "Not for long."

2

PERSEPHONE

This is fine.

I repeated the words over and over in my head as I calmly collected pieces of clothing scattered across the hotel room. *My* clothing.

A silk blouse here.

A sleek pencil skirt there.

My strappy black pumps over in the corner.

Sweet heavens, why *had I hung my red lace bralette on the doorknob?*

I clenched my eyes shut as I slipped the damning evidence in my bag, my mind a fuzzy mess of fog and forgotten dreams.

A flash of me sliding the bra off through the sleeves of my silk slip—the slip I'd awoken in this morning—fizzled behind my eyes. The reason for doing so? Totally a blank. As was the rest of the night.

My wedding night, apparently.

And I knew from the lack of soreness between my thighs and my perfectly untouched lipstick that nothing worth remembering had happened—despite waking up beneath the sexiest and most infuriating man I'd ever set eyes on. I'd thought I'd been dreaming when I'd felt his delicious weight atop me, his lips caressing my neck, his strong thigh between my legs. Thought it was one of my most creative dreams yet until...well, until we both realized we were *awake*.

My fingers trembled as I gathered the rest of my things, the only lack of composure I'd allow to show. Because I was Persephone VanDoren and I'd be damned if I gave control to the gathering panic coiling in my chest.

Cannon spoke on the phone in the sitting room attached to the hotel's bedroom, and his deep tenor skittered over my body, leaving a warm chill in its wake. I sucked in a sharp breath and once again tried to recall the events of the night prior.

The plane ride had been pleasant, a quiet sort of comfortable as Cannon read his book. Nathan Noble and his twin brother Nixon had offered a subdued source of constant chatter on the plane's opposite side, Nathan's fiancé, Harper content with her research on her laptop. And Nixon's date, Liberty—the auction winner—seemed more than happy to simply stare at him with an awestruck sense of disbelief as he'd chatted with his brother.

I *did* remember the headache Sterling had mentioned, and the pain pills which both Cannon and I had obviously assumed were harmless.

But *after* the plane ride?

Nothing.

Blank.

A thick, wet blanket of darkness buried the memory.

Once again, that cold, building panic pulsed in my chest, threatening to break my composure. How could I have let myself get into this situation? What would my father think? And my mother—

My cell phone rang from my purse on the nightstand, and

I hurried over to it. As if I'd conjured her out of thin air, my mother's picture flashed over my screen. For a few seconds too long, I debated not answering. But she was my mama, and I'd never shut her out.

"Hello, Mama," I answered, forcing warmth and grace into my tone. "How are you feeling? Everything all right?"

"It most certainly isn't all right, Sephie," she said, her voice anything but unhappy. "How could you possibly elope and not tell me?"

My blood ran cold.

"What? How? I—" For once, words spewed from my mouth in a shocked state of confusion.

"Well, darling, it's all over the media. And, naturally, I must say. What with your status and the popularity of that hockey star of yours."

He's not my anything.

"He's—"

"Honey, I'm not upset," Mama cut me off.

"Well, I damn sure am!" my father's voice shouted in the background.

"Oh, hush now," Mama scolded him before returning focus to me. "Darling, I am so thrilled, honestly."

I sank onto the edge of the bed, still unmade from our abrupt awakening this morning.

"What?" It seemed to be the only word capable of leaving my mouth this morning.

"You know I probably don't have much time left on this earth," she said, her voice softening. My chest constricted, tears biting the backs of my eyes. "And, well, it's always been a dream of mine to see you walk down the aisle. To see you truly happy."

The truth of the situation clogged my throat, choking my airways. The joy in her tone, the compassion in her words stilled my tongue.

"Happy?" my father surged in the background. "She'll be *happy* when I approve of the son of a bitch! The nerve! What kind of coward doesn't—"

"Harold!" Mama used the *tone* only proper southern women could conjure—the one that could silence *and* scare the living daylights out of any person on the planet, including ones as hardheaded and strict as my father. "Come by the house when you return, please? We have so much to talk about. And bring that man of yours!"

The line went dead with more grumblings from my father, and it took me a few seconds to realize I didn't need to hold the cell to my ear anymore.

Cannon stomped into the room, his massive presence like a vacuum for all the air in the room, not to mention my lungs. My heart raced as I watched him, tracked his movements as he pocketed his cell and hurriedly shoved shirts and slacks and a hardback into his bag. "Spoke to my lawyer," he grumbled, not even bothering to meet my eyes. "We'll annul this thing on Monday."

A sharp, hot something stabbed the center of my chest.

Not that I wanted to be married to Cannon Price, but the cold tone, his harsh words—God, was I so awful a mistake to wake up married to?

No, not going down that road.

Of course, we had to annul.

I knew Cannon only in the basest levels of acquaintances, and ninety percent of our exchanges were arguments. Sizzling debates that sparked life into my blood where I hadn't realized I'd been lacking, but *still*.

I gripped the phone in my hand a little harder than necessary. Tears were inevitable, but I sure as hell wouldn't cry in front of him.

He slid to a stop before me, finally noticing my lack of movement or response.

"Hey," he said, the word sharp.

I refused to look up at him. I'd have to arch my neck from my seated position, and I honestly thought if I had to look into those dark eyes and see the utter rejection…well, I might very well crumble into a thousand pieces.

He dropped to his knees, forcing me to catch his gaze. "Are you in shock?"

The serious set of his features made a laugh rip from my chest, so fast and hard that he jolted a little before me.

"What ever would I be in shock for, Cannon?"

He cocked an eyebrow as if to say *don't test me, woman.*

I blew out a breath, then straightened my spine.

He nodded, as if something had settled between us.

"We're leaving," he said, his voice dropping to that normal, irresistible tenor that made my blood heat. "Now." He rose to standing, his gaze lingering on me for a few seconds where I remained seated. "Don't worry. I won't mar your reputation for long." He grabbed our bags and hurried from the room like I might slap him or curse him or cry on his shoulder. I had yet to figure out which of those actions would unnerve him most.

What an absolute mess.

One I'd gotten myself into, sure, but for what? Because I couldn't resist the tall, dark, and terrifying man? Because when I saw the other women bidding on him for the charity auction, something had snapped inside me? The thought of him with anyone else became a sharp, near unbearable pain I couldn't possibly explain or soothe.

A passing flutter of unwarranted jealousy, of course.

A sting of loneliness and desire.

A mistake, certainly.

One made on instinct as opposed to composed thinking. And perhaps that was the crux of it. Because when it came to Cannon Price, I rarely thought rationally.

* * *

Mama swung open the door to the home I grew up in—and technically *still* lived in, if you counted the guest house on the back five acres. She stepped onto the front porch, her modest pumps clicking against the stonework as she craned her head back and forth. She even went as far to walk behind me, as if I were hiding Cannon in some invisible pocket, and he might materialize at her search.

She sighed but smiled as she hooked her arm in mine and walked me into the house.

Despite growing up in the painstakingly restored 1903 Neoclassical home, it never ceased to steal my breath when entering. I'd grown so accustomed to my cozy guest house that I'd forgotten how high the sweeping ceilings were, how polished the hardwood floors were, and how astoundingly *grand* each room and piece of furniture was. My mother always had an eye for restoration and decoration, and she'd outfitted the estate brilliantly—from the rich leather furniture to vintage pieces hand-plucked from dusty antique stores—she'd created a near-magical home for us.

And now, she couldn't do those things she loved—spending long hours hunting for the perfect piece.

Not with her condition.

"You just missed your sister," she whispered as if someone might hear us as we slowly made our way to the main sitting room. The floor-to-ceiling windows drenched the room and velvet chairs in golden sun, the heat enriching the leather-bound-book smell that permeated from the first editions perfectly lining the shelves making up the entirety of the east wall.

"I didn't realize she was in town," I said, settling into the farthest chair on the right—a favorite of mine because it offered an unobstructed view of the ancient oaks and whispering pines that dotted the estate grounds. As a little girl, I'd curl up with a book and open the windows to let in the southern breeze, the soft hissing of the wind blowing through the trees the perfect background noise when getting lost in a fictional world.

"I didn't either," Mama said, drawing me back to the present. I focused on her as she sat across from me. She looked tired. Paler than the last time I'd seen her. "Of course, you know I'm always happy to house my firstborn…"

Her words trailed off as she wrung her hands, and I reached over to squeeze one.

"What is it this time, Mama?"

A long, slow breath left her lips. "It's nothing, really." She waved me off with her free hand. I fixed her with the look she'd raised me on, the one that said I wouldn't be lied to. "Well," she relented. "I had hoped her surprise return was because she simply *missed* us. She's been on her travels for months now."

Her travels. A kind way of sugar-coating what my older sister *actually* did on a day-to-day basis, which was blowing through her inheritance, usually on luxury items, resorts, or booze.

"But she got into a bit of a bind in one of the clubs in Morocco, and she needed Harold to clean it up."

"Not surprising," I said, trying to keep my tone even. I loved my sister, but she'd never been considerate of other's feelings and continuously lived her life like she needed to outrun herself. I'd wasted many a night fearful of the day I'd get a call from Mama, tear-soaked and grief-stricken due to my sister's untimely demise—it'd be drunk driving or overdosing or being hit too hard by one of her many ex-husbands or lovers or something equally awful.

I surveyed my mother's features, the sadness clinging to her frame and guilt chipping away at the eyes that were an identical shade of blue to mine. Something punched me in the chest.

"She didn't get the test, did she?"

Mama shook her head. "Not that she's required to. Lord knows I had a hard enough time when you tested. Even if you'd been a match, honey, I don't know if I could've accepted the offer." She patted my hand.

I swallowed the lump in my throat.

When we'd found out my mother's kidneys were failing, I'd immediately gotten tested as a potential donor. As did my father, a few of our close cousins, and several friends from my parent's inner circle. None of us were a match, and I lived with that grief and anger every single day. It raged and roared in the tight box I kept it in, locked deep inside me as to not let anyone ever know how helpless I felt to save my mother. My favorite person in the entire world—the woman who'd raised me to be independent, to think for myself, to love fiercely, and to never take a single day for granted.

"If I would've been a match," I finally said. "You would've taken it willingly, or I'd have Daddy haul you into the hospital kicking and screaming."

She gaped at me, a smile lighting up her eyes. "I would *never!*"

I laughed softly and shrugged. "Either way, I would've given it to you."

She squeezed my hand again. "I know, darling. You've always had such a big heart. You get that from your father, though most wouldn't know it."

"How long is Andromeda staying this time?" I tried to keep the contempt from my tone, but even my grace had its limits. My older sister had refused to get the test when I'd tracked her down to ask her—claimed if I wasn't a match, then she wouldn't be either, so it would be a waste of time.

She'd stuck to that excuse even after I'd explained to her it didn't work like that.

That familiar rage bubbled in my chest, and it took a great deal of time to stop it from boiling over. My mother didn't deserve to see my contempt for my sister, didn't deserve to see her two daughters fight. Not when she had so little time left.

Which is why it would be even harder to tell her the truth about Cannon. Something I planned to do, after a few more deep breaths.

"A few weeks, I believe," Mama answered me. "I've drawn up the guest room for her the way she likes. Had Harold put up those ghastly black-out curtains she simply can't sleep without."

Have patience. Exude grace. Be forever grateful for your lot in life.

I repeated the words my mother raised me on while taking a deep breath. I *was* grateful for all we'd been given. It was no secret us VanDoren girls were blessed at birth. We were born into the money and privilege my family had worked hard for, and I'd spent my entire life ensuring I didn't take a second of it for granted. My sole focus since grade school had been to spread our wealth to those who needed it more, and the endless charity work I'd done simply because I love doing it landed me the career I had today. I'd never dreamed of being able to do what I'm passionate about and get paid for it until the day Asher Silas—owner of the Carolina Reapers—offered me the job as the head of his charity foundation. And he'd surprised me even more when he agreed to my request for my salary to be spread among the charities we chose together each year.

A sizzle of heat licked right up my spine as the thought of the *home* I'd made with the Reapers raced through my mind.

Tattoos—ink and color and designs everywhere. Swirling or jagged, the ink covered nearly every inch of his skin.

The memory flashed, cloudy and distant, as quick as a blink.

Had I dreamed of seeing him without his shirt? Or had that actually happened?

Heaven save me, I was in a world of trouble.

And that trouble would triple once I said what I'd come here to say.

"You didn't bring your hockey star," Mama said, a chiding look in her eyes.

"No," I said on a breath of air. "I didn't."

"I did make your father lock the guns up," she said, leaning closer. "I'm not so foolish as to invite the husband we've never met and not take some precautions."

A half-panicked, half-sincere laugh tumbled from my lips. The idea of my father pointing a shotgun at Cannon…a cold chill raced across my skin. I don't believe the man would even flinch. Cannon kept himself locked in a hard exterior as impenetrable as Fort Knox, and yet, *somehow*, he'd allowed himself to get so far gone we'd gotten married. I still couldn't make sense of it.

"You see, Mama—"

"You don't have to be ashamed, darling," she cut me off. "I know how love takes hold of us in unexpected ways and never lets go. I understand the strength of passion and how it can push us to do terrifying yet beautiful things." She flashed me a conspirator smile. "That's how you know it's good."

My lips parted, the words getting tangled somewhere between the shock of my mother's approval of such a rash decision and her romanticized talk of passion.

"Can I ask one thing, though? Beyond meeting him, of course."

I tilted my head, speechless.

"Please let me plan a real wedding." The hope in her eyes hit me like a hammer—the big kind that took no issue cracking fissures down a line of concrete. "Lord knows I'll never be able to do it for Andromeda. I've lost count of how many marriages and annulments she's acquired on her travels." Mama leaned a bit closer, lowering her voice. "I believe that is the source of your father's...frustration with this Vegas business. But I told him it's not fair to punish you for your sister's mistakes."

"Thank you," I choked out.

She nodded and continued. "Anyway, with the donor waiting list being so long and my health deteriorating so fast...well, I know how to do the math. It would bring my heart so much joy if I could plan a real wedding for you and your man. Watch you walk down that aisle and take your vows."

The only thing that kept me from dropping my jaw was years of practice at schooling my features—being a proper VanDoren, we never showed our hand before we had to.

"Is it too much to ask?" Mama asked sincerely. "I mean, who doesn't love a party? And we would obviously work around his schedule, unless..." her eyes dropped to my stomach. "Unless there was a pressing reason you tied the knot in Vegas."

I laughed, shaking my head at the absurdity of that claim.

Difficult to conceive a child when you've never had sex before.

"Of course not, Mama," I said, shaking my head.

"Well, I wouldn't have said no to a grandbaby, but just as well." She shifted in her seat, an alarm softly ringing from the crisp white watch on her left wrist. "Walk me to my room?"

I stood from my chair, my heart racing and breaking at the same time as I helped her to stand. I walked her through the house, grateful when we didn't run into my father, or my sister returning no doubt from wherever she'd run off to shop for clothes. It was beyond me how she constantly started over with every city she traveled to, but I suppose endless means could do that to a person.

I turned into Mama's bedroom, forgoing the main portion with their canopied king and instead settled her into a simple but elegant leather chair near the window. A gray box half the size of the chair sat next to it, a white machine with an array of tubing atop it.

"Here," I said as she settled into the chair. "Let me." She remained silent as I gently hooked her up to the at-home dialysis machine, and once again thanked the good lord that we were able to afford the at-home care. My mother was one of the strongest women I knew, and she wanted everyone to see her as such. Not that this made her weak, not in the slightest, but she was a private woman when it came to her illness.

"How is that?" I asked as I placed a pillow under her arm.

"Wonderful," she said, resting her head back against the chair, the whir of the machine humming beside her. "So, what do you think?"

I could barely breathe around the ache in my chest. Around the split in my heart. I never lied to my Mama, but this...she deserved any joy I could give her before...

"Let me speak with Cannon," I said finally.

A wide smile shaped her lips, then she raised her brows. "Well, what are you waiting for? Go ask him." She shooed me away with her free arm.

I kissed her forehead, swallowing down the tears that were desperate for release. But I kept my smile firmly planted on my lips as I left the estate, because with what I had to do? Convince Cannon Price to marry me...*again*? I needed all the strength I could get.

3
CANNON

The sounds of the weight room brought a little balance back to my very fucked up reality. I'd always liked to work out. The shape of my body was something in my direct control through the diet I chose and the work I was willing to put into it. I liked things I could control.

"So, not to address the elephant in the room or anything," Logan said as he appeared overhead as I bench pressed. "But what exactly are you going to do about that whole wedding ring thing?"

"Do you see it on my hand?" I growled as I pushed through a rep.

"Well, none of us wear rings in the weight room. You know exactly what I'm trying to say." He folded his arms across his chest.

I set the bar back on the rack and sat up with a heavy sigh. The last thing I wanted to do was talk about this right now. Or ever. "Can we just not right now?"

"Sure. Or you could have called me back any of the nine times I called you." He shrugged.

The sounds around me ceased, and a quick glance showed that all six other Reapers in the room had halted their workouts and were staring at me. Lukas, Axel, Connell, Noble, Sterling, and yep, Ward was still staring, too.

"If you guys are looking for me to empty my heart out on the gym floor, you've all lost your fucking minds."

"That's assuming you have a heart to empty…" Lukas teased with a smirk.

"Leave him alone," Axel warned. As our team captain, the man took his responsibilities seriously, both on and off the ice, and apparently during the off-season, too.

"Come on, it's natural for us to be curious," Connell argued in his thick Scottish brogue. "You went to Vegas and married Persephone."

"Which he thought was a prank you'd devised," Sterling said as he wiped the sweat off his face with a towel. "Seriously, it would have been funny if it hadn't been so…well, out of character for everyone involved."

"Och, that would have been a good one," Connell admitted thoughtfully. "But since I had no hand in your impetuous acts, I feel a little bereft and need you to fill the hole in my soul with the knowledge of what you're going to do."

"We're getting an annulment," I announced, avoiding the hollow feeling that burrowed inside my chest and set up house. "That's what you do when you accidentally marry the queen of the debutante ball in a drug-and-alcohol-induced bout of Vegas insanity. Hell, I'm pretty sure Vegas is the reason annulments exist in the first place."

The guys glanced at each other as if they were privy to some secret.

"Oh, for fuck's sake. You're all going to stand here like a bunch of moping matchmakers until you have your say, so just say it." I rested my elbows on my knees and settled in for one of their life-is-great-when-you're-in-love pep talks that they usually gave each other.

"You actually want our opinions?" Noble asked as he climbed out of the leg press.

"No, but I know that's not going to stop you from giving them to me, so feel free." Maybe if I sat through this shit once, they'd leave me alone to deal with it.

"I think you should give it a try," Axel stated with a nod.

Every head turned his direction, and most had the same disbelieving look of *what the fuck* that I did.

"I'm sorry, but you think that giant, scary-ass man should stay married to the cute, fragile-looking woman who runs our charitable foundation?" Lukas questioned.

"I do." He stood there with his arms folded across his chest, confident in his statement. "Look, I'm the only man in this room who had a quickie wedding—under some really false pretenses, I might add—and look how we ended up? I fucking love my wife and wouldn't change a thing about how we got to this point."

"Right, but you wanted that marriage," Noble argued. "You were the one who asked Langley for it, if I remember correctly. You didn't just wake up married to the woman and think, well, let's make the best of it."

"If I had woken up next to Langley—" Sterling started with a smirk.

"Don't finish that fucking sentence," Axel warned, leveling a glare on the kid.

"I'm with Noble on this one, Cannon," Connell said as he rubbed the back of his neck. "That lass is no match for you."

"Hey, she's not exactly weak," Logan countered.

"I didn't mean it that way," Connell argued. "She's sweet and kind, and he's…" He gestured at me.

"The surliest bastard on the entire planet?" Lukas offered.

"Exactly." Connell nodded. "I think you're making the

right decision with an annulment. I say set the lass free before you hurt her, because whether you mean to or not, she's going to get scraped up."

He was right, which was exactly the reason I'd called my lawyer in the first place.

"Oh, come on. Do you see the way they look at each other?" Sterling stepped into the fray.

The group muttered.

"What the fuck are you talking about?" I asked since no one wanted to offer an answer to that ridiculous question.

"He's right." Axel nodded. "When you two aren't fighting over something ridiculous, or generally pissing each other off, you do...well...*look* at each other."

My gaze narrowed on the man, and he had the nerve to grin at me.

"She looks at you like you're... I don't know. I guess a mixture of devil and dessert," Sterling said with a shrug. "When you're *not* looking, of course."

"Right? Like that time she fell into his lap on the plane?" Logan added.

"You're not helping my cause here," I told my best friend.

"Sorry," he muttered.

"And sorry to tell you, but you look at her like you're torn between worshipping her and carrying her off to *worship* her, if you get my meaning," Sterling said. "You know, in the hot, sweaty way of—"

"We get it!" Lukas shouted. "Christ, you're talking about a woman we work with."

"A hot woman we work with," Sterling muttered. "And it's not like I was saying that I wanted to—"

"Enough." I shot a glare at the kid to make sure he understood my meaning.

"Are we talking about the sudden marriage of one Cannon Price to Persephone VanDoren?" Sawyer asked as he walked into the weight room. "Because I can hear that shit all the way down the hall."

Great, now I had to listen to the resident newlywed weigh in.

"You have an opinion?" Noble asked him.

"Me?" Sawyer's eyebrows shot up. "Hell no. Cannon, I love you like a brother, and you deserve to be happy. Persephone is pretty fucking awesome, but if she isn't the one, and this is really some giant fuck-up, then exit with grace, my man." He took a seat on the bench across from mine.

"And do you have an opinion?" I asked Logan as he stood beside me, just like he always did.

He sighed and ripped his hand across his hair. "Honestly, you know I'm going to back whatever decision you make. That's my job as your friend."

"And I appreciate that. But if everyone in here is giving me their best Dr. Phil, I wouldn't mind hearing your actual thoughts." I'm not sure how I managed to say it, but I did. The more they all talked, the higher my blood pressure spiked.

"I think you guys have something. I think we've all seen it since that first moment you met, and we've watched you two dance around each other for almost two years. You want to explore that? Cool. There are six men in here who will testify that our happiness is dependent on the way we feel about our women."

The guys muttered an ascent.

"Sterling will tell you that his happiness is dependent on the way a plethora of women feel about him." Logan arched a brow at the resident playboy of the Reapers, but hey, none of us were perfect our rookie years. "I also think that girl is a good one. She's the kind of woman you don't fuck around on. The woman you hold on to for the rest of your life. And you, my friend, are carrying about three tons of damage like it's nothing. I'm not saying that she won't help you dig through your shit, because I think she will. But I *am* saying that if you're going to use that damage as an excuse to run, then you do it now before either of you gets hurt."

I nodded, knowing that what he said made the most sense out of any of them. Then I stood and headed for the door.

"Hey, are you going to tell us what you decided?" Connell asked.

I turned in the doorway to face down the friends that had become my family over the last two seasons. "Really?"

"We could vote," Sterling suggested. "But I should get to show everyone the videos of you guys in Vegas. It seems only right to put the evidence out there."

"Everyone's already seen the videos," Axel countered.

My temper snapped.

"Sure, we could vote. You know, if my life was a fucking democracy that you guys ran." I folded my arms over my chest and glared them down. "But it's not. It's my life to fuck up, so while I value everyone's thoughts, let's just all agree that you'll never give them to me again unless I ask, okay? Because the last time I checked, there are only two people in my marriage, and lucky for me, none of you are my wife."

My wife. While part of me rebelled against the term, kicking and screaming in all of my stubborn glory, there was an annoying warmth that filled my chest, too.

"You're a little too dominant for me," Connell replied with a smirk.

"You don't have to listen to us," Axel agreed. "Hell, I'm not really sure you've listened to anyone in your entire life. But I hope you give this a chance. You deserve your shot at happiness, too."

And that warmth shriveled and died.

"It's not about what I deserve. It's about what she deserves. I am more fucked up than any of you know. You think she's going to want me all tatted up and hair-triggered at her fucking country club? I'm the guy you fuck on a spring break weekend so you can brag about it to your sorority sisters, and the only reason a woman would ever introduce me to her daddy is to piss him off so she can work out her own issues. Trust me, she wants this annulment just as badly as I do, and the press has to be killing her."

"She wants the annulment too?" Logan asked, concern shining through his eyes.

"Of course she does! Who the fuck would ever want to stay married to me? Definitely not someone like her, who's been raised on her daddy's money and high society. That woman is everything I loathed growing up. I got shipped from foster home to foster home praying that I'd get placed with my sister in the next one. Hoping they wouldn't mind feeding a teenage boy, let alone clothing me during a growth spurt. Don't even get me started on trying to play hockey during those years."

"Cannon," Axel started, but I cut him off.

"Persephone hasn't struggled for a single thing in her life. She's been handed whatever she wanted the minute she wanted it. She has no idea what it's like to come from my background or deal with my damage. You honestly think two people that different have any business sharing a last name?"

By the time I finished my tirade, the guys were all looking anywhere but at me. Or the doorway behind me.

My stomach hit the fucking floor.

"She's standing right behind me, isn't she?" I snapped.

They had the nerve to mutter and nod.

"Well, now that you've covered every reason I'll never be what you want, do you think you have a couple of minutes to talk, *husband*?"

I turned around slowly, steeling myself for what I'd find.

Persephone stared me down despite my height advantage.

She wore a different dress than the one she'd worn home on the plane a few hours ago. It was pink, like the color rising in her cheeks, and the simple sheath clung to every elegant line the woman had.

"If we must," I agreed, then walked right past her, heading for the locker room.

How the fuck was I married to her? Of every fantasy I'd ever allowed myself to have, my ring on her finger had not been one of them.

"Can you please slow down?" she called after me. "Not all of us are six feet tall!"

"Six five," I threw over my shoulder. "Wait here." I slipped into the team locker room and grabbed my bag. She'd caught up to me by the time I exited. "Follow me."

I led her down the hall a bit to the away locker room, then flipped the light switch and held the door open for her.

"Well, at least I'm getting two-word sentences," she muttered as she passed under my arm. God, everything about the woman was petite except her curves. Those were fully fleshed out, as my brain liked to remind me every five fucking seconds since waking up in bed next to her.

"What can I do for you, wife?" Why the fuck did I say that? Just because I could? Because as soon as the annulment went through, she'd be free to have someone else call her that? A rage bubble rose in my throat at the thought.

"I just need to talk to you for a second." Oh great, now she was pulling on her pearls, which was a definite sign that she was stressed.

"Okay." I stripped off my shirt and threw it on the bench.

Her eyes widened, and her lips parted as her gaze skimmed my chest, no doubt horrified by the amount of ink I had going on there. Hadn't she gotten an eyeful in that hotel room?

I kicked off my shoes, peeled off my socks, and tossed

them in the same direction as my shirt. Then I dropped my athletic shorts, leaving me in nothing but my black boxer briefs.

The fact that I was semi-hard didn't faze me. That was pretty much my constant state around Persephone, and I'd gotten used to it. Apparently, she hadn't, though, because her eyes had graduated from wide to *fucking huge*.

"You're not talking." I grabbed my shower bag and walked right past her slackened jaw.

Of course, my ink shocked her. The guys she'd been with probably had their frat symbols inked on their arms, and that was it. Hell, if that.

"Right. Um. Sorry. It's just that you're naked." Her voice pitched ridiculously high, and I grinned as I headed for the shower, knowing she couldn't see it.

"Not yet, but soon, sweetheart." I reached the showers and started to lower my boxer briefs.

"Oh my God! Right! I'll just wait out here!"

I glanced over my shoulder to see her covering her eyes with her hand, backing away like she'd stumbled onto the set of a porn.

"You do that," I called out before turning on the shower and getting to business. I took my time, careful not to give my already-eager cock too much attention as I washed. The last thing I needed was to sport a full hard on while trying to deal with whatever shit she wanted to talk about.

She'd probably faint right on the spot.

I finished my shower, then wrapped myself in a towel, tucking it in at the waist before walking back into the locker room.

She sat next to my gym bag and meticulously folded pile of laundry. God, the woman couldn't even stand to have dirty clothes out of place, so how the hell had she ever thought marrying me was a good idea?

"You said you wanted to talk. So, talk."

"Right. I did." She stood like it would somehow put us on an even playing ground when I was a good foot or more taller than she was. I momentarily thought about lifting her to the bench so she wouldn't have to crane her neck. "Look, about our marriage..."

"The one I already promised to get annulled first thing Monday?"

"Monday?" She looked stricken.

"Damn, Princess, I know people jump at your command, but we literally got married on a Friday. I can't exactly ask my lawyer to file papers at a court that isn't open until Monday. I'm sorry I can't wave a magic wand and make the last forty-eight hours disappear, but I'm trying my hardest."

"What? No. That's not what I meant." She shook her head, sending her hair moving in a ripple.

Fuck, she was beautiful. Fucking flawless.

"Then please tell me what you meant."

Her gaze lingered on my abs before she dragged it up to meet mine. "It's really hard to think when you're not wearing any clothes," she snapped.

"I think just fine. I'd even go as far to say that I do my best work without my clothes."

She seethed. "Cannon, *please!* I'm trying to talk about something serious, and I can't very well do that when you're standing there all..." She stepped forward, her gaze locked on my stomach, and she reached forward, almost absent-minded.

"Don't." I stepped out of her reach, and her eyes flew to mine, wide and embarrassed. "Standing here all what?" I dared her. "Inked? Scary? Scandalous?"

"Gorgeous!" she snapped, then blinked. "Scary? You're not scary. You're distracting the shit out of me, but you're not scary."

Gorgeous? I took in the flush of her cheeks and the rapid rise and fall of her breasts against that modest neckline. Huh. Maybe I wasn't the only one fighting an attraction here.

"Turn around," I ordered.

"What?"

"Turn around unless you want an eyeful."

Our eyes locked as the room filled with a potent electricity. Fuck me, but one tug of this towel, and a simple tug of her panties to the side, and I could be so deep inside this woman that she'd be ruined for every man who came after me.

The thought had its appeal.

She broke the connection, turning her back on me, and I went about getting dressed.

"I don't think we can get this annulled."

I paused momentarily, then jerked my boxer briefs up and reached for my shorts. "Why? It's not like we had sex."

"You don't know that," she said primly.

I pulled on my shorts and shirt. "It's safe to turn around now."

She did, and I felt an odd sense of satisfaction that she looked disappointed when she saw I had my shirt on.

"I do know that we didn't have sex," I reiterated, sitting to get my socks and shoes on.

"You can't possibly know that!" She repeated.

"No condoms in the trash can. Trust me, even drunk, there's no way I'd forget to use one."

"Well, maybe you did this time. I mean, we both did things completely out of character, right?" She ran her tongue across her lips, and I quelled the urge to pull her toward me and suck it into my mouth.

My gaze narrowed. What the hell was she getting at?

"Are you sore?" I bent to tie my shoes, and by the time I looked up, she still hadn't answered me. "Well, are you?

Because if we'd had sex, trust me, you'd still feel it. You're fucking tiny, and I'm not."

"Well, no." She looked away. "But that doesn't mean anything, either."

It what? My gaze narrowed. "Okay, then how about this. It wouldn't matter if I was drugged out of my goddamned mind. If I ever got my hands on your body, I'd remember. We didn't have sex. Trust me. What the hell is this really about, Persephone?"

She swallowed and took a deep breath. "I need us to stay married."

My jaw dropped. "I'm sorry?"

"My mom is really sick. She's dying. She has a super rare blood type, and her kidneys are failing. We've tried for the last five years to find her a match and can't. The doctors are giving her months, Cannon. That's it. Just months." She took a seat beside me on the bench.

"God, I'm sorry." Losing my mother had been the worst moment of my life. I wouldn't wish that shit on my worst enemy. Persephone was a lot of things, but she wasn't even close to being an enemy.

"Thank you. I guess it just goes to show you that money can't buy everything, right?" She forced a smile. "I thought she was going to lose it when the press got ahold of our wedding pictures."

"Fucking chapel," I muttered.

"We should definitely report them to the Better Business Bureau," she said with a nod.

The corners of my mouth lifted.

"Anyway, instead of being angry at me, she was thrilled." Her voice shook a little.

"Thrilled?" I examined her profile, but there wasn't any hint that she was lying.

"She was so happy. She said she just wanted to see me

happy. To see me find love. And then she mentioned the dozen or so times my older sister has been married and annulled within a month, and I felt so…slimy."

"Slimy," I repeated because I didn't have any other words.

"Right." She turned slightly and looked up at me.

Fuuuuuuck, those eyes hit me right in the heart. I threw up every defense I'd managed to construct in my twenty-seven years, and those baby blues sliced right through them like butter.

"Cannon, I know you hate me and hate how I was raised and pretty much everything I stand for, but would you consider staying married to me? At least until…" She drifted off.

At least until my mother dies. I heard her unspoken words loud and clear.

"Persephone, I'm the last person your family would *ever* want you married to, even for a few months. Look at me."

She didn't flinch. "I am looking at you, Cannon. My mother has seen your pictures. She knows you're an NHL star. She knows, and she's still so happy for me, and the idea of taking that happiness away from her when she's already lost so much…" She shook her head.

It would only be for a few months. Holy shit, was I actually considering this? "There are a thousand reasons this is a shit idea."

Her eyes flared with hope. "But one really *good* reason that it's not. And I wouldn't ask much of you, I promise. Well, there's one thing." She cringed.

"There's something bigger than asking me to stay married to you when we both know we're completely wrong for each other?"

"Mom wants to plan a wedding."

"Fuck that—"

"She said she can't die knowing that I was married by a

singing Elvis and she wasn't even there to see me, or have my dad give me away. And it would be a really small affair, and it wouldn't hurt anyone because we're already married, right?" She pressed her lips in a thin line and flat-out begged. "Please, Cannon? Please?"

Those eyes. They were my fucking kryptonite.

But marry her again? This time for real? Just to turn around and annul it months later? Months of living with her? Struggling to keep my hands off her?

"Persephone, I don't know. I really respect what you're trying to do for your mom. You have no idea how much I respect you for it but do you really want her last months on this earth—her last months with you—to be consumed by a lie?"

She stood slowly and turned to face me. "I want her last months on this earth to be consumed by happiness, and if I have to lie to give her that, then I hope she'll forgive me when I eventually join her. I hate having to ask *you* to lie. I've honestly never known you to even tell a lie. But I can't give that kind of happiness to my mother without your help. I know it's unfair of me to ask, but there's nothing I wouldn't do for her."

She raised her chin and stilled, waiting for my verdict.

"I need some time to think. Can you give me that?" I asked her.

Hope flared in her eyes again, and she nodded enthusiastically. "Absolutely. I can give you that." She gifted me with a smile that would have knocked me on my ass if I hadn't been sitting down. "I'll talk to you later."

She was almost out the door when I called her name.

"Persephone."

"Yes?"

"I don't hate you," I assured her gently. Her posture softened. "I might hate everything your wealth stands for, but I don't hate *you*. There's a difference." I needed her to know that. Why? Who the hell knew.

"Thank you. And don't stress about the wedding thing. Really. I'll even buy your tux. You know, a real one. Not like the tux and T-shirt you wore to the Vegas wedding."

My eyes widened, and she waved her goodbye and ran.

Smart woman.

I headed home to Reaper Village, where the team all had houses in the same suburban neighborhood, and called the only woman I trusted.

My sister answered and filled me in on life with my nephew before dropping the bomb that she'd already seen the gossip sites.

"I figured you'd tell me when you wanted to."

She was seriously the best. I caught her up on everything, from waking up in Vegas to Persephone's plea in the locker room.

"What do I do?" I asked as I pulled into my driveway.

"You're asking me for advice on marriage?" She laughed. "God, I think mine lasted, what? Six months?"

"I'm serious, Lillian. I need advice, and you're the only one who really knows me well enough to give it."

She sighed. "Okay. All I can say is to follow your heart. And honestly, what would you give to go back and make Mom that blissfully happy during her last months?"

"Anything," I replied. "I would give anything."

I guess I had my answer.

4

PERSEPHONE

I paced the length of my foyer, my cream pumps keeping time with the ancient grandfather clock that decorated the space. The second hand ticked louder than it had when it was originally constructed, or so I'd been told, but I'd become accustomed to the steady click of it. And right now, that second hand felt like it counted down my very life's breath.

Because Cannon Price would be here any minute.

My heart raced despite my efforts to calm it. Gerald—head of security and currently on gate duty tonight—had phoned down moments ago informing me Mr. Price would like to see me. Lord, bless Gerald. He'd been like a second father to me growing up, and he was just as protective.

I'd barely been able to manage a full sentence when Cannon had called me the hour prior, saying he wanted to talk. And rattling off my address had never been harder.

"You honestly think two people that different have any business sharing a last name?"

Cannon's words echoed in my head, stinging just as much now as they had the first time I'd heard them. Of all the things I'd expected walking to the weight room in search of him, those cold words were the last. Cannon was many things—grumpy, guarded, and infuriatingly teasing—but he'd never been outright icy toward me.

And yet, when I'd told him about my mother, something in him had *melted* toward our predicament. That softness I sometimes caught in his hard, dark gaze had surfaced.

"I don't hate you."

The memory sent a warm chill over my skin.

The breath in my lungs halted as two strong thuds sounded against my front door. I swore even the grandfather clock paused as my fingers reached for the knob. This moment would either make or break me, and it was all in Cannon's hands.

After a deep breath, I straightened my spine and slowly opened the door.

Cannon wore a black pair of Reaper athletic pants, and a tight black T-shirt covered his incredibly muscled chest and torso. Those damn arms were on display, though, enough to make heat sizzle in my blood. The whorls of ink created patterns and pictures—a story I desperately wanted to understand.

"You live with your parents?" Cannon tucked his hands into his pockets, leaning against the doorframe like he'd be content to speak to me about our future on the porch.

I shook my head, pointing behind him and to the east. "No," I said. "They live on the eastward portion of the estate."

Cannon arched a brow, his jet-black hair falling slightly over his forehead as he waited. Silent, yet with the churning ferocity of a storm building over the ocean. Damn this man, why did he make me feel so small? I'd never had that problem my entire life, *despite* being short.

"Would you please come in?" I motioned behind me. "I have a pitcher of ice tea in the study."

He snorted, likely at my southern manners, but elected to come all the way into my home. The heat from his body seemed charged as he passed me, like running my fingers over staticky fabric.

He checked out my clock for a heartbeat before saying, "Lead the way, Princess."

I ignored the pet name and nodded, heading toward the study and not daring to look back. I needed Cannon, whether I wanted to admit it or not. I'd quell the instinct that only manifested in this man's presence—the one that told me to push him back and pull him in all at the same time.

Cannon ignored the leather chairs situated near the bay windows and instead went straight to my study's farthest wall. His eyes danced over the ancient spines of my personal collection of books, those hands still secured in his pockets—as if he were afraid of what he'd touch if he let them out.

A grunt was all he deemed to voice after his perusal.

"Thank you for coming," I said, hating that my voice quivered. There had been countless times I'd needed something from others—charity donations, business mergers, event spaces—but never once had I been so afraid as I was now. Perhaps that was due to the circumstances—our untimely marriage—made the situation a shade different than a donation request.

"Tea?" I asked, my fingers gripping the ice-cold pitcher resting on my desk in the far-right corner.

"No," he said, finally facing me. "Thank you," he added, likely for my benefit.

A small smile ticked at the corner of my lips at that *thank you*. I poured myself a glass and took a sip, the cold liquid hushing some of that heat that sizzled in my veins.

"Must be nice," he said, motioning his head behind him toward the shelves.

I flashed him a confused look.

"To have first editions handed to you like candy canes on Christmas Eve."

I set my tea down and plopped my hands on my hips. "Handed to me?" The bite in my tone practically had Cannon's name on it since it only surfaced when he was in the room.

A smirk and a nod.

I sucked my teeth, my tongue sharp and ready to sting.

The image of my mother—the hope in her eyes and the fatigue—quashed the retort. Instead, I shifted out of my fighting stance, allowing my hands to hang loose at my sides. "I appreciate you coming," I said, completely ignoring the game we usually played—the one where he taunted me until I ignited. I gripped the back of the leather chair for support. "Have you considered my offer?" I tried not to let the nerves —the *desperation*—show on my face.

He pursed his lips, those dark eyes trailing me up and down, questioning. Perhaps the jab had been an effort to bring us back to common ground—that space where we danced so viciously with each other yet never touched. I hadn't taken the bait, not because I didn't enjoy our little spats, but because this was important to me. More important than the thrill arguing with Cannon Price offered.

"I have," he said, his deep tenor skating across my skin as fast as he moved on the ice. "And I have rules."

The breath rushed out of my lungs, my shoulders curling inward slightly at his mention of rules. Rules meant he would agree. And *I'd* agree to anything that allowed my mother a few months joy before she—

"One," he said, finally taking his hands out of his pockets and ticking the items off on his fingers. "You have to move in with me, because I sure as hell won't live with your parents."

"It's a guest house," I groaned, but he ignored me, pushing on.

"Two. You can have access to *all* of my accounts, but I want nothing of yours. You understand? Nothing." He took a step toward me, then another. "I've worked hard for every single thing I've earned. I don't need a handout—"

"Understood," I cut him off, tipping my head back to meet his eyes. He stood so close I could smell him—a sharp, almost mossy green scent, edged with a lighter hint of citrus.

He cocked a brow at the interruption, but a lick of fire churned in those dark eyes, some sense of relief that I'd brought my bite back.

"Three," he continued, not bothering to move back an inch. "The only people from my family invited to this wedding are my sister and my nephew—"

"Of course," I cut in again. "I adore Lillian and would love to meet her son."

A low huff, and I'd sealed my lips again. "Four," he said, his eyes doing their best to scorch every inch of my body. A modest yet elegant sundress allowed my skin to breathe during the sweltering southern summer, but the way he looked at me? I may as well have been naked. Those damn eyes saw straight to the heart of me. "Don't go falling in love with me, Princess. Because I'm sure as hell not your happily ever after."

I glared up at him, my fingers trembling as I gripped the back of the chair even harder. "Not an issue," I snapped, but instantly regretted it. Damn him. He knew how to get under my skin. Knew how to make me hiss. And it wasn't fair to him. Because I could see it in the settled, broken pieces in his eyes, those jagged edges I don't think anyone ever noticed because they were too afraid to get that close to him—I could *see* it. The truth he believed—that he wasn't worth loving anyway—and some deep, aching part of me lurched at that notion. Again, I wanted to reach between us, wanted to touch him, hold his hand, or simply wrap my arms around the beast and tell him he was worth more than he allowed himself to believe.

"Five," he growled, likely noting my train of thought with his infuriating ability to read me. "No sex. Zero sex."

My lips popped open.

"Six," he pushed on. "No sex with anyone else either because—"

"Won't be difficult," I grumbled.

He tilted his head. "I mean it, Princess. Just because I don't scratch your itch doesn't mean that trust-fund-douche is allowed to either." The primal ownership in his tone uncoiled something hot and hungry in my core. I backed away from the safety of the chair, folding my arms over my chest. "Persephone." He growled my name, and every nerve ending in my body stood at attention. "This is a deal-breaker for me. If you think you can't handle not—"

"I haven't had sex for twenty-four years, Cannon," I cut him off, the breath rushing from my lungs. "I think I can handle another few months!"

Cannon's lips parted, and he took a step away from me.

I held his gaze, not daring to be ashamed.

"You're a...you've never had..." The words stumbled from his lips in the first show of shock and vulnerability I'd ever seen from him. The sight made a chuckle burst through my lips.

"A virgin, Cannon." I grinned at him. "Not a bad word," I said. "Certainly not foreign to you, I'm sure."

"You're a virgin." The words were a whisper. "I thought that trust-fund—"

"Oh, Michael has *tried*," I said, waving off the declaration. "But I don't love him. Barely even like him."

Could big scary NHL stars break? Because the way Cannon froze, the way he couldn't gather his words...it sure looked like I'd broken him. I boldly took a step forward, so close I could've touched him if I wanted to. "When I *do* give myself to someone?" I mimicked his earlier appraisal of my body, taking in all the gloriousness of his. "It will be because I trust that man. Because I *want* that man more than I want myself. When I get that *hungry*? Then I'll know the man I choose will be worth it."

The bob of his Adam's apple was his only response.

"Any other rules?"

A subtle shake of his head.

"Good, I agree to those rules. Now, I have a few of mine."

"You're not really in a position to be making rules here. I'm doing this for you—"

"And I appreciate that," I said honestly. "I don't know if I made myself clear in the locker room, but this will mean the world to my mother. And I'll do whatever it takes to bring her joy in her last months on this earth."

Cannon's tense shoulders loosened just a fraction. "I do," he said the words so softly I almost didn't hear him. "I do understand," he spoke up. "More than you know."

I bit my bottom lip, studying the well of pain in his eyes. "Did you lose someone?"

A muscle in his jaw ticked, and that familiar iron wall dropped over his eyes. "What are your rules?"

I sighed. Fine. Fair enough. He wasn't obligated to share, to open up. That didn't mean I'd stop trying, though.

"You can't get into any fights," I said, ticking the first item off on my finger. The mimicked position from his earlier stance earned me the tiniest, if not briefest, of smiles. "No public scenes, violent or otherwise."

Cannon folded his massive arms over his chest.

"And you can't have sex with anyone else either." The final rule came out firmer than the other two, and it dawned on me how this rule held more importance. To *me,* this one was the deal-breaker. The idea of him with another woman...I cringed. That inward swirling mount of jealousy is what urged me to buy him in that damned auction in the first place. I didn't take one more second to ponder on it and instead pushed on. "Because, Cannon, for all *pretend* purposes, you're mine."

His lips curved at the edges—more bite than smile.

"And I do ask if you feel the...urge...feel like you might be on the brink of breaking that rule, that you ask *me* to satisfy it first."

His eyebrows perked up at that, and the look made me tremble inside.

"I'll be just fine without it," he said. "And I won't break my own rules. No sex."

"Perfect," I said, though a bit of disappointment fluttered through my chest. Not that I particularly wanted him to fight for the right to come between my thighs, but...

Well, it didn't matter anyway.

This was clearly business, and at least on this end, we knew why we were going through with another marriage.

For the life of me, I wished I could remember my reasoning for the first time.

"So, we have a deal?" I offered my hand between us. Cannon eyed it for a few moments like I might have hidden some sort of taser between my fingers. "Oh, for goodness' sake," I said, and grabbed his hand.

A jolt of heat pulsed through me at the contact of his skin on mine—the roughness against my smoothness, the strength in his fingers yet the gentleness in which he held my hand.

Cannon shook it once, twice, and then released me and went so far as to take another step back.

Well, if this marriage wasn't off to a most *pleasant* start.

* * *

"How many garment bags do you truly need, Princess?" Cannon grumbled as he carried in three more of the dozen or so said bags.

I shifted the box of cosmetics in my arms, clicking across the hardwood that lined his Reaper Village home. "With as many events, galas, and charity fundraisers as I attend, not to mention the meetings with Silas and his owner friends, how many appropriate dresses and gowns would *you* deem enough?"

He shook his head, moving past me and down the hall, toward my designated room—down the hall from his. "I think you'd be just as powerful in jeans and a T-shirt, *more* so maybe because you wouldn't need all this fancy armor to hide behind." He lifted the bags draped over his arms before shoving past me and depositing them on the bed.

I sat the box on the ottoman at the foot of the bed and whirled on him, my blonde hair snapping behind me. "I happen to enjoy wearing nice clothes, and that isn't a crime, Cannon," I snapped. This wasn't the first time since I'd brought my things over to move in that he'd made a jab at my wealth. "And I don't *need* fancy armor."

"Sure thing, Princess." He shook his head. "How many more ten-thousand-dollar dresses do we need to haul in?"

My eyes flared, and adrenaline pumped in my veins. It had been a long fucking week, and I was done with his attitude. "You're one to talk. You have a closet full of fancy suits—"

"Coach makes us wear them to and from games."

I rolled my eyes. "I'm sure that's the only reason you wear them, too. I'm sure you only took a modeling gig with Connell for that same reason, hmm? Because *coach made you*." I scoffed. "Also made you buy that expensive beast of a car too? And this home and everything in it?"

He pressed his lips into a hard line, but his anger didn't give me pause for one second.

"You may think it's fine for you to have nice things because you've worked your butt off for it, but don't for one moment presume to know me, Cannon Price." I stepped closer to him, arching my neck to meet his eyes. "I may have been born with wealth, but I had as much say in that as anyone else who is born into whatever situation their family has brought them into the world under. But everything in *my* accounts? Every piece of clothing or possession you've hauled in here today? I worked for it. I earned it. I accumulated this wealth by waking up and busting my butt every single day. Just because I don't do it on the ice or in the gym doesn't make it less valuable." Hot tears welled behind my eyes—a curse of mine, being an angry crier—but I didn't dare let them fall.

"I didn't say your work had no value." The edge in his tone told me I'd hit him where it hurt.

Good. He deserved it.

He's doing you a favor.

My fire soothed a bit at the voice in my head. I kept forgetting.

Kept forgetting this situation was for *my* benefit and not his.

But still, it didn't give him free rein to stick it to me every time he felt like it.

My cheeks reddened at the train of thought until I was a jumble of nerves with images of a shirtless Cannon making me hot in *so* many other ways.

"Are there more?" he asked more gently, eyeing the bags and boxes strewn across the room.

"I don't need your help. I can get them," I said, striding past him. I made it to the end of the hallway before he blocked my path.

"Don't," he said, hands braced on either wall, preventing me from reaching the entryway of his home.

"Don't what?" I sighed, pinching the bridge of my nose. A headache formed behind my eyes—a side effect from concocting this massive lie, most certainly. Fighting with Cannon, while most of the time was fun, had become exhausting today, like I was trying to hold my own against a tornado. A silent tornado.

"Don't push me out like that," he said. "I'm here. I want to help." He shrugged, slowly dropping his hands and letting them hang at his sides. "Even if it doesn't seem like it."

I knew that. I truly did. I was just tired. So, so damn tired. I'd had to stick our official marriage license in the safe he'd shown me earlier, and part of me was heavy with the lie it represented. The other part? A mess of emotions I couldn't begin to understand.

I studied Cannon for a moment, my eyes tracing the lines of ink decorating his neck. I itched to get closer, to run my fingers over the artwork covering his body. To understand the choices behind the patterns, the images. To understand the man before me.

"I know," I finally said. "And I apologize if I don't seem grateful. I am...indebted to you. For life. And possibly the next."

A small, low laugh escaped his lips, the sound jarring me with its rawness, like he didn't do it often enough.

Why? The question burned my tongue.

Why didn't he laugh more? He had a family of brothers on the ice, had a wonderful sister who loved him, a nephew who adored him, and countless fans who cheered for him. What darkness had sunk its claws so deep in this man that he could find such little joy in life? What fueled the fights and the intimidating-as-hell exterior?

I parted my lips, almost brave enough to ask the questions haunting my mind.

"Why did you put me in the guest room?"

Almost brave enough.

But I knew him better than he thought I did. Well enough to know he wouldn't let me in or tell me until he deemed me worthy enough. I simply hoped that day would come.

"Rule number five," he said. "No sex."

I laughed again. "And you think if I slept in the same bed as you I'd...what? Fall helpless to your spell? Lose myself with desire?"

Fire churned behind those dark eyes, and his tongue darted out to wet his lips.

The desire I joked about roared and thrashed.

"Of course not, Princess," he said. "You're much too strong for that."

"Then why?" I pressed. "I'm your wife, after all. I could stand to sleep next to you. Sleep, and nothing more."

Was I truly so repulsive to him that he couldn't even stand that?

His gaze was like a brand as he surveyed me, some inner battle raging inside.

Too long. The silence between us became my every mortification. So I switched back to sass and anger, our common ground.

"Snobbery isn't contagious, you know," I said, and pushed past him, heading for the door. I wanted to get my last two boxes and lock myself in my sweet little guest room and pretend none of this was happening. Pretend like I didn't want to dig beneath the surface with Cannon. Pretend like his proximity to me was anything more than a business arrangement.

Cannon beat me to the front door, his hand on the knob. "I think it's funny," he said, swinging the door open.

"What?" I asked when he didn't elaborate. I followed him outside, where the last of my things awaited. He scooped up the two boxes like they weren't filled with books and pumps, and paused where I stood at the edge of his porch. He glanced down at me and shook his head.

"That you think *you're* the dangerous one."

I narrowed my gaze, giving him a good glare before he stalked back into the house.

I remained outside, breathing in the fresh air because I knew the moment I stepped into his house, it would become *mine* for the foreseeable future.

Mrs. Cannon Price—sequestered to the guest room because her terrifying husband couldn't and *wouldn't* stand to let her in.

5

CANNON

My pain tolerance was something I'd honed over a decade in foster care and another decade pushing myself on the ice, and yet somehow, I'd reached my limit within the first thirty minutes of this engagement party. When Persephone had described the plans, she'd used words like intimate, small, simple, and my favorite—*thrown together* at her parent's house.

This was none of those things.

A string quartet played Mozart in the corner of what could only be called a ballroom. Who the fuck had an actual ballroom in their house? Oh, that's right—the VanDorens did. As for *small*, there were at least a hundred *intimate* acquaintances here in suits entirely too stuffy for the oppressive July heat. This was anything but simple. It was a goddamned three-ring circus, and I was the main attraction.

I'd never felt so out of place in my life.

"It really was so lovely to see you," Persephone said to yet another couple as we *worked the room*, as she called it.

With her hand hooked lightly in the crook of my elbow, we finished making our excuses and walked away.

"You're doing great." Her praise came with a smile that had the same knee-wobbling effect it had a month ago when we'd woken up in Vegas.

I grunted in response.

I'd been married to Persephone for a month. We lived together, ate breakfast together, and even read together in the evenings. It was…fine, it was awkward as hell, and yet as natural as breathing. She didn't put the TV on to fill the silence, or chatter incessantly, which put her at the top of my list for females I could tolerate spending more than a night with.

And at night, we parted in the hallway, and each went to our respective bedrooms, where, gauging by the glow of her skin and peppy early morning attitude, she slept like a baby. I, however, did not. I'd put her down the hall to keep as much physical space between us as possible, but that didn't stop my mind from crossing that distance every single fucking night. I'd woken up hard and aching every morning for the last month, and it wasn't getting any easier. Mostly because I was married to a fairytale Barbie with the body of a Playboy bunny.

"Oh, sweet heavens have mercy on my soul, please tell me —" Persephone whispered.

"Sephie!" The obnoxious cry sounded from across the ballroom, only to be repeated while a blonde wearing a white dress bounced up and down and waved her hand.

I took one look at my wife's stricken face and put the other woman on my don't-like-her list. Persephone schooled her features within a heartbeat and flashed a smile that didn't reach her eyes.

"We can escape through the side door," I offered in a low tone.

She laughed softly. "While I appreciate the offer, it would only delay the inevitable. My sister would simply follow us."

Her sister? That woman was the black sheep of the family?

"So it's onward into battle we go?" I asked, mimicking her southern accent.

This time her smile was real. "Prepare yourself," she warned as she straightened her shoulders. The move highlighted her breasts in the strapless, fifties-style, knee-length, white cocktail dress she wore. I'd wanted to remove it with my teeth the second she'd walked down our stairs in it. Instead, I'd told her she looked great and kept my damn hands to myself.

Rule number five was still in effect.

We moved through the crowd, heading toward the small group of people by the wall of windows who, shockingly, looked to be our age. Persephone's sister held out her hands and wiggled her fingers, which must have been some type of rich-girl summoning because my wife slipped her hand from my elbow and walked straight into her sister's arms.

"Sephie!" she cried, pulling away long enough to scan down Persephone's dress. "You look so lovely tonight!"

"Andromeda," Persephone greeted her with a smile, but her shoulders were still tense.

Andromeda. Thank God I wasn't actually marrying into this family. They'd probably force Persephone to name her first kid Hercules or some shit.

"You surviving?" Sawyer asked as he appeared on my left with his wife, Echo.

"Barely," I muttered, keeping my attention on Persephone.

"This might be the most uptight room I've ever been in," Logan muttered as he slapped my shoulder and stood next to Echo with his girlfriend, Delaney, who also happened to be my favorite librarian.

"I can't believe Mama let you wear that dress," Andromeda noted with a heavy undertone of pity. "You know it just washes you out without a little color." She held out her tanned arm to Persephone's sun-kissed one and shook her head.

"I don't spend my days by the pool anymore, Andromeda. I have a job," Persephone replied, lowering her arm. "And besides, it's tradition for the bride to wear white to her engagement party."

"You look radiant." I snuck my hand around my wife's tiny waist and tugged her to my side in a move that almost felt natural. She looked up at me with grateful eyes.

"So does that mean you're getting married too?" Echo asked, using her champagne flute to motion toward Andromeda's straight, short, white dress.

"Oh. Um. Of course not." Andromeda shrugged and beckoned a waiter with a snap of her fingers.

My pain threshold was discovering a new level.

"I'm actually just coming off a ridiculously painful annulment that I'm simply not ready to discuss yet," she said as she took a glass of champagne from the waiter's tray and then waved him off like he was a nuisance. "But at least I'm single, right? I mean, who wouldn't want to be single when there are so many excellent specimens of manhood around?" She batted her eyes at me, then glanced over at Logan and Sawyer.

My warning bells went off. Loudly.

"Who's looking for excellent specimens of manhood?" Michael Carlisle, trust-fund douche extraordinaire, entered our little circle with three of his friends. Guys looked like they belonged in an investment banking club or some shit. A kernel of annoyance grew in my chest.

"Michael!" Andromeda tilted her head and looped her arm through his. "I was just saying that I'm glad I'm single, seeing as my baby sister decided to marry one of Charleston's prized Reapers."

"So she did," he muttered, raking his gaze down Persephone appreciatively. "Caught us all off guard with this little move, Sephie."

She stiffened, and my hand tightened at her waist to keep from punching those roving eyes out of his head.

"Yeah, we all thought it would be you and Carlisle celebrating eventually," one of his friends agreed. "Imagine our surprise when this invitation appeared." His eyebrows rose.

"Don't be ridiculous, Andrew. You knew about Sephie's indiscretion the morning after when it hit the press, just like the rest of us," Andromeda chided.

"I'm not sure I'd call getting married an indiscretion," Persephone countered as the quartet started a new movement.

"Oh, I didn't mean to ruffle your feathers, honey." Andromeda shot another pity glance at Persephone. "God knows I've had my share of impetuous liaisons with incredible men that just didn't…work out. Not that I'd been bold enough to wear white to a post-wedding-night engagement party, but I always did love that spirit of yours!" Her grin dripped with saccharine sweetness.

Holy shit. I'd rather be on the ice, where we battled with sticks, boards, and bodies, than in this ballroom. This outright combat via sharp words and fake smiles was bullshit.

"Are you serious?" That little kernel of annoyance transformed to rage in a heartbeat. Persephone was still a virgin. Not that any of them knew that. Hell, I was still grappling with that fact, myself. I wasn't one of those assholes who prized virginity in their women, and the logical side of my brain listed her untouched state as reason number four billion and eight that we'd stick to rule number five. I'd never been with a virgin, and sure as hell wasn't about to make her my first by being her first. No fucking way.

But the primal side of my brain? Holy shit did it have a

field day knowing that no other man had been inside her. That I'd be the man she compared every other lover to...not that I was ever going to make love to her. *Make love?*

Let's call that little slip of the tongue reason four billion and nine I wouldn't ever know what this woman looked like when she came.

"What? She knows I meant no offense." Andromeda assured me in the sweetest voice imaginable. "We're all so happy for you, Sephie. Though, Andrew's right. I think we were all a little shocked that you ended up with a *hockey player.*"

Both Sawyer and Logan's eyebrows hit the ceiling.

"Holy shit," Echo muttered, then drained her champagne.

"And why exactly would that shock you?" Persephone challenged. "After all, I run the charitable foundation for the Reapers, so it's only natural that I would befriend them. I've known these men for almost two years now."

"Well," Andromeda looked me over with a ravenous glimmer in her eyes.

I was going to need a shower to scrub away her intentions.

"We can all see why you'd *get to know them*. I mean, of course, their bodies are perfect. They're professional athletes, but the fact that he's also gorgeous must have been quite the enticement to spend a little more time at the office, hmmm?"

"I'm standing right here," I said slowly.

"That is *not* why—" Persephone started.

"And don't you look good doing it?" She gave me a little shoulder-shrugging grin. "Honestly, Michael, you didn't see this coming from a mile away?"

"We've met," he answered, clearing his throat, then facing Persephone. "Though I can admit, I thought you'd fall for one of us." He arced his glass in front of him, as if she should have chosen someone from her own social circle.

Fuck that. I might not have been the right man for Persephone, but she was far better than any of these clowns.

"I've had quite enough investment bankers in my life," Persephone fired back with a shrug and a smile. Fuck, if that didn't make me want to lean down and kiss the shit out of her, audience and all.

"For now, maybe," he said softly.

It's not smart to wave the red cape at the bull, douchebag. I reined my temper in tight. Persephone's first rule was that I not get into any fights or make any scenes, and I wasn't about to break it in the middle of our fucking engagement party, even it was fake.

"You're an investment banker?" A smirk rose on my face. I'd been right.

"What of it?" His eyes narrowed on mine. "I work with millions of dollars every day, using my Harvard education, not my body to move upward in life. After all, one day my body might give out, but my mind never will." He dared me with a smirk of his own.

Logan's mouth opened, but Delaney's hand flew to grip his, effectively silencing my best friend. The girl was as southern as Persephone and recognized warfare when she saw it.

"It's impossible for your body to give out when it hasn't shown up in the first place," Sawyer glanced meaningfully toward the bankers and nodded at the passing waiter. He thanked him as he replaced his and Echo's empties with full glasses.

I pressed my lips into a flat line to keep a dark laugh down at Sawyer's obvious shade.

"How do you guys survive so many blows to the head, anyway?" Andrew asked with a perplexed expression on his pompous face. "You must have really thick skulls."

"Well, you know what Sartre said." Michael lifted his glass. "What doesn't kill you makes you stronger."

His buddies chuckled, along with Andromeda. Persephone jolted forward, but I kept my grip on her waist and subtly lifted so her feet were an inch off the floor. She gasped softly, and I set her back down in a move so subtle no one noticed it had happened except my wife, who hopefully got the point that I didn't need her to fight my battles for me.

"Sartre, huh?" I questioned. "Your Harvard education cover philosophy?

He arched an eyebrow and tilted his head. "Among other things. Where did you matriculate from? Assuming you went to college. I know so many young athletes get pressured to go pro too early and miss out on the benefits of a good school."

"University of Michigan," I answered. "They offered me a full-ride scholarship for hockey and threw one in for my little sister." That last part had been off the books, but a handshake later, Lillian had early acceptance.

Persephone looked up at me with such a tender expression that I couldn't help but return it, knocking loose one of the bricks that held up my emotional defenses. God, she was beautiful, and for the next couple of months, she was mine.

"Scholarship, huh? Guess they don't care about your grades up in Michigan as long as you're racking up the points on the scoreboard," Michael snapped, losing the edge off his civilized mask. Guy was outright pissed that I'd married the woman he'd set his sights on.

Made sense, really. Persephone was flawless in every way, even as she arched a delicate eyebrow at me as if asking what I was going to do about the outright shot he'd just fired at me. I winked at her, and her eyes flared bright with amusement and something else I couldn't let myself ponder.

Managing to rip my gaze away from hers, I turned back toward the douchebag brigade.

"Well, it's not Harvard up there, but at least they taught me that it was Nietzsche who said, "What doesn't kill *me* makes *me* stronger." Not Sartre."

Persephone's arm slid around my waist like she was claiming me, too.

Everyone looked at Michael like this was some kind of fucked-up tennis match, and I'd fired the ball back across the net.

He scoffed. "Bullshit. It's Sartre. I minored in Philosophy."

All the eyes turned back toward me.

"You're wrong." I shrugged as Andromeda gasped. Guess I stepped across the line of southern manners. "It's in *Twilight of the Idols*."

Ball's in your court, asshole.

He blinked. "I'm not wrong. You're wrong."

And now we were back in kindergarten. Phenomenal.

"Guy reads a lot, and I mean *a lot*. My vote goes to Cannon," Delaney announced with a nod.

"It's Sartre!" Michael snapped. "He believed that we had to be aware of existence and our own strengths."

"You're close," I admitted with a nod. "Sartre believed that we should be aware of our existence without the assumptions we naturally inherit through our routines, but Nietzsche authored the other quote."

Michael's face turned red. "You're wrong!"

"I'm not." I shrugged.

"Someone look it up!" His hand shook slightly. And somehow *I* was the one with a temper problem?

Cell phones appeared in various hands, but neither Michael, Persephone, or myself moved an inch.

"Oh man," Andrew muttered, looking at his phone.

"Ha! We win," Sawyer announced with a grin, turning his

phone so the others could see. "Nietzsche. *Twilight of the Idols. 1888.*"

The blood drained from Michael's face.

"Both were great philosophers." A corner of my lips lifted. "But have to say that I'm a bigger fan of Nietzsche's concept of the Ubermensch, the man capable of rising above life's hardships. Then again, Sartre's concept of bad faith is pretty great, too."

His jaw locked and flexed, and I couldn't help but continue.

"Bad faith? Come on, you know it. That's the one where we tell ourselves that things have to be a certain way because that's the way it's always been, and therefore close our eyes to the other options that exist around us. For example, by marrying me, Persephone has proven herself enlightened by Sartre's standard."

Every gaze turned back to him, to see how he'd respond to my volley but he remained silent.

"Our guy is smarter than yours," Sawyer whispered at Andrew.

Persephone yanked on my suit-coat, and I leaned down slightly just in time to see her rise up on her toes to brush a kiss over my lips.

It was quick. Soft and chaste, but the meaning behind it punched me in the gut and stoked the carefully contained fire of need that raged in my belly. She pulled back with a wide, pleased smile.

I was so fucked.

"This won't last," Michael's tone dropped low. "You'll never make it to the altar. Eventually she'll see that she's made the wrong choice—took the bad deal, so to say, and she'll back out." He nodded slowly.

I grinned at him with lips still humming from Persephone's kiss. Jesus, the woman *kissed* me. "Harvard, huh?

What? Daddy couldn't get you into Wharton?"

He blanched. Apparently, I'd struck a nerve.

"First off, we're *already* married, just in case you missed that memo. Two, you're right." Persephone stiffened next to me, but I kept going. "One day she'll see that I'm not good enough for her, but I somehow don't think that's going to help you, considering she *already* knows that about you. And lastly, you get to play with millions of dollars all day because men like me—" I gestured toward Logan and Sawyer, "—and my friends, make those millions with our talent, drive, and sheer fucking willpower. But don't worry, the first thing I'll do on Monday is make sure none of my *millions* are in any of your banks or hedge funds. I don't trust morons with my money any more than I trust douchebag assholes with my wife. So if you'll excuse us." I turned abruptly from the group, taking Persephone with me.

"Thank you for coming! It's always a pleasure to see you!" She fired over her shoulder as I ushered us toward the door. "Cannon, where are we going?"

"I need to talk to you." It came out more growl than statement.

"Oh. Okay. Here, this way, then." She took my hand and led me past a tuxedoed attendant into a dark hallway.

I counted to thirty, trying to cool the fire in my blood, and she pushed open a heavy door on our left once we were halfway down the hall. The smell of old books hit me as she flipped on the light switch and closed the door behind us.

The room was massive, with fifteen-foot high bookcases and a ladder that ran down each side of the wall. There was a sitting area on our left, complete with a fireplace, and a massive mahogany desk in the center of the room.

"Dad's study," she said simply. "He does most of his work in Charleston, of course."

"Of course," I repeated dutifully, taking in the clean expanse of his desk.

"What did you want to talk about? I thought you handled Michael quite masterfully." She toyed with her fingers, spinning her engagement ring as she placed herself in front of me.

"You kissed me," I accused.

She blinked, her lips parting. "Oh, that."

"Yes, *that*." I backed up a step to give us some space, but she took it right back.

"I wanted to show you my support." She turned those eyes on me with a pursed, worried set to her mouth. The same mouth that had been on mine moments ago.

"Then you pat my arm or give me a high five," I snapped.

She pressed her lips in a line as laughter danced across her face. "A high five? What am I, one of your teammates? Because if that's the case, I should at least get to pat your ass, not your arm."

I shoved my hands in my pockets to keep them off her. I'd never wanted a woman like I wanted Persephone. Never been taken to the maddening edge of obsessive need without so much as a kiss…except she *had* kissed me, and it wasn't enough. It was too much. It was all fucked up.

"Rule number five specifically states—"

She scoffed. "Rule number five says no sex. It certainly doesn't say anything about kissing you. Are you saying we need to negotiate our verbal contract?"

"It should be covered *under* rule five," I argued.

Her eyebrows popped high. "What? Why? It's not like I gave you a handjob or oral—"

"Oh my God, stop talking," I begged, spinning around so I could get the hell away from her. The imagery in my head was sinful, and I couldn't help but wonder if her fingers would manage to wrap all the way around my cock, or if she'd come up just a little short. I parked my ass at the edge of her dad's desk and gripped the heavy wood of the top.

"For being one of the NHL's baddest boys, you sure are a prude." She folded her arms under her breasts, drawing my eyes to her impressive cleavage and the single strand of pearls that nestled at her collarbone.

"Prude?" I snapped.

"What else would you call all this fuss over a little kiss?" She walked closer.

"I'd call it looking out for your best interest."

She arched an eyebrow in challenge but kept moving toward me.

"Persephone, if you had any idea of the things that go through my mind regarding that mouth, that body, you wouldn't just casually kiss me. You'd run the other fucking direction," I warned.

"Oh, really?" She stopped right next to me, her thigh inches from brushing mine. "You don't scare me, Cannon."

"I should." How many times did I have to warn her? Did I have to spell it out for her?

"Tell me why I can't kiss you." Her gaze darted to my lips, and I muttered a curse.

"Why? Because it's not just a kiss. Hell, I wouldn't even call what happened in there a kiss. It was an invitation to things that you don't want and aren't ready for." My grip tightened on the wood as she tucked a strand of hair behind her ears.

"You don't know what I want," she accused softly. "Tell me why I can't kiss you," she repeated.

Guess she really did need me to scare her off. Being platonic and careful around her had given her some misguided sense that I was one of the good guys. Fine. That was an easy enough mistake to remedy.

"Why can't you kiss me? Because I don't want a kiss. Not from you."

Her face fell. Good.

"I want way more than just your lips on mine, Persephone. I want your body splayed out naked beneath me, bared for feasting, begging for my mouth and hands. I want your mouth open for my tongue, and then I want to see those pretty pink lips wrapped around my cock."

She gasped, her lips parting, and her eyes widening slightly. Excellent. She was starting to understand.

"I don't want you to give me some little peck of approval in front of your friends so we can play out a lie. I don't want your feigned interest and fake, polite sighs of appreciation. I won't lie about need, and I won't let you, either. Not when I want you screaming my name with your legs wrapped around my hips as I drive into you, so fucking lost to your own desire that you don't care who the hell hears you or what your friends think because all you need is one. More. Thrust. To get you there." I stared at her lips, letting everything I'd said show in my eyes, letting the leash slip just enough to scare her off.

"Cannon," she whispered.

We locked eyes, and the temperature in the room rose by at least five degrees. God, I wanted her in every way I'd just detailed and so much more. I'd wanted her from the moment she'd fallen into my arms almost two years ago. She was everything right and good and pure in a world that had only shown me unimaginable cruelty.

"Cannon," she whispered again, moving that inch so our thighs touched through layers of clothing. She may as well have branded me.

"Persephone." I shook my head slowly, warning her not to do what her eyes already told me she was planning.

She leaned forward, giving me every chance to back away.

I should have. I needed to. I didn't. Instead, I watched her lips part and her eyes close a second before she kissed me. Her lips met mine in a gentle recreation of the kiss she'd given me in the ballroom. This time she lingered, her lips incredibly soft against mine. I meant to hold back, to teach her with my lack of reciprocation.

Instead, I kissed her back, gently sucking on her lower lip.

She cupped my face and leaned in for more. Fuck me, I could fall into this woman and never resurface for air. The thought jarred me, and I grasped her wrists lightly and pulled them from my cheeks as I broke the kiss.

Hurt flashed in her eyes, but it didn't overpower the desire I saw there. Or was that my own reflected back at me?

Bad idea. Horrible idea. Really fucking awful idea.

I abandoned her wrists, took her waist in one hand, and the nape of her neck in the other, and kissed her. She gasped with surprise, and I ran my tongue along the soft skin inside her lower lip. Then I took total possession of her mouth, stroking my tongue over the roof of her mouth and the line just behind her teeth. Fuck, she tasted like strawberries and champagne—all sweet and heady.

I groaned when her tongue rubbed against mine and nearly lost my shit when she licked that sweet little tongue into my mouth, exploring me the same way I'd just done with her. I tilted her head so I could kiss her deeper, then took her over and over. It wasn't enough. I needed more.

As if she'd heard my thoughts, she shifted her legs, looped her hands around my neck, and used me as leverage to climb. My grip shifted to her silk-clad ass as she settled in my lap like she'd been there a thousand times, her knees braced on either side of my hips.

Our mouths met in a fury of want and desire too long ignored. We were ravenous, as if we could sate the need of the last two years in this single kiss. Her fingers shifted to my hair as her hips ground over mine, drawing a groan from my throat as my cock swelled.

I wanted to touch her, to find out if her skin felt as soft as the fabric of her dress, but my hands were occupied keeping her from falling on her ass. I stood, carrying her slight weight, then spun to deposit her on the desk.

She didn't blink at the switch in positions, but merely took hold of the tie we'd fought over earlier in the evening, and pulled me down to her as she lay back against the expanse of cherry. Holy fucking turn on.

I sent one hand into her hair and closed my eyes in surrender as my lips found hers again. She was hot, spun silk, from the skin of her shoulder to the hair that spilled over my hand as I sank into her kiss. She was better than I'd ever imagined. How had I lived this long without knowing her taste?

She arched up against me, and my mouth traveled a path from her lips to the impossibly soft skin of her neck. She whimpered, her hips rolling over mine as I kissed her pulse. My girl had a button, and I'd just found it.

I tongued that little patch of skin, and she cried out, her fingernails biting into the back of my neck. When she rocked against my hips, sending shockwaves of pleasure through my cock that shot through the rest of my nerve endings, I switched my grip, sending one hand to her knee.

As I traveled south, caressing each millimeter of her neck as I went, my hand journeyed north, following the silk of her stockings until I reached a lace band and—

"You wear garters?" I growled against the base of her throat.

"Are you complaining?" She shifted so my hand slid further up her thigh, following the small strap that connected her stockings to the lingerie above.

"Fuck no. Everything about you is incredible." I lifted my head.

Her smile was the sexiest thing I'd ever seen in my life.

Our mouths met in a kiss that was even hotter than the last, our tongues as urgent as our breathing. My hand reached the top of her thigh and nearly trembled with restraint. How the hell had I not known she'd worn this under all that prim and proper fabric all night? I grazed the line where thigh met hip with my thumb, then followed it down until I found the edge of her panties—they felt like lace.

My mouth watered at the thought of burying my head between those thighs and finding out if she tasted this sweet *everywhere*. Instead, I dragged my thumb down the very center of her, using the friction against the lace to drive her higher in her need.

She yanked her mouth free, sucking in lungfuls of air as her eyes locked with mine, which narrowed slightly, daring her to stop me, to tell me she'd had enough.

The woman rocked against my fucking hand.

I hissed, feeling the lace grow damp beneath my fingers.

"More, Cannon," she pled, then rocked again so I knew exactly what she was asking for. Then she gripped my neck and pulled me back into her kiss.

Fuck, the woman kissed with a reckless hedonism that had thoroughly intoxicated me. My thumb drifted to the band that separated lace from flesh—

A soft click sounded, and I jerked my hand to her knee as the door opened behind me. I moved to instinctively cover Persephone, only to realize she was fully clothed. We both were.

The woman had driven me to the brink of madness with just a kiss.

"Oh!" Her mother laughed from the doorway. "There you two are!"

"Kill me now," Persephone mumbled, burying her face in my neck and holding me against her.

"We'll be right out," I replied, hoping I didn't sound as turned on as I felt. Fuck, my dick was harder than the desk.

"Oh, don't rush. I know how young lovers are!"

I felt Persephone cringe.

"It's just that your sister started in on the Hampshire boy and now she's…well…she's already broken three champagne flutes…"

"I'll be right there, Mama. Just give me a second to right myself," Persephone called out over my shoulder.

"Take your time, love birds! I mean, of course we want a grandbaby, but do be careful with the desk! It's an antique, you know!" The door clicked shut.

"Is she gone?" Persephone asked.

"She is."

She released the death grip on my neck, and I backed away like she'd bitten me. Space. I needed space, or I'd be right back on that desk, finishing what we'd started. Where the fuck was my self-control? My ability to shut it all off?

She just kissed it out of you.

I held out my hand against my better judgment, and congratulated myself when I managed to step away after helping Persephone off the desk. She smoothed the lines of her dress and ran her fingers through her hair.

"Do I look okay?" she asked, her eyes wide with worry.

"You look exquisite."

She offered me a tentative smile, but it faded as she looked me over. "Umm. Are you going to be…okay?" She glanced at my beltline.

"I've had worse. I'll be fine. Get out there and help your mom." My cock throbbed, calling out my lie.

She hesitated.

"Persephone, go. Before someone else marches in here."

She nodded, then walked out of the study, taking a second to lift her chin and transform into the VanDoren everyone expected.

Thank God I'd met her mother two weeks ago, or I might never have recovered the first impression. I got my body under control and headed out of the study, barely dodging the man I'd had yet to meet as he walked into the room.

"Mr. VanDoren." I held out my hand.

The older man was fit, and rather distinguished, with hair that leaned more toward salt than pepper and with a grimace where a smile should have been. He looked over the tattoos that sprawled from my wrist to my knuckles and tensed before meeting my gaze.

"Mr. Price." He ignored my outstretched hand. "Let's forgo usual pleasantries, shall we?"

"I prefer it that way," I answered, lowering my arm.

"Good. Let's get one thing straight. You're not good enough to marry my daughter." His eyes narrowed in challenge.

"You'll get no argument from me on that." He may as well have said that the sky was blue. *Duh, asshole.*

"Any man who spirits a young girl off to Vegas for some Elvis wedding without asking her father's permission for her hand or letting her mother attend isn't worthy of being a VanDoren." He folded his arms over his chest.

"I'm a Price, but you do have my apology for that. I'm afraid we got carried away." It was the most I was going to back down, and I only did it for her.

"Well, you're done getting carried away. I know all about your temper. I've read all about your lack of control, and I'm telling you that if you harm one hair on Persephone's head, I'll destroy everything and everyone you love."

Well, that turned all Godfather with a quickness.

"Mr. VanDoren, I would never hurt Persephone. You have my permission to cut me limb from limb if I ever so much as touch her in a way she doesn't appreciate." *For the few months I'll be married to her.*

He bristled, but his shoulders relaxed a little. "Good. Fine. Your purpose here is to make my little girl happy and keep her mother ecstatic for all the time she has left. Then I'll deal with the legal mess you two have created with your recklessness."

He turned and left me standing in the doorway of the study as he headed back to the party.

People like him with their preconceived judgments were the reason Persephone and I would never happen. Not for real. They'd remind me at every possible turn that I wasn't good enough for their first-class life because I'd been born into steerage.

It didn't matter how Persephone and I fit together, or how our chemistry ignited on a nuclear level. Nothing that happened between us back in that study would do us any good in the long haul, and yet it hadn't mattered when she'd been in my hands. The world could have burned down, and I wouldn't have cared. That was dangerous to both of us.

I had to keep my fucking hands off my wife if I wanted to come out of this marriage as sane as I'd been before going in.

6

PERSEPHONE

"*I want way more than just your lips on mine, Persephone.*"

Cannon's words replayed in my head over and over.

As did the memory of his lips on mine. His body pressed against me, winding me up like a coiled spring. The way he'd effortlessly lifted me and splayed me out on the desk as if we had all the time in the world to explore each other, taste each other. And *sweet heavens* did he taste so good. I hadn't been able to *stop* thinking about that kiss. About the way his touch had seared me to my very soul. And I wanted more. So much more—

"Why are you staring at me like that?" Cannon asked around a mouthful of cereal. "You've never seen a grown man eat Rice Krispies before?"

I blinked a few times, backing out of the memory but losing none of the heat pulsing in my blood. Hunger, fierce and brutal, nipped at every inch of my body. A need I never knew existed until Cannon had set his lips on me.

Lips that currently closed around another spoonful of cereal as he leaned over the kitchen island, eating breakfast.

It had been a week of this—a week of pretending like that kiss in my father's study didn't happen.

But it *did* happen, and try as I might, I couldn't stop thinking about it.

He continued to stare at me from over his bowl, eyebrows raised.

Waiting for an answer.

Oh, right.

I situated on my barstool, my phone with an email pulled up on the screen in my hand. "I was thinking of how to respond to this email," I said. "But naturally, you would think eating cereal makes you irresistible." I doubted my eye roll was very convincing because he gave me one of those rare laughs I'd started to look forward to.

"I never said anything about me being irresistible, Princess," he said, swirling that spoon along the edge of the bowl. "But I'm glad to know this does it for you." He brought the spoon to his mouth and somehow—though I didn't think it possible—he ate the bite in a sinfully seductive way that made me want to throw the cereal box at his head.

I scoffed and returned my focus to the unread email—despite having read it three times. I couldn't focus. Not with him and his spoon licking.

My cell vibrated in my hand, a text flashing over the screen.

Sister: The parents kicked me out. I need a place to crash. Be at your new hubby's in ten.

I jolted in my seat, the phone dropping from my hand.

"Shit!"

"What?" Cannon was instantly at my side, so quickly I hadn't seen him move, his cereal bowl forgotten on the other side of the island.

"My sister," I said, my heart racing, "is on her way here!" I bolted off the stool, my bare feet padding against the hardwood as I hurried to my room. "Help me, Cannon!" I hollered behind me, though I knew he'd followed.

"Help you what?" he asked as I darted into my room and into the en-suite bathroom.

I grabbed everything I used daily, cradling it against my chest as I booked it past Cannon and toward his room down the hall.

Cannon blocked my entry. "Oh, no, Princess, I said—"

"To *hell* with your rules, Cannon! Andromeda is nearly here, and if she finds out I'm sleeping in a guest room despite being blissfully married to your gorgeous ass, what do you think she'll say? You witnessed how she acted at the engagement party," I said. "She'll twist the information to her advantage." I paused, my heart sinking. "What do you think she'll tell my mother?"

He furrowed his brow. "She'd do that?"

"Yes. She'd do that and more." I sighed. "My parents kicked her out—it's not the first time—and she needs a place to stay."

"And you want her here, even though she could potentially betray you?"

"It's complicated."

"Obviously," he said, but he didn't move. "I don't understand the upper-class-gossip-war."

"She's my sister," I said, eyes pleading. "What would you do for Lillian?"

He moved and opened the door to his room, allowing me inside. All at once, I was hit with an essence of *him*—his smell, his books stacked on the nightstand by his bed and strewn across the dark wood dresser across the room. "What do you need from me?"

I swore I melted a bit at his words.

"Grab the clothes out of the dresser in my room, please? You can just toss them in here anywhere. I don't care. The gowns and dresses are fine hanging in the guest closet, since we can always say we were saving space in here. It's just the daily stuff—"

"I'm on it," he said, cutting off my ramble. He disappeared as I found my way into his bathroom and dumped the contents of my facial régime into a random drawer. I'd organize later. Or I wouldn't. I didn't know how long she'd be staying.

At least a night.

Which means...

I stared at the massive bed tucked against the back wall, a hot thrill rushing through me at the knowledge that I'd share that bed with Cannon tonight. His body next to mine, only inches separating—

"Clothes are done. Anything else?" Cannon's voice cut into my fantasy, grounding me in the present.

Right. So *not the time.*

"Thank you," I said as he finished shoving my clothes into a pair of empty drawers in the dresser on the opposite side of the bed. "I'll just go make the bed—"

"Done," he said, and I sighed.

"Thank you."

"You don't have to keep saying that," he said. "What else?"

"Well, if it isn't too much trouble," I said, wringing my hands. I heard a car screech to a stop outside. "If you could do that thing again."

He cocked a brow at me, and my skin flushed.

"Where you pretend to love me? Like at the engagement party? I know it'll take more effort on your part since she'll be staying here, but I'm not sure how long and I just—"

"We'll figure it out." He reached out, grazing his knuckles ever so gently over my cheek. The sweet, innocent gesture sent a white-hot tremor down the center of me.

I leaned into that caress, biting down on my gratitude since he'd told me to stop.

A firm pounding on the door broke the tension buzzing between us, and I jolted out of his touch. He dropped his hand, a muscle in his jaw ticking as I brushed past him and out of his room.

"You would not *believe* the way Waze took me to get here!" Anne said by way of greeting, stomping past me and dropping her two large Louis Vuitton bags on the floor. "This is such a cute little town! And an even cuter little house!" She scanned the interior—taking in the clean lines, open floorplan, and simple yet comfortable furniture Cannon had outfitted the place with. Little was the last thing I'd call the house, but my sister had much more lavish tastes than I ever had.

"Please, come in," I said, a bit sarcastically as she made herself at home. She found the kitchen and plopped on a barstool, reaching for the bowl of fruit I'd replenished this morning. Cannon loved a banana before his morning run.

She fiddled with an apple, crossing one leg over the other as she chomped into it.

I took a seat across from her, and Cannon elected to remain on the other side of the island as if he needed the distance.

"What happened?" I asked after she'd had a few more bites.

"Did you get these here?"

I nodded. "Sweet Water Farmer's Market."

"They're so much better than the ones in Charleston."

I raised my brows, not at all amused by the evasion. "What. Happened."

She huffed and sat her half-eaten apple on the island, not even bothering to reach for the small fruit plates I had next to the bowl.

Patience. Kindness. Compassion.

"Mother and Father totally overreacted," she said.

I waited, silent.

"They *did*," she insisted. The black from her mascara had smudged underneath her eyes, whether from tears or staying out too late, I wasn't sure. "I got kicked out of one itsy-bitsy club—"

"Which club?" I cringed when she didn't answer right away. "Not *the* club?"

A slow nod. Then she rolled her eyes. "I was drunk, and I got into a fight with Brittany. She tried to say...well, it doesn't matter what she said. She deserved a few slaps for it. Then she pulled my hair, and I don't remember much after that. Except that Gerald *threw* me over his shoulder! Can you believe that? The *nerve*." She sucked her teeth. "I should have Father fire him."

Anger bubbled beneath my calm exterior as I counted my breaths. I couldn't speak, not at the moment, because if I did, I would say—

"You get in a drunken fight so intense at your parents' country club that your head of security has to haul you out, likely for your own safety and that of the other guests, and *you* threaten to have him fired?" Cannon's voice was all hard edge, none of the softness from earlier. "Sounds to me like your parents kicked you to the curb for good reason."

My lips parted, but Anne's mouth dropped.

Yes, I'd been thinking the same exact thing, but she was *my* sister.

"Are you going to just sit there and let that inked-up creep speak to me like that?"

I raised my hands, palms up. "First things first, Anne," I said, surprised at the amount of control I held over my tone. "Don't ever speak about my husband like that. This is his home. And despite his lack of bedside manner, you *will* respect him while under his roof. If you can't accept that, you know I'll be happy to put you up at the Seasons."

She gaped at me like she'd never seen me before. I spared Cannon a glance, his eyes fixated on me in much the same way.

"Secondly," I said, returning my focus to her. "Did you try and apologize for your behavior?"

"Of course, you blame me." She shook her head. "I don't know why I thought I could come here and vent and simply be like normal sisters."

I flinched at the jab. The one she knew would hit home. Because we weren't normal sisters. We hadn't been for quite some time. Kind of hard to build a relationship with someone who constantly disappeared—usually right after destroying some family event. She'd broken my mother's heart so many times, and I honestly didn't know if I could take one more reckless decision from her.

"Fuck the Seasons," Cannon said. "Maybe we should put your ass on the street. Maybe then you'd learn you shouldn't bite the hand that—"

"Cannon," I chided, despite a piece of my heart lifting at his defense of me. I sighed, but he stopped talking. "Anne," I said, looking back at her. "You admitted you were the one who was drunk and got into the altercation. What happened after that? Because I know Father wouldn't have kicked you out if you had apologized."

"I may have kicked Gerald in the junk."

Cannon hissed.

"And accused him of copping a feel."

I cringed.

"I tried saying I was sorry this morning," she continued. "First to Gerald, then to Mother and Father. They weren't having it. Said they needed to issue tough love. They've kicked me out and cut me off. I have nothing but my car and those two bags."

"Good thing the bags are worth more than some people's cars," Cannon grumbled.

"Darling?" I said, my voice dripping with sarcasm.

"Yes, Princess?" He mimicked my tone.

"Could you give us a moment?"

"Gladly." He pushed off the island and disappeared, likely to his personal library. The one place he ever truly seemed happy.

"He's not intimidating at all," Anne muttered.

"He's not," I said. "Not when you get to know him." Which I was doing my best to do. "Anyway," I said. "What's your plan?"

"Ugh!" She rolled her eyes. "Why are you always on me about having a plan?"

"Well, do you have one?"

"No!"

"This is why I always told you to go to college. I told you to get a job, a project, something to give yourself independent funds—"

"Yes, you did," she cut me off. "But why should I do that? Why should I work and grind and be boring like you? When we have the means to go anywhere? Do anything? Anyone?"

"Because of situations like this, that's why!" I snapped. "And just because I don't country hop doesn't mean I'm boring! I happen to love my career and my friends and my family—"

"Career, ha, what a joke." She shook her head. "All you do is spend other people's money."

I sucked in a sharp breath, cooling the fire inside me. "Perhaps you *would* be more comfortable somewhere else."

The reality of her situation seemed to catch up with her because fear flashed in her eyes. "I have nowhere else to go."

"Fine. You can stay here until you've found a way to make it up to Mother and Father." I scooted off the barstool. "But, Anne, so help me if you insult me one more time—"

"I'm sorry," she said, her voice a bit quieter than before. "It's a habit."

"Why?" I folded my arms over my chest.

"Because you're the perfect one. The *good* sister. The one everybody admires and loves and favors."

"I'm far from perfect." I sighed. "And I'm far from the favorite. Mom can barely ever tell you no, and she's told me no plenty of times. Plus, Father would do anything for you."

"They kicked me out and cut me off!"

"Have you ever, for one second, thought they did that because of their love for you? Because they're tired of seeing you waste your potential, your life, drinking, and over-indulging, and who knows what else? Maybe once you have nothing, you'll realize what is worth giving up everything for."

A few tense moments passed before she stood. "Can you show me to my room? I'd like to crash until next week."

I nodded. "You carry your own bags here."

She snorted but retrieved her bags.

* * *

CANNON HAD MADE himself scarce the rest of the day, going as far to have a long lunch with the boys that turned into a dinner, and then after-dinner hockey gossip. Langley had been right, they were as bad or worse when it came to team melodrama, eating it up like candy.

I finally gave up on him coming home for the night and took a good long soak in his enormously deep tub, a favorite audiobook of mine playing from my phone on the table next to the tub. I figured the idea of actually sleeping in the same bed with me was so repulsive to Cannon that he'd crashed at Logan's or Connell's, but he'd kissed me so passionately at the engagement party. Played my body so perfectly, like he'd known all the sensitive areas even I didn't know existed. And yet, he wasn't *here*. My heart sank, but I swallowed the emotion as I climbed out of the tub an hour later.

After drying and lotioning up, I slid into one of my dark red slips, the silk cool against my heated skin, ready to sink under the covers and sleep off the strain of such a long day.

I froze upon exiting the bathroom, the steam from the room following me into the bedroom.

"What in God's name are you wearing?" Cannon snapped from where he was already tucked under the covers, a hardback clutched between his fingers.

"When did you get home?" I popped a hand on my hip.

"In the middle of your bath," he said. "I didn't want to interrupt. The audiobook you were listening to sounded...*interesting*." He cocked a brow at me, and my skin flushed. The romance novel I was currently listening to had just come to the incredible part where the hero and the heroine make love for the first time.

"You could've told me you were home."

"Were you worried about me?"

Yes.

"Do you need to be worried over?" I countered. "Figured there was nothing you couldn't handle."

He eyed my slip again, his opened book resting against a chest. A chest I now noticed was *bare*. I'd only seen it that one time in the locker room and now with him so close...sweet heavens, I wanted to pull those sheets back and see where those tattoos led.

"Again," he said. "What the fuck are you wearing?"

I glanced down at my slip—sure, my cleavage was on

display, but the length cleared my rear with a lace hem. "I sleep in this."

"No, you don't."

"Yes, I do. It's *hot*." I stepped toward the bed, and he snapped his book shut, the motion halting my progression.

"We have air conditioning. Rule number seven, you do *not* wear that to bed."

I huffed. "It's a southern July, Cannon Price! What would you suggest I wear?"

"Anything!" he growled. "Anything but that." He flung his arm toward his closet. "Grab literally anything in there, and it would be better than that."

A laugh escaped my lips—the intensity in his eyes, the crazed sort of panic in the tenseness of his body. "I didn't think I was your type," I whispered to ensure the words didn't carry across the hall to where my sister likely was sleeping or taking selfies. "Didn't think you found me attractive." My voice wavered a bit on that one, the truth and rejection fueling the tremble. His kiss had definitely said otherwise…but had he done that to prove a point? Prove that I could wind up underneath him, out of my mind with lust, just like every other girl he'd ever been with?

"Put. Something. Else. On." He cocked a brow at me.

The demand in his tone, the primal urgency in it, had me rushing toward his closet. Because damn it, I *liked* that tone. I liked that I made him uncomfortable. And I'd been thinking about his mouth on mine for a week straight.

I grabbed one of his T-shirts at random, tossing the silk in a corner as I yanked the soft cotton over my head. The gray material felt well-worn and nearly paper-thin, instantly melting against my shoulders and stopping mid-thigh. Some dark blue logo of a Viking rested atop my breasts, now peaked against the material as I walked out of the closet.

"Fucking hell," Cannon grumbled, sitting his book down again. "That's even worse."

I glanced down at the shirt and shrugged. "High school?" I asked.

He nodded, gripping the edges of his book a bit tighter. "The only one I ever liked."

"You went to several?" I asked, using the casual question to walk around to my side of the bed. I peeled the sheets back with the careful fingers of one defusing a bomb. My heart stalled as I sank into it, worried Cannon might bolt at a moment's notice.

"Yes," he said, the word clipped. "After Mom…" he cleared his throat. "I moved around a lot. One year I was in three different schools." He nodded toward the shirt as I tucked my bare legs underneath the sheet. "That school was the longest and my favorite. One year straight."

"It's important," I said.

Another nod.

"I should take it off." I moved toward the edge of the bed, but a gentle hand on my wrist stopped me.

"Don't," he said and groaned as he closed his eyes. "For the love of God, don't take anything off."

I laughed softly and turned to lay on my side, facing him.

He swallowed hard before marking the page in his book and setting it on the nightstand next to him. After he clicked off the lamp, he lay on his side, facing me, to my utter shock and delight. It took a few moments for my eyes to adjust to the dark, but once they did, Cannon's were intently on mine.

Mere inches separated us, and every beat of my racing heart was a plea to cross that invisible line. Heat sizzled in that space between us, and it flicked and licked the edges of my skin so much I had to shift my legs in an attempt to soothe the ache.

"Why did you make rule number five?" I whispered into the dark.

"You're a virgin," he whispered back.

"You didn't know that," I countered. "You came to my house with a list of rules you'd already made. Why that one?"

"Persephone," he groaned, and the use of my name instead of *Princess* had my toes curling.

"Because you've never...wanted me?"

"I'm pretty sure I answered that in your father's study."

Another breath, another stuttered beat of my heart. "Because I'm not your type?"

"No."

His answers were so sharp, but I liked the sting.

"Because you think you'd break me?"

He loosed a breath and dared to breach that distance between us, just enough to graze a fingertip along the line of my jaw. I arched into that feather-light touch, aching for *more*.

Cannon drew his hand back and tucked it under his pillow. He closed his eyes then, his breathing evening out so much I was sure he'd fallen asleep. I turned over to my back, unable to gather enough courage to touch him in return.

"Because I'd ruin you," he whispered just as the heavy blanket of sleep fell over me, his words settling between us like an anchor in a stormy sea.

7

CANNON

*H*ow the fuck did I wind up here?

"Hmmm. Okay, I think that should do it," the tailor said as he removed his tape measure from the area of my junk, and got off the little dais he had me standing on. "We're definitely going to have to let out an inch here at the inseam."

"Sounds good." No one liked having their cock strangled by their obnoxious dress clothes.

"If you'll wait here, Mr. Price, we have the vest in the back." The man took his flirty little assistant and headed for the back of the shop.

I wasn't against custom-tailored suits. I owned a shit ton of them. My objection stemmed from the fact that my mother-in-law, as fake as that title was, currently occupied the fancy-ass couch behind me.

"Cannon, dear, do you have a preference between the notched lapel or the peak?" Mrs. VanDoren asked as she flipped through the tailor's book of options.

"No, ma'am, I don't," I replied.

"Hmmm..." Her brow crinkled as she flipped between

two pages. She reminded me so much of Persephone. She had the same willowy, petite frame and blue eyes, but she kept her silver-streaked blonde hair up in a French twist. The woman was classic, but even better, she was kind. "I think the notched will look better with those broad shoulders of yours." She held the book up as if she could picture me in it.

"What are we discussing?" Andromeda flounced into the fitting area, flipping her gold-blonde hair over her shoulder.

"Oh, hello, darling. Why don't you sit next to me?" Mrs. VanDoren patted the seat next to her.

"Hi there, Cannon. Don't you look dashing in a tux." She gave me an appraising look that made my skin crawl. I'd seen that look far too many times on the faces of women who saw me as a challenge. They wanted to climb Mt. Everest once in their lifetime, but it wasn't like they wanted to set up a home at altitude or anything.

"Thanks, Anne." She'd demanded I use the nickname on her second day in my home. We were going on day eight, and she had both Persephone and me on edge with her constant whining and demands.

How the hell had such a graceful, dignified woman like Mrs. VanDoren raised such different daughters? Then again, how could a woman with such life in her eyes be terminally ill?

Anne plopped down next to her mother and looked over at the book. "Such good options. You know, from what Sephie has told me, you're not really a fan of tuxes."

"I'm not a fan of anything tight around my neck," I answered, glad that the tailor had given me an extra half inch at my collar when I'd asked for it.

"And you're still willing to wear a tux for the wedding?" Mrs. VanDoren asked with concern in her eyes.

"It's what Persephone wants," I answered simply. If the woman asked me to show up wearing a G-string and pasties,

I'd probably do it just to see her smile. She was so sad lately. Frustrated with her sister's overwhelming presence and the doctor's inability to find her mother a donor. I found myself joining her in that department.

"You two are going to have such a beautiful life together," Mrs. VanDoren remarked with a little sigh. "I'm so glad you're letting me do this—plan this little affair. It means so much to me to see my little Sephie walk down the aisle." She smiled up at me with a slight tremble. "Now if she'd just make time to get to the tux fitting," she teased.

"She said she'd make it if she could. Persephone is an incredibly busy woman," I replied with a nod as the tailor came back in. "She loves her career and does a lot of good around Charleston with the foundation."

"Aren't we all just proud of her," Anne quipped with a tight smile.

"Of course we are," her mother said softly. "And Cannon, I really appreciate you letting us be here. Seeing as you don't have your mother with you."

"Where is mommy dearest, anyway?" Anne asked, taking a bottle of water from the end table.

My stomach clenched.

"She died when I was younger. Is that for me?" I asked the tailor, hoping the abrupt change of subject would signal that my mother's death wasn't up for discussion.

"Yes, Mr. Price." The tailor handed me the vest, and I put it on, then buttoned the avocado green fabric over the tuxedo shirt.

"The color's all wrong!" Mrs. VanDoren chided as she stood.

"This is the color you ordered, Mrs. VanDoren," the tailor assured her.

"It most certainly is not. Maybe if this was nineteen

seventy four, or we were looking for baby-vomit, but I assure you, that is not the color we ordered."

"I have the order right here," his assistant said, flipping through her notebook. "The color was called in last week by Andromeda VanDoren?"

Anne stood and folded her arms. "I ordered silver like you asked, Mama."

"Oh," the assistant's brow furrowed. "Well, there's only two numbers different from silver, so maybe I took it down wrong?"

"Of course you did." Anne arched an eyebrow. "And you'd better get it fixed before the wedding."

I would have bet my entire year's salary that Anne had called in the number wrong on purpose. She'd been a bitter little witch the entire week whenever Persephone brought up the wedding.

"Okay," Mrs. VanDoren put her hand out to her daughter to settle her down. "I'm sure something can be done. Let's not panic. Claude, why don't we step into the back and see what fabric you might have on hand. Cannon, do you mind waiting for just a second?"

"No, ma'am. I'll be right here." This entire shitstorm my life was wrapped up in was to make the woman happy, so I'd stand here until the shop closed if that accomplished the mission.

"Thank you, dear." The three of them walked out of the fitting area, leaving me with Anne and a massive headache.

"Why don't you call her Sephie? I've been meaning to ask you." Anne asked as she walked closer.

"Because Sephie is the name of a child, and Persephone is a grown-ass woman," I replied, examining the cuffs of the shirt.

"Hmmm. Is she, really?" Anne challenged as she walked

around the dais, studying my pants. "The fit is good." She grabbed a handful of my ass and squeezed. "*Really* good."

"What the hell do you think you're doing?" I seethed, stepping away from her. Was it the first time a woman had grabbed at me without my permission? No. Boundaries were something that some fans didn't quite understand. However, it was the first time the sister of a woman I was involved with had done it.

Are you really involved with Persephone? Or just married to her?

"What does it look like I'm doing?" Anne stepped up on the dais and immediately came at me like I was going to welcome her advance.

"Back the fuck down," I warned her as I stepped off the platform. "I'm married to your sister." Jesus, Persephone was going to be crushed when I told her.

She scoffed. "Married? So what? Sisters share." She shrugged.

"I'm not a fucking sweater from the GAP," I hissed softly, hoping her mother wouldn't hear. That would definitely fuck up mission Keep-Mom-Happy. I folded my arms across my chest and stood my ground. I wasn't letting her chase me all over the goddamned shop.

"Like I'd shop at the GAP." She stalked forward, eyeing me like prey. "And come on, Cannon. I know your rep, both on the ice and with the women. There's no way a man like you could be satisfied with a frigid, fragile little princess like my sister." She smirked. "Because I'm well aware that she doesn't know how to please a man. And honestly, no man would look as frustrated as you do *all* the time if he was getting what he needed at home."

"Are you out of your fucking mind?" Rage blossomed in my chest, fierce and undeniable. I'd never put my hands on a woman in my life, but I'd never encountered a snake like

Anne, even living in some of the shittiest situations a kid could be put in.

"I'm sorry?" She looked genuinely confused.

"Holy shit, are you that used to getting your way that you can't understand that I don't want you? That there's zero fucking chance I'd ever touch you willingly? Persephone is *everything* I've *ever* wanted. Everything I will *ever* want. So I'll ask you again—are you out of your fucking mind?" It didn't matter if I really was as sexually frustrated as she'd accused. Hell yes, I was on edge. I slept next to Persephone every single night, wondering if it would be the night I finally snapped and took everything she'd offered back in the library—took everything I wanted. My control was a single, thin, fraying thread when it came to my wife, but there wasn't anyone else I wanted.

Anne's eyes flew wide, but she stepped the fuck away from me, so I counted it as a victory.

"She sure as hell is!" Persephone stood in the doorway, looking furious as hell and all the more beautiful for it. And *shit*, her mother occupied the other.

"Sephie…" Anne turned with her palms facing outward. "You misheard—"

Persephone marched forward. "I didn't mishear *shit*."

"Girls," their mother beseeched softly.

"No, Mama," Persephone shook her head but didn't look away from Anne. "She's fucked up her last three marriages, and that's on her. I'll be damned if she's going to try to come between my husband and me."

Damn, my wife had bite. She wasn't some docile little kitten, though her looks advertised otherwise. She was a fullgrown tigress with the claws to match. She was holding her own in a situation where I would have stepped in front of her and handled a year ago. That emotion welling up through me? It was pride.

"That wasn't—" Anne started.

"I heard it *all*!" Persephone snapped. "Now in the interest of our mother, I'm telling you to get in my car so I can take you back to my house, where you will promptly pack your shit." Even with her sweet, southern drawl, the words packed a punch.

A corner of my mouth lifted at my wife's use of *shit*, *fucked*, and *damned* in front of her mother.

"Oh...but..." Anne looked at her mother, who shook her head. Then she turned to me.

"What? Like I'm going to help you? What my *wife* says goes in our home." I shrugged.

Defeated, Anne raised her chin in the air, plucked her bag off the couch, and walked out of the shop ahead of Persephone.

"I'll see you at home?" I called out.

She turned and offered me a sad smile. "Don't stay out too late."

"I'm right behind you."

With that promise, Persephone left the shop. The silence was broken by Mrs. VanDoren's stuttered sigh.

"Don't worry about them," I assured her, sitting her down and cracking open a bottle of water for her.

She sipped at the water with a straight back and a shaky grip. "I'm so sorry, Cannon. Andromeda...she's..." Her eyes squeezed shut.

"You don't owe me an apology."

"I do. I just...I love both of my girls. I need you to know that."

"I do. They know it, too. And they'll work it out. Don't worry." I spotted her driver lurking near the doorway.

"How do you know?"

"Well, first, Persephone agreed to drive her home. She's

not making her walk, and second, they're sisters. I would do anything for my sister."

She pressed her lips in a thin line but nodded. "Right. You're one of the good ones, you know that? Persephone's own knight in shining armor." She patted my cheek, and I let her.

I muttered my thanks and made sure she got to the car safely with her driver, keeping my thoughts to myself.

I wasn't Persephone's knight. I was her personal devil.

I ditched the tux, then picked up takeout from Persephone's favorite comfort food restaurant and headed back home. It had to have been about an hour and a half after she'd stormed out with Anne, which meant she'd had an hour to deal with her sister.

Carrying the takeout bag in one hand, I walked into the house through the garage, unsure of what was waiting for me.

The smell of bleach stung my nostrils as I hung my keys by the door. But it wasn't Monday or Thursday, which meant Margaret, our housekeeper, hadn't been here.

"Persephone?" I called out as I walked into the kitchen, where the bleach smelled the strongest. "Are you trying to get rid of a body? Because I've heard lye is the way to go."

"Right here." She was scrubbing the shit out of the counter in the corner of the kitchen.

"Everything okay?" I set the food on the counter and approached my wife carefully. For all the time I'd known Persephone, I'd never seen her so…frenzied.

"Of course, everything is okay!" she snapped, working an area of granite so hard I wondered if we'd have a permanent divot there. "Why wouldn't it be okay?"

"Princess…"

"Don't call me that! Not after she called me…what was it?

A *frigid, fragile little princess?*" She moved slightly to her left and started scrubbing even harder.

"You're not any of those things," I said softly.

"You should have heard her once we got home." She shook her head, flipped the sponge over, and started again. "Saying that I'd never keep you. That a man like you needed more than a woman like me. That I should have let her have you, because then at least you'd be satisfied enough to stick around with me, and the worst part is maybe she's right!"

I reached my arms around her and captured a wrist in each hand. "Drop the sponge. You're murdering our counter."

"It's not our counter!" she cried as the sponge slapped against the granite. "It's yours because we're not really married! I don't care what that license in the safe says!"

My heart didn't just hurt. It ached at the raw pain in her voice. I made quick work of removing her rubber gloves, then turned her in my arms and caged her against the counter so she wouldn't run off before I'd had my say.

"Persephone."

When she wouldn't look at me, I tipped her chin up and found her blue eyes sparkling with tears and rage. Now that was a feeling I knew all too well.

"I don't want your sister." She looked away, and I waited until she dragged her gaze back to mine. "I wouldn't want her even if I wasn't married to you."

"I appreciate that." So ladylike.

"We're legally married. That counter is half yours. It's going to be *all* yours if you keep scrubbing it like it's personally offended you."

Her lips twitched in a smile, but it faded fast. "I'm just so mad. So *fucking* mad."

"Damn, it's hot when you swear," I muttered with a grin. "You're beautiful when you smile."

I blinked. Gorgeous, hot, fuckable…those were the compliments I was used to getting. "You're always beautiful."

Her lips parted.

I cleared my throat and backed up. "I know how to work out the rage."

She arched an eyebrow. "Does it include removing my clothes so I can prove I'm not frigid?"

Damn, that word must have really hit home for her to dwell on it like this. "No, but it involves you getting cold."

Her brow puckered, and I motioned for her to follow me. I led us through the kitchen and down the hall toward the steps that led to the basement. I flipped the switch and shut the door behind us as we descended, then opened the door at the bottom of the staircase as we approached.

Cold air smacked us in the face as I shut the rink door.

Persephone's jaw dropped as she saw why this house only had two bedrooms. The entire basement was a half sheet of ice. "This is amazing."

"Cost me a pretty penny, but it keeps me from punching the shit out of people when I get mad, so I figure it's out-earned itself bail money." I led her down the rubber-floored walkway to the alcove that served as my personal locker room. It was lined with four giant, wooden lockers. "You never realized it was here?"

She shook her head as I handed her a pair of brand new skates. "When you gave me the tour, you pointed to the basement door and grunted, '*mine*,' so I steered clear."

Had to love a girl who respected a man's privacy. *Love*? I wiped that thought straight out of my head.

"Those are your size. I had them made for you when you moved in." I quickly got my skates and sat on the wide wooden bench.

"That's so sweet," she whispered, running her fingers over the lavender laces. "Thank you."

"You're welcome." I motioned to the locker behind me. "I have a clean sweatshirt in there so you don't freeze."

She glanced down at her yoga pants and tank top. "Oh. Right. I changed right after I threw Anne in a cab."

I quirked a brow as I started lacing my skates under my athletic pants. "No driver?"

"Nope. She can kiss my ass."

I laughed, then helped her get her skates tied once she had my sweatshirt on. "They're stiff when they're new. You'll have to break them in."

"Are you saying I can skate down here?" she asked as we walked toward the ice. Her steps were steady. Good, she'd spent some time on skates.

"Any time you want." I grabbed one of my sticks and one I'd bought for her, then picked up the bucket of pucks and stepped onto the ice. "Can you skate?"

"A little." She glided out onto the ice easily. "I've never been in hockey skates, though. Only figure skating ones."

I dumped the pucks in a pile about ten feet from the net as she made a small loop around the rink, testing out her skates. My sweatshirt dwarfed her, almost reaching her knees. She was pretty much shapeless in that thing, and yet I'd never seen her look sexier. Her hair was up in a knot, showing off the line of her neck, and something primal sat up and took notice when I saw her skate away with my number on her back.

"Okay, get over here and vent your rage," I ordered, holding out her stick.

"Oh, I'm left-handed," she remarked.

"I know. It's a left-handed stick."

Her eyes flared. "You notice way more than people give you credit for."

"Not really. I just happen to notice everything about *you*. Now start shooting." I moved over and took a few shots myself so I didn't have to see her face after that comment. I wasn't even sure why I'd said it, other than knowing that she needed to feel desirable, to know that her sister was an evil, wrong bitch for what she'd said.

"Lower," I pointed to her hand. "You can't grip it like a golf club."

She swung again, and I cringed as the thousand dollar stick struck the ice at the completely wrong angle. "I can't even do this right!"

I skated over and stopped a few inches from her. "Let me help."

"How the hell do you skate like that?" She shook her head. "I mean, I know you're the fastest skater in the NHL or whatever, but you seriously move like those things are part of your feet."

"Fastest skater or *whatever*," I muttered with another grin as I spun her around. "Leave it to you to minimize my number one selling point." Wrapping my arms around her from behind, I put my hands over hers to give her the right grip.

"It's just never been what I think of when you come to mind." She turned her head so her lips nearly grazed my cheek.

Fuck, she smelled like apple blossoms again, and the scent went straight to my dick. After living with the woman for the past six weeks, I'd hoped that her effect on me would lessen, but that wasn't the case. I just found more things to like about her and had more chances to stare at her, which led back to finding more things I liked about her.

"Okay, then what comes to mind when you think about me?" I challenged her, working her arms through the shot.

"Well, first impression was your reflexes." She smiled, and I swore to God, I felt my chest crack open. "Because you caught me."

"In the hallway. I remember." I backed away after the second shot she took, letting her find her own rhythm.

"And then I realized how smart you are. Stubborn closely followed." She shrugged at me, but she was still smiling when she turned to fire more and more shots at the net.

"Hmmm."

"That's a lie…" She turned to me, wobbling for a second on her skates, but catching her balance.

"I'm not stubborn?" I fired a puck at the net, hitting the top right pocket.

She followed my shot and rolled her eyes. "Oh, no. You're as stubborn as a mule. I mean, I recognized your reflexes first, but then I looked up at you and thought you were the most beautiful man I'd ever seen."

My grip slackened on my stick, and I nearly dropped it.

"I still think that."

"Figured the tattoos would have scared you off." My fingers spread over my sternum, trying to rub away the glow that her words sparked.

"Nope." She skated closer, running into me slightly when she couldn't stop. I gripped her elbows to steady her, then let go. "You've never scared me. Infuriated me? Absolutely. Frustrated me? Daily. But I've always known I was safe with you."

"You are." The words came out embarrassingly gruff.

"I know. The artwork doesn't hide the man you are, Cannon." She swallowed and looked away. "Thanks for bringing me down here. You definitely worked off the anger to a manageable level." She gave me a half-hearted, fake smile, and skated off the ice.

We'd left a mess on the ice that I'd have to clean up later, but that little stomp of frustration coming from the bench area told me Persephone was the bigger mess, so I skated her way.

I came off the ice and propped my stick in the rack next

to hers. "Why don't we scrap the dinner I brought home and eat out—hey, what's wrong?"

"Nothing. Go skate." Her muffled voice came through her hands, where she sat on the bench, holding her head.

"Bullshit." I dropped to my knees in front of her and lifted one of her skates into my lap. Her feet were so small compared to mine. "Start talking." My fingers made quick work of the unlacing.

"Why?" She raised an eyebrow at me and pursed those kissable lips. "It's not like you talk to me."

"I'm also not the one who needs to do the talking." I gripped her calf lightly and removed the skate.

"Because you're such a well-balanced, open book."

She had a point. Fuck, this was why I avoided relationships at all costs. I liked my life the way it was and didn't want to drag out old shit by talking about it. But I didn't mind her knowing a little more about me as long as she didn't mind when she found something she didn't like.

"Fine. I'll answer one of your questions if you answer mine," I offered as I picked up the next skate and put it in my lap.

"What was your first impression of me?" she questioned softly.

I glanced up at her, then focused on untying her skate. "That you were clumsy as hell."

She scoffed. "Seriously? I give you *beautiful,* and you give me clumsy? This game sucks."

I smiled as my fingers yanked her laces free easily. Then I did the same move with her leg, cupping her calf and taking off the skate, but this time I didn't let her leg go when the skate hit the floor. "I couldn't let you fall. You looked tiny and as delicate as glass, and I was afraid you'd shatter if you hit the floor. Irrational, but that was my first thought."

I dragged my gaze up over my Reaper hoodie and found

her eyes already on me, searching for something I didn't know how to give her. But I wanted to. For the first time in my life, I wanted to please someone who wasn't in a position of power. Old childhood habits died hard.

"Tiny. Well, I guess I *am* short." She shrugged.

"You guess?"

"Anyone is short next to someone who's six-five." Her nose crinkled as a smile spread across her face.

"True." It was the smile that broke me. "I thought you looked like an angel."

She sucked in a breath, her eyes flaring.

"I got you back on your feet, and your eyes…" I slammed mine shut for a second, remembering the moment. "Everything about you cut me to the quick because I knew you were the kind of woman I could never have."

The air between us thickened with that electrical charge I only felt around her.

"Okay." She nodded, not asking why I could never have her. Somehow this woman knew exactly when to push and when to let something go when it came to me. "I was thinking about what Andromeda said."

I nodded, figuring that had been it. "And?"

"Maybe I am frigid. Maybe that's how I wound up a twenty-four-year-old virgin." She gave me a self-deprecating little chuckle. "I just never felt that hunger for someone before, you know? Not that I haven't been to third base. I have. I'm not *completely* inexperienced or anything. But when my boyfriends would press me for sex, I'd just break off the relationship, because let's face it. If you've been dating someone for six months and still don't want to sleep with them, something's wrong."

Suddenly I wanted to know the name of the guy who'd made it to third base with her and permanently remove his hands. *Jealous much?*

"I agree. And you're not frigid." My hands moved to her knees.

"You can tell that from one little kiss?"

"Yes. But I knew that the minute you bought me at the date auction."

Her cheeks colored. "Right. That. I was just trying to save you from—"

"From the hot brunette in the second row?" I teased.

"Was she hot?" Persephone blinked at me with mock innocence. "I guess I didn't notice."

"Right. Look, no woman who's frigid or scared of sex climbs a man like a tree in her dad's study and then begs him to keep going when his hand is one scrap of lace away from her pussy." There. I said it.

Her jaw dropped.

"I couldn't think of a less vulgar way to put it." I shrugged.

"You put it just fine." Her hands gripped the edge of the bench on either side of her knees. "I didn't want you to stop."

"Persephone." It came out as a strangled plea. For what? For her to stop? Or for her to continue?

"Was my sister right? Am I keeping you from finding… satisfaction because I've got you tangled up in this marriage?"

"I haven't been satisfied since the day I met you," I admitted, knowing my honesty would eventually come back to bite me in the ass. "But if you're asking if I'm going to lose control of my cock because I haven't gotten laid in the last few months, then the answer is no. And as for what your sister said—I got more satisfaction from kissing you than I have from any sexual encounter I've ever had." It was true. Sex had stopped being fulfilling once I'd laid eyes on Persephone. Once I started seeking out brunettes so I couldn't give in to the fantasy and pretend I had her beneath me.

"I bought you because I didn't want to see you leave with another woman," she admitted in a whisper.

"No." My hands flexed, sliding up to her mid-thigh as need pooled, thick and heavy in my dick. This was a bad idea. We had to put the walls up. Had to ignore the attraction. This could only end in two ways—badly or fucking horribly.

"It's true," she snapped. "I didn't want to think about you on a date with someone else. Not that I didn't hear about your escapades from the gossip mill, but that night I just couldn't stand to know I'd sent you on a date with someone else."

I rose on my knees, bringing us level. "No. You bought me because you couldn't stand to think about me *fucking* someone else. It had nothing to do with the date." I pushed her thighs apart and filled the space between them, leaving only inches between us.

"Maybe." Her breath hitched.

"No maybe about it, Princess." My hands rose on her thighs until I gripped her hips.

"Don't—"

"I call you *Princess* because to me, you're untouchable. You're so far out of my fucking league that you might as well be royalty. Not because you're cold or fragile, because you're not. I've felt the passion in you, and you prove to me every single day that you're anything but delicate. Don't punish me for shit your sister says and stop letting her in your head. I call you *Princess* because you're fucking flawless. That's what I saw that day in the hallway. What I see every time I look at you. You. Are. Fucking. Flawless."

Her mouth was on mine before I could comprehend what I'd just admitted to her. Her tongue licked at the seam of my lips, and I opened on instinct, then groaned at the taste and feel of her. Fuck, I hadn't imagined it, hadn't blown it out of proportion. Our chemistry was combustible.

I raised a hand to the nape of her neck, then slid my fingers into her hair, not caring that I was fucking up her little messy bun. Then I tilted her head and kissed her hard and deep, pouring every single ounce of my need and frustration from the last week into it. I kissed her like I'd wanted to when she'd walked out of my bathroom in that damned silk nightgown. Like I'd wanted to every morning when I found her sleeping peacefully next to me.

She gripped the back of my neck and held me tight against her, whimpering slightly when I'd pull back, just to fall into her again. How the hell was I going to walk away from this woman when I was already addicted to her?

I'd been addicted since the moment we met.

Her hands slid down my torso, and I felt my shirt rise over my stomach. I broke our kiss and raised my arms as she took it off. She looked over my body with hungry eyes that showed nothing but appreciation. Then her fingers followed just *above* my skin, no doubt remembering how I'd reacted in the locker room, air-tracing my tattoos from the dragon that breathed fire from my left shoulder to the inked hands that looked as though they were reaching across my pecs to grip the flaming, crowned heart detailed in the center of my chest.

"It's the only empty place," she whispered as her fingers framed the colorless, empty heart. "Why?"

"To remind me that no one owns me."

Her gaze flickered to mine, but I let her finish her exploration up my neck, where the tats ended until she cupped my face. "You are extraordinary."

I kissed her in reply, pulling her against my chest, then lifted myself in the same motion to spin her back on the bench so she sprawled out beneath me. This thing was three feet wide, and I was suddenly thankful for every inch. She broke away, sending my hoodie, then her tank top to the floor, leaving her in a cream-colored lace bra that cupped her breasts.

"God. Persephone. Don't—" I shook my head, but she was already tugging me back down to her mouth, to her kiss that stole my words away.

I trailed kisses down her jaw, then skimmed her neck, pausing just above that magical little place that had driven her mad in the study. I tested my little theory, kissing, then sucking lightly on the spot.

She arched beneath me as goosebumps rose down her arms, so I did it again and again until her fingers threaded through my hair, and she sighed my name.

One day I'd make her scream it.

Ignoring the caution lights in my brain, I kissed my way down to her collarbone, then to the valley between her breasts. Persephone might have been petite, but her breasts weren't—they were the perfect size to fill my hands, but not overflow them. The pale, soft orbs rose with every breath, and my mouth fucking watered as I lowered my lips to the nipple that showed through the lace.

"Persephone?" I asked, hovering above her.

"God, yes!" She arched, bringing her breast to my lips. I licked and sucked her through the fabric while I palmed its partner, then groaned when she filled my hand exactly like I thought she would. She was so responsive beneath me, like a living flame, and I wanted to feel her skin under my tongue, not this lace.

I reached under her back and unfastened her bra with one hand. She stripped it off herself, leaving her bare to the cool air of the rink. Perfect breasts. Perfect, pink nipples. Perfect Persephone.

"I told you. Fucking flawless." Our eyes locked for an instant, hers glazed with want.

She cried out when I sucked her into my mouth, my tongue swirling over her as her hips rose beneath me. I let myself rock against her once, my cock hard and insistent at the seam of her pants.

"Cannon," she moaned, sending another jolt of white-hot need down my spine. Her hand reached across my abdomen, and I barely caught her before she got to my cock. "Please? Let me."

I rose above her. "You touch me, and we'll violate rule number five," I growled against her mouth.

"Then fuck rule number five." She stared up at me with heavy, crystal blue eyes. "Please, Cannon. I want you. I've never wanted anyone the way I want you." She nipped at my lower lip to make her point.

Her first time wasn't going to be on a goddamned bench. It wasn't even going to be with *me*. Pain, sharp and vicious, ripped through my chest at the thought, but it was true. The only way to get us out of this thing unscathed was to hold to that fucking rule.

"Please," she repeated, rocking her hips so my cock gave her the friction she sought. "God, you feel good. You make *me* feel good. Please don't stop."

I groaned from both the pleasure screaming through my body and the heady nature of her words. Fuck, her breaths were coming faster, her thighs were tight around my hips, and she was flushed from cheeks to breasts. Getting her off would be so fucking easy, and then at least one of us would get some relief.

I sank into her kiss and sent my hand down her belly, savoring the dips and hollows of her curves until I reached her waistband.

"This is up to you," I reminded her in the softest voice I could manage.

"Teach me." She placed her own hand on top of mine and then guided me under that fabric, and then the soft lace of her thong. Holy shit, the woman wore garters and thongs. I wasn't just fucked, I was royally, completely fucked.

"Take whatever you want," she whispered in my ear as she slipped her hand free, then sucked on my lobe gently.

I shuddered at the simple caress. "I'm not taking. I'm giving," I promised.

Then I braced my weight carefully on my elbow, rolling slightly to the side, and kissed her senseless while my fingers trailed down, down, and found her wet and slick.

"Fuck," I growled. "Persephone." She was ready. So fucking ready. My cock pulsed in time with my heartbeat as I parted her, then slid my finger from her pussy to her clit.

She cried out, gripping my neck and my arm, her eyes flying to mine. "Again," she demanded. "Do it again."

So I did. I circled her clit and teased every nerve ending until she swelled beneath my fingers, and she soaked the fabric of her thong. Her hips rose and fell with my touch, trying to gain enough control to ride my hand. I gave her a touch then backed away, barely brushing her clit, then retreated as she started to writhe beneath me. Pure fucking fire.

"Cannon! Touch me!" she shouted.

"I am touching you." I swirled two fingers around her opening, then dragged them up and around her clit. I could play this woman all goddamn night and never get bored. Fuck that, I could play her body for the rest of my *life*.

"You know what I mean!" She kissed me, and I nearly gave in as her tongue worked over mine. Her hips bucked under my hand, and I flicked her clit once. She cried out again.

"Tell me why you bought me." I kissed the edge of her mouth. "Tell me why you didn't send me out with someone else."

Her eyes locked on mine, fierce and wild. Then she softened. "Because I wanted you, damn it! Because I didn't want you to fuck another woman. I wanted you to fuck *me*, and it was the closest—"

I pressed down on her clit as satisfaction roared through my veins. She'd wanted me. Not the hotshot, douchebag banker. *Me*.

She moaned, loud and long as I stroked her over and over. "Yes. God, yes. More. Cannon, *more*."

If she ever realized the power she held over me every time she said my name like that, I'd be done for. I circled her pussy, and slid one finger in slowly.

"Is that what you want?" I asked, sucking at that spot on her neck.

"Yes!" she shouted.

She was so fucking tight, her muscles constricting around that one finger. *Virgin*, I reminded myself, and slowed even more, stroking her walls as I began to pump her slowly while my thumb worked her clit. When she started to ride that finger, I nearly came in my fucking pants like a teenager. Her sensuality was off the charts. How could she ever believe she was cold?

I carefully added a second finger and ground my dick against the bench to keep myself under control. God, she would feel so good around me—all hot, wet silk when I—

No. Because I wasn't *ever* going there.

Her breath came in stuttered gasps as she kissed me, her fingernails digging into my skin, reminding me that this wasn't a dream. I had her beneath me. Her tongue was in my mouth. My fingers were in her pussy. For this exquisite moment, she was mine.

Her thighs began to tremble, and she keened a cry that was half pleasure, half plea. I found that spot inside her and rubbed at her while my thumb gave her the pressure she needed.

"I would have bought you, too," I admitted in a harsh whisper before she exploded beneath me.

She screamed my name, her hands gripping me tight as her pussy convulsed around me, clamping down on my fingers as she rode out her orgasm. It was the most beautiful sight I'd ever seen.

I stroked her down until she was through the aftershocks. Then I slipped my finger free of her heat as she gasped for breath, going limp beneath me.

"Holy shit," she muttered as her head rolled toward mine. Her eyes were even bluer, the shade somehow clearer as she looked at me.

I lifted my fingers to my mouth and licked the taste of her clean, knowing her in the only way I'd let myself. Sweet and salty and decadent, just like the woman herself.

She whimpered. "That's really…God, that's hot." She leaned up on her elbows. "Now you."

"No." I stood, somewhat surprised that my skates were still on. "Never me. I won't go there with you."

"What?" Hurt flashed in her eyes. "Why?"

"Because it would ruin us both." I found my shirt and pulled it on, not caring that it was inside out.

"That's not true. You want me. It's pretty damned obvious." She looked at my cock, then looked again, her eyes widening.

"It's not about wanting. It's about making sure we both survive this…marriage." I ripped my hands over my hair. "Now, please, for both our sakes, walk away."

"I don't want to walk away. I want *you*."

She sat up completely, her perfect breasts swaying with the motion.

I groaned but managed to back up farther toward the ice. "I have never asked you for anything, Persephone, but I'm asking you this. Don't push me. Have mercy on us both and walk up those stairs."

I turned abruptly and skated onto the ice, grabbing my stick as I went. I slammed at least twenty pucks into the net before I found the willpower to turn around.

Thank God, she was gone.

But I could still taste her.

8

PERSEPHONE

"And then I told the officer that I *would* be pressing charges." Angela finished her tale by lifting her glass of white wine to the table and taking a sip.

I didn't lift my glass—the only one at this miserable table who didn't.

"You'd think you'd have a little more compassion," I said, then blinked as every set of eyes landed on me. I shrugged. "You don't know the woman's backstory or situation. Perhaps she truly was asking for help."

Michael patted my shoulder from where he sat on my right, and I subtly shifted away from under his touch. "That's our Sephie," he said to the luncheon. "Always using her heart instead of her head."

I bit down on my response, exhaustion settling over me. These lunches had become more taxing in recent months. Since I returned from college and started my own career. Since my socialite friends had become colder and more crass and more…well, snobby. The tale Angela had recanted—a homeless woman approaching her on the street corner and asking for money to feed her child—had spurned a sadness in me. It most certainly wasn't a story to laugh about, and the woman hadn't deserved to have the cops called on her either.

"Not everyone is born with money," I snapped, glaring at Michael in the special southern way I'd learned from my mother—the look was equal parts sugar and salt.

"How *is* Cannon?" Michael asked.

I swallowed hard. Flashes of our moments near his personal rink, on that bench, raced through my mind. The way his mouth had claimed mine. The way he'd touched me, stroked me into a wild mess of tangled tension. The way he'd effortlessly brought me to that edge and made me shatter for him. The man drove me crazy in the best of ways, and I wanted so much more. But I would never force him, never push him beyond his limits. He'd asked me to walk away, and I did. But it had been one of the hardest things to do in my life.

It'd been a week, and he hadn't touched me in that way since. Sure, we spent our nights reading together in bed, our bodies *almost* touching but never quite. Sometimes he'd graze my hand as we lost ourselves in conversations—like the one where he admitted how badly he'd wanted a dog as a child, but out of all the foster homes he'd went into, they never had one. Or the time he'd told me about Lillian's boy band phase and how he'd worked as a busboy after school to save up to buy her the new albums when they dropped. Or the small pieces he'd given me about his time with his mother—the way she'd been trapped in an abusive marriage and when she'd finally gotten the courage to leave, it had been too late. She'd had no resources, no money, no family, nothing to cling to. Nothing to help her take care of her children. Glimpses—he'd given me mere pieces of the life he'd lived.

The memories brought a sad smile to my lips. He'd let me in a little—his story inspiring my current charitable focus, one I would be discussing with Mr. Silas in a little over two hours.

"OMG," Angela said, drawing my thoughts back to the luncheon. "Yes! How is that tall drink of badass?"

"Please give us all the details!" Brittany chimed in from Angela's left. You wouldn't know she'd been in a slap-fight with my sister mere weeks ago. No, everything about her was a concocted mask of perfection, an outward pretty package for every passerby to admire. I wondered what she'd said to my sister to set her off, but Anne had never told me. She claimed it was because she was too drunk, but I gathered there was more to it than that.

Michael groaned into his wine, rolling his eyes.

"He's at a pickup game," I answered. "And he's incredible," I answered honestly. The man had enchanted me, not only with his lips but with his words, his soul. The way he could see straight to the heart of me, the way he could slip his way into places I hadn't let anyone in—my mom's illness being one of them. I could talk to him about it for hours and afterward feel all the better for it. Because he *listened*.

Outsiders took in his rough exterior and his stoic silence and deemed him dangerous or uninviting, but the truth was Cannon was an observer. More perceptive than anyone I'd ever met. He could read a room, a person, a group, and know the mood. Know how to navigate *out* of it if need be. And he used that same skill set to hone in on my needs these past weeks, satisfying them and beyond, even if that was merely a hot bath and a quiet night.

Not that he'd take the hot bath with me.

No, *that* I was still working on.

Because while I wouldn't push him, I wanted to *prove* to him that my intentions were real—I wanted him on every level. I had to earn his trust first. Had to show him nothing about it was a passing whim, a fantasy I wanted to play out.

Cannon—though he'd never admit it—craved depth and truth and unflinching loyalty. I would prove to him that it wasn't his perfect body or his bad-boy exterior that I hungered for, but *him*. The man he was and the happiness he brought to my life—for however long I was allowed to keep him.

Chatter continued around me, aimless and this side of haughty. I wondered how I'd ever managed these luncheons before, but figured it was mostly for Father's benefit. He'd always urged me to maintain close relations with club members. Though, just because some of his best friends originated from here didn't mean mine had to.

No, I had found myself friends with a much different group of people—people who laughed freely and loved deeply. People who were fiercely loyal and equally as kind.

My *Reaper* family. And after two years of being surrounded by that family, I was quickly realizing they were the ones I found myself needing to be around more and more.

An hour later, I happily walked to the parking lot, ready to drive to my meeting with Mr. Silas—partly because of my excitement to discuss a new venture and partly because I knew Cannon would be there.

Sweaty.

In hockey gear.

Sliding across the ice like a lightning strike.

"Sephie!"

I jolted at the sound of my name, so lost in my thoughts I hadn't heard Michael behind me.

"Yes?" I asked, turning toward him as he approached my car.

"What was that back there?" He motioned toward the club.

"What do you mean?"

He lowered his voice, dipping his head slightly toward mine. "You were distracted. Downright rude to your friends who haven't seen you—"

"Excuse me?"

"I'm sorry, but someone has to tell you." He raised his hands. "You've changed."

A small smile played at the corners of my mouth.

"I mean, seriously, Sephie. What the hell?"

I raised my brows, clicking the unlock button on my car.

"We had a plan," he continued. "And you up and married some...some piece of trash like that?"

"Careful," I said with unnerving calm. "I adore my husband," the truth of that statement filled my heart. "And I have no qualms about smacking that mouth into place when it rattles off insults like that."

"We had a plan," he repeated, totally ignoring my words.

"*You* had a plan," I snapped. "I was never, not once, involved in that plan. Just you and your parents and your wild dreams. Well, if you knew me at all, you would know I'd never marry someone for money, let alone connections as old family friends."

He gaped at me like I'd grown another head.

"And," I continued, "if you knew me at all, you'd know I'd never laugh at the expense of others like that crap up there was." I pointed toward the club. "And I'd never stand for you calling my husband trash." I sucked my teeth, shaking my head. "We're done here, Michael. I'll kindly ask that you leave, or I'll just have to run your ass over on my way out."

I sank into my car and slammed the door, the force of which made him jump. I revved the engine, more than prepared to reverse if he didn't get out of my way.

He did, though, because he was a bit smarter than he acted.

Thirty minutes later, I greeted Mr. Silas with open arms.

"Silas," I said as he tucked me gently into his side. He wore an all-black Armani suit today, the lone pop of color a blood-red silk handkerchief folded into a perfect triangle peeking out of his breast pocket. "Good to see you," I said as he released me.

"And you," he said, smiling down at me. It was shocking to me how identical his eyes were to his sister Harper's—Nathan Noble's fiancée and one of those newly formed friendships I'd been waxing poetic about earlier. The sharp angle of his jaw was dusted with a five o'clock shadow, his dark hair ruffled in a way that suggested he'd run his hands through it a few too many times. Handsome, powerful, and with endless connections and intelligence, this man should be the feared Reaper, not my Cannon.

My Cannon.

I smirked a bit at the claiming in my mind.

Though it was true. I should be weak in the knees for a man like Asher Silas, but nothing but true friendship rang between us. And yet, one brief instant in the arena hallway with Cannon Price and I sparked for no one else.

Silas settled himself into one of the many chairs situated around the table in our designated meeting room. "What do you have for me today?"

I grinned at his straight-to-business attitude, something I admired and appreciated when most people loved to talk and talk until the cows came home. I sat across from him, drawing the folder from my bag and sliding it toward him.

"I believe this charity should be this season's focus." I tapped the folder before he opened it. He leafed through the pages, nodding at some text, tilting his head at others.

"This looks solid," he said after a few minutes. "Though, I wouldn't expect any less from you. That's why I hired you."

"To which I'm eternally grateful," I said, smiling at him. "Do you like the direction?"

"I do," he said, but there seemed to be something left unsaid from the furrowed features of his face.

"But?"

He grinned. "I suppose I'm wondering what inspired you to choose this one. Beyond the statistics, that is. Clearly, I see the need in the numbers."

I pursed my lips a bit. Silas was a friend, but he was also my boss, and technically Cannon's as well. Though, I supposed a bit of truth wouldn't hurt anyone.

"Cannon," I said, his name rolling off my tongue with an admiration I couldn't hide.

"Ah," he said, leaning back in his chair. "I thought so, but I wasn't certain."

"His story," I said, swallowing a bit. "Touched me. Opened my eyes to the need of more successful women's shelters, as well as accessibility. There are so many women who have been in domestically violent relationships for so long that once they have the courage to leave, they leave with absolutely nothing but hungry children in tow. We need to focus funding on expanding the shelters so there are fewer women turned away due to lack of space. And we need to up the security of the shelters too."

Cannon's story flooded my mind, my heart, my blood. If his mother had had access, more help, more confidence to get free...would he be here now? Would he be different?

Would you want him to be?

No. I adored him for who he was, but...the pain. I wouldn't mind erasing that, despite my lack of ability to do so.

Silas tapped the table. "I agree completely, though I don't know Cannon's story."

"He's a private man." Even I didn't know all the details, and I was married to him.

"That he is." Silas grinned. "Though, it makes a bit of sense now."

"What does?"

"Why he donates so much of his earnings to particular charities." He eyed the paperwork before him and noted the look of surprise on my face. "Private man," he said. "But hard to be private about that when I'm the one who pays those earnings."

"Indeed," I said, my heart swelling just a bit more, though I wasn't surprised one bit. Cannon needed little to satisfy his material needs, and he'd earned enough money for the rest of his life in his last contract.

"Well, as usual, I grant you full permissions. Just copy me on the specifics, yes?" Silas pushed back from the table, re-buttoning his suit jacket.

"Of course," I said, standing too.

Silas glanced at his watch. "I'd wager they're out of the locker room by now," he said, and winked at me before exiting the room.

I may have walked with a bit more speed in the hopes of catching Cannon coming out of that locker room.

Freshly showered and in nothing but athletic pants, a tight T-shirt, and a massive gear bag thrown over his shoulder, the man looked like a wet dream.

"Hey, Princess," he said as he greeted me in the hallway.

Sounded like a wet dream too.

Damn him.

"You want to ride home with me?" He reached his free hand toward me but dropped it before he could touch my face. A motion I was getting unnervingly used to.

"I'd love to," I said. "But I drove here." My shoulders dropped, and without any really good reason. I lived with the man. I'd see him at home.

"We'll get your car in the morning when I bring you

back," he said, and jerked his head toward the exit. I fell into step beside him, an easy quiet settling between us.

"How'd the pickup game go?" I asked after he'd ensured I was secured into the passenger seat of his massive car.

He pulled onto the street with a grunt. "I was a few seconds slower than Connell today."

"*Seconds*," I gasped. "That bad?" I teased.

He growled from the driver's seat but kept his eyes on the road.

"Are you hurt?" I asked, eying the length of his body as if I could answer the question by merely looking.

"No," he said. "Top shape."

"Then what's with the slowness?"

He spared me a glance of shock, but that rough laugh escaped his lips, causing all kinds of delicious chills to tickle my skin. "*Slowness*, she says." He shook his head.

"Well, you are the faster skater in the NHL."

"Says who?"

"Everyone."

Another small laugh.

The car filled with a familiar quiet, the sweet weight of comfort draping around my shoulders. We'd settled into a rhythm I rather enjoyed, and it didn't occur to me until today how beautiful our normal could be...if we'd let it. If *he'd* allow it.

And it wasn't until he'd pulled into home that he finally admitted, "I was distracted."

"By what?" I asked as I followed him into the house. I headed to the kitchen island as he dropped off his bag in the mudroom.

"Things," he grumbled.

I pulled out the grilled chicken and veggie plates I'd prepped this morning and stuck them in the oven to heat them up.

"Care to share?" I asked, eying him as he took a seat at the island.

A debate raged in his eyes, one I knew could take hours, even days. That was Cannon...calculative, thoughtful—unless someone lit his fuse, then all bets were off. Except for me, I suppose. Because despite our ability to crash against each other in verbal waves of sass, he never once snapped on me.

We shared a quiet dinner, something we'd settled into the past weeks together, and he cleaned up while I got ready for bed. I didn't push the subject, not when I knew Cannon had to come to me—like some wild feral jungle cat. If I pushed, he'd retreat so far I'd never see him again. Luckily for him, I had the patience of a saint.

I slipped into another one of Cannon's shirts—this one a freshly washed Reaper shirt with his number on the back—and delighted in my newest nightly satisfaction, watching Cannon struggle with the sight.

"Damn you, Princess," he growled from his spot in bed.

"What?" I asked innocently and spun around to show him the name scrawled across my back.

Another low growl.

I practically pranced to my side of the bed, alight with the game we'd been playing.

He grabbed the book off his nightstand, opening it to the page where we'd left off last night.

"You didn't even want to take a gander at the book I brought home?" I teased.

He refused to look at me as I settled in next to him, close, but not close enough to touch.

"I saw it."

"Did you find anything interesting in it?" My heart raced.

He gave me a good side-eye before returning focus to the book. "I didn't find it funny if that's what you mean."

I gaped at him in faux shock. "Well, I would hope not. *The Kama Sutra* is no laughing matter."

He laid the book against his chest, glaring at me.

I raised my hands. "I wouldn't need a book if I had a teacher."

A muscle in his jaw flexed before his tongue darted out to wet his lips. God, that little tick. It made heat pulse between my thighs.

"You don't need a book, Princess."

"Then you'll do it?" I asked, breathless. "You'll teach me?"

He swallowed hard and shook his head.

I pretended not to deflate, and instead nodded toward the book on his chest. "Where did we leave off?"

He scooped up the book, the breath rushing from his lungs like he was equally glad and disappointed I'd given up the fight.

Tomorrow I might push a little harder, but for now?

For now, I reveled in *this.*

The sound of his voice as he read from the pages of the book he'd decided to share with me. The feel of his warm body next to mine, the scent of him drenching the sheets and my skin despite not touching. I fell into this sweet, deep sense of happiness with Cannon beside me—something beyond lust, beyond forced proximity.

Happiness.

A true happiness I'd never experienced before, and I had Vegas and a mishap to thank for it, but *damn* I loved my new normal.

9

CANNON

"I have to say," Logan began as he rubbed the back of his neck as we stood outside our favorite restaurant in downtown Charleston, "it's not as weird seeing you two together as I initially thought it would be."

"Thanks?" I glanced toward Persephone as she talked with Delaney and Annabelle a few feet away and waited for that sense of dread to fill me—that deep, empty ache that this was all headed toward disaster...but it never came. We'd been married almost two months, and instead of it becoming more and more obvious that we were absolutely wrong for each other, it somehow got easier. Which was a good thing, considering Mrs. VanDoren had set our wedding date for October twenty-first, dragging this little lie out a couple of months longer than planned.

At least she was feeling better. Doctor called it a *miraculous surge of health*, which Mr. VanDoren attributed to our wedding plans, though he still glared at me whenever the girls weren't looking. Did the asshole really think a good glaring was the worst I'd been through?

"He's right." Connell shrugged. "You two seem to balance each other out."

"Like an opposites attract kind of thing," Logan added.

"Exactly! And the way she took all the olives off your salad?" Connell gave a giant, mocking sigh while he thumped his chest.

"Or the way you ordered her a second sweet tea before she'd finished her first?" Logan chimed in with an equally absurd expression.

My eye roll could not have been stronger.

"What are you two going on about?" Persephone asked, sliding her arm through mine. That same electric jolt I felt whenever she was near zinged up my spine at the contact, and I suddenly wished I'd chosen a long-sleeved shirt. Maybe I would have sweat to death in the August heat, but it would have protected me from the immediate, intense flashbacks to having my hands elsewhere on her bare skin.

I was losing my fucking mind a little more every day as I fought my need for this woman.

"Oh, just telling your husband how cute you guys are together." Connell winked at my wife.

Good thing I liked him.

"And on that note, we're leaving before I end up thrashing you two idiots." I gave them a wave, and Persephone did the same as she said goodbye to the girls.

We walked down the block in relative peace and quiet. The best thing about living in Charleston was the relative anonymity we had. I'd been hounded by reporters and paparazzi back in Detroit, all of them waiting for me to inevitably lose my temper and fuck up royally.

"That was nice," Persephone said as we turned the corner to where I'd parked the car. "I had a lot of fun."

"Me, too." I wrapped my arm around her shoulder, shifting her to the inside of the sidewalk, farther from any traffic, and pressed a kiss to the top of her head simply because she smelled so damn good and felt so right tucked against me.

"You ready for preseason to start up?"

"I'm always ready. Plus, I hammered Connell's ass at the pick-up game yesterday, so I know my speed is back." I spotted my Hummer a few cars away and hit the unlock button. "The morning runs are helping."

"Good." She patted my stomach, and the muscles tensed under her touch. "I was a little worried there that you were putting on a few pounds."

My jaw dropped, but she just winked, then laughed.

"I've heard about an excellent workout for that," she assured me as we reached my car. "It happens to involve two people and minimal workout gear." She turned to face me and lifted her eyebrows.

"Did you now?" Every fucking day she proposed that I teach her about sex…through experience, of course, and every day, I shook my head in refusal, wondering when I'd eventually break. The problem was, giving in to what we both so obviously wanted would only make it hurt all the more when this ended. Not to mention that I wasn't gentle or careful enough to be any woman's first—let alone Persephone's.

A shadow moved over her shoulder, and my head snapped up as a man pushed himself off the wall and moved toward us.

Holy shit. The man stepped out under the street light, and every molecule in my body hardened in response. I stepped to the side and pulled Persephone behind me, putting myself between her and…him.

"What the fuck do you want?" I seethed, ignoring Persephone's gasp of surprise behind me.

"Is that any way for you to talk to your dad?" he asked with a grin, his arms outstretched like he was Jesus Christ. Like the fucker came in peace when all he'd ever brought me was pain.

"It's the *only* way to talk to you," I ground out through clenched teeth. What the hell was he doing here in Charleston?

"Hi there. I'm guessing you must be Cannon's wife?" He cocked his head to the side.

"You don't speak to her. *Ever.*" I'd never put her in his path. Hell, I wasn't even putting my back to him for the length of time it would take to get her into the car.

His grin fell. "Cannon. I was hoping we could talk."

"So, you ambushed me outside my car?"

"It's not like you take my calls." He stopped a few feet away from me, and I noted the changes since I'd last seen him. He was still a handful of inches shorter than I was, but he'd put on some weight. His belly hung over his jeans and stretched his Red Wings T-shirt to capacity, and while he still wore his hair slicked back, the dark color no longer mirrored mine, but was streaked with silver.

"Nor will I ever. My agent, my publicist, my coach, and my team's owner all know you're not allowed to have my phone number."

"See? And you wonder why I have to resort to stalking my own son." Rage filled his eyes before he blinked it back. I knew that rage well. It was the same, all-consuming anger that put out cigarettes on my skin when I was too young to run and welts the same size as his belt when I was old enough to protect Lillian. It was the same rage that lived inside me—an insidious, infectious disease I could never completely cure.

"Is that how you found me?" I felt Persephone lean against my elbow, where I still had her locked against my back, no doubt peeking around my arm to get a look at the man who'd sired me.

"It's not hard when the internet knows what car you drive. I just had to wait outside the Reaper Village gates long enough to spot you."

Ice dripped down my spine.

"What the hell do you want? Because whatever it is, you may as well get back in your car and go. I'm not giving you shit."

"Cannon." His eyes softened, and his face fell. It was the same expression he'd used on Mom every time he'd apologized for beating her, swearing it would never happen again, that this time it would be different. "I've gotten myself into a little trouble."

I snorted. "Of course you did. Why exactly should I care?"

"Because I need your help, son."

"Don't call me son, and the answer is no." My empty hand clenched at the familiar term, but I kept the other splayed over Persephone's back. She was the reason I would hold my shit together instead of crushing this piece of shit like he deserved.

"Please? Cannon, it's not that much. It's just a hundred for this loan shark—"

A scoff burst from my mouth. "A hundred grand? You're out of your fucking mind."

"Cannon." His shoulders dropped dejectedly, and I felt Persephone soften behind me.

She was definitely peeking. I glanced her way. Yep, she was. Was she falling for his same line of bullshit that Mom had? Were his pity-inducing puppy eyes playing her?

"No. Walk away." I bit out the words.

Anger flashed in his eyes, but he locked it down. Impressive. "It's nothing to you! Just a drop in your massive bank account. But it's the difference between life and death for me!"

The rage drained from my body, leaving me iced out and numb. My sister called it *the killing calm*. "Death? You want to talk about death? Then how about this. You've been dead to me for *years*. The day you killed my mother was the day I wrote you off."

Persephone sucked in a breath, and I felt her hands clasp my sides. Even at my worst, the woman did her best to comfort me.

Dad transformed from the kicked puppy to the monster he hid just beneath the surface. His mouth twisted, his fists clenched, and his eyes narrowed. "I served my time for that! You think it's easy with a vehicular manslaughter conviction on my record? I can't get a good job, and I sure as hell don't have an NHL contract. Now, I'm giving you one more chance to do the right thing and help me."

"Or what? You'll hit me? I'm not some scrawny little kid cowering in the corner of the kitchen anymore. I've got four inches and fifty pounds of muscle on you now, asshole." Those very muscles were on alert, ready for whatever he'd try.

He tilted his head again, and his gaze dropped to my wife. *Fuck, no.*

"Pretty little wife you have there. I heard she's rich as Midas, too. A real southern belle. You'd better be careful with her, Cannon. We Price men have tempers. Can't help what's in the blood, son, and she looks a hell of a lot more fragile than your mother was." He slowly dragged his gaze back to mine. "I'd hate for something to happen to her because you let that temper get the best of you."

My stomach lurched, threatening to send my dinner up.

"Walk the fuck away."

He clucked his tongue at me and tucked his thumbs in his

jeans, going close enough to his belt that my head immediately filled with the sounds of my own screaming when he'd last used it on me. "You'll regret this. I swear to God, I'll make you regret it."

"I regret every moment I spend in your company."

He shook his head slowly and turned around, then began walking up the block, away from us. "It was nice to meet you, *Mrs. Price.*"

"I can't say likewise," she muttered behind me.

As soon as he was out of sight, I loaded Persephone into the car, going so far as to buckle her seat belt for her. Nothing was getting to her. Nothing. Not even me.

"Cannon," Persephone started as we pulled into the driveway, breaking the strained silence that had been our constant companion on the drive home.

"Don't," I snapped, pulling the car into the garage.

"I just—"

"No. Not with this. Not with him. You have *no* idea what that man is capable of or what he's done. Do you know how many scars these tattoos cover up? How many burns and cuts I've masked with all this ink? Don't you realize there's a reason I don't like people to touch me?"

Her mouth softened, but before she could speak, I climbed out of the car.

"Cannon!" She caught up to me in the kitchen. "How can I know any of that stuff when you don't talk to me about it!"

"You knew he beat my mother. I told you that." I threw my keys on the counter.

"In really vague terms, yes, but you never told me that he killed her." She moved toward me, then thought better of it and stayed on the other side of the island. Good. It was dangerous to be close to me when I felt like this.

"She packed the car and told his drunk ass that she was leaving him. At least, that's what we think happened in the house. Then he stumbled out to the driveway and got into the driver's seat, shouting that she wasn't taking his kids anywhere, and when she ran after us, he *accidentally* hit the gas instead of the brakes and hit her." God, I could still feel the abrupt motion of the car, the sound of her screaming.

Persephone gasped, her hands flying over her mouth as her eyes flared in horror.

"Accident my ass, right? But Lillian and I didn't know what happened inside, so we couldn't prove that he did it out of anger, and it wasn't some accident like his slimy lawyer professed. The man did fifteen years for murdering my mother. Fifteen. That's it. So, I'll be damned if I give him a dime of what I've earned. He can rot in hell for all I care."

I pushed away from the counter and walked away, heading straight for our bedroom. No amount of shooting or skating in the basement was going to wash him away. I felt the dirt of it all on my skin, impossible to see, but oily to the touch.

My clothes hit the floor in a scattered path as I walked to the massive shower. I turned on the water, then shed everything else until I wore nothing but the art I'd chosen over the scars I'd had no say over.

When the water steamed, clouding the air of the stone-walled, doorless shower and the rest of the bathroom, I stepped under the heavy spray, letting it scald me to the point of pain, begging for my nerve endings to come alive and kill the numbness. When I'd burned enough of him away, I turned, letting the water singe my back.

At least he was in Charleston, which meant he wasn't near Lillian. I'd have to call her later and warn her that he'd reappeared, but she never held the same appeal for him that I did—she didn't have the money he always needed. She was safe.

Persephone wasn't. Not while she was still married to me.

He was right. That was the real kicker. She was in danger every moment she stayed near. She was so breakable. So fragile. What the fuck would happen if I snapped one day the way he did? My heart stopped at the thought of anything happening to her.

The bathroom door opened, and Persephone walked in. Her steps were slow but deliberate. She had that look on her face she wore when she needed something done and wasn't going to leave the locker room until we'd all agreed to whatever her plan was.

I watched silently as she pulled her hair up into a knot on the top of her head, then pulled down the zipper of her dress that ran down her side. The blue silk fluttered to the floor, leaving her in a matching set of underwear that almost made me flip the handle and change the water to freezing. Every line of the woman was so fucking flawless that all I could do was stare as she reached behind her and unsnapped her bra, then shrugged out of it.

Her breasts were just as perfect as I remembered. I'd done my best to keep my damned hands off her for the past two weeks, to keep away the memory of the feel of her on my fingers and the taste of her on my tongue. For having the reputation of the very devil, I'd been a fucking saint when it came to my wife.

My wife. Even thinking that term had my cock rising. She was mine to protect. Mine to care for. Mine to adore. At least for now.

She tucked her thumbs into the sides of her thong, and my breath stilled. Our eyes locked, and she bit her lower lip with indecision. I sighed with relief when she left the little scrap of fabric in place. I was already on edge, fraying by the minute, and the last thing I needed was the delectable temptation of Persephone—

Wait. What the fuck was she doing?

She walked into the shower, keeping her eyes on mine, craning her neck when only inches separated our bodies. A single jet reached her skin, and she jolted, sucking in a breath with a slight yelp.

My hand flew to the knob on my right, and I dialed it back so the water wouldn't burn her. Never her.

Her brow scrunched momentarily, and she swallowed, then she reached for the dark blue loofah she'd bought me when she moved in. It hung, untouched, next to the frequently used pink one that she favored.

I tensed as she put shower gel on the scratchy nylon then raised it to my chest. She paused before she made contact and looked up at me for permission.

That act alone made me give it to her with a curt nod.

She washed my chest gently, then ran the loofah down both of my arms before turning it on my stomach. Her lips parted, and her breath quickened as she watched her own motions, tracing the lines of my abs. She was so fucking sexy. A heady mixture of sensuality and innocence that pushed my control to the very limit of existence.

She hesitated when she drifted lower, and her eyes flew impossibly wide when she accidentally brushed over the head of my cock with her wrist.

I groaned, clenching my hands into fists to keep them off her.

Her cheeks flushed pink, and her gaze flew up, enough heat in those baby blues to tell me she hadn't been afraid of what she'd seen there. Her lips trembled slightly, that motion telling me she was aware that she'd bitten off a little more than she was ready to chew.

I cocked an eyebrow at her, then turned around, giving her my back.

She washed the expanse of my back, and it took every ounce of willpower I had not to arch back into her touch.

Fuck, I wanted her. The need I felt for her was more than these months of abstinence, and more than the temptation of a fantasy that had come to life. It was so much deeper than that. My very soul wanted this woman, not just physically, but in every way possible.

I ached for her.

She lingered over a scar that was hidden in the pin of a grenade along my shoulder blade.

"Belt buckle." The words echoed off the stone, and I braced my hands on the wall in front of me.

She simply stroked over that scar again, then moved to one on the left of my spine, disguised in the scales of a sugar-skulled mermaid.

"Edge of a table."

She washed that spot gently, then continued her trek, soaping down my spine, over my ass, and down my thighs and calves. When she stood and reached the loofah around to my chest, I turned and stepped through the spray so it ran down my back.

Drops of water clung to her skin in a way I longed to, lingering before giving in to gravity and racing down the curves of her body. Fuck, I had to get out of here—had to get away before—

She ran her fingertips over the small, circular scar on my right pec, hidden in the inked ribs that led to the hands and heart in the center of my chest. Her eyes met mine in question.

"Cigarette," I answered simply.

Her eyes squeezed shut as she drew a ragged breath.

I took her hand in mine as the loofah hit the floor, then pressed her fingertips to the half dozen others that raised the skin around the same spot.

Her lips pursed tight, but she followed each and every burn scar. Then she pressed her mouth to the centermost one and erased some of the pain in that memory with a simple kiss. My heart slammed so hard that I knew she had to be able to hear it as she kissed each scar in that region.

Her fingers quested over my rib cage on the opposite side, finding the raised, puckered flesh that formed a tight spiral.

"Stove burner."

I expected to see pity in her eyes, but there was none there when she lifted her face to mine. No, they were filled with anger and a touch of the rage that lived inside me.

"He pushed. I fell." I shrugged.

She lowered her head and ran her lips over the horrific pattern that the tornado disguised within its swooping vortex. Again, some of the memory felt lighter to carry, as if she had somehow washed me clean.

When she rose, she moved forward until my cock rested against the smooth, warm skin of her belly. I hissed at the contact, pleasure shooting through me, sharp and sweet.

"You're still the most beautiful man I've ever seen," she said as her hands rested on my chest. "I get it now. You didn't just cover them up. You reclaimed your body. You took back control."

"Yes." My hands cupped her face. "But I have little to no control when it comes to you."

Her gaze flickered to my lips, and my blood heated another degree. She rose on the balls of her feet as her hands traveled to my shoulders, and she tilted her face back slightly, waiting for my choice.

I should have walked away. The better man would have.

I was never the better man.

That last tether on my self-control unraveled, and I brought my mouth to hers. The kiss started soft, but then she opened under me. I growled, sinking into her kiss with deep, swirling thrusts of my tongue against hers. She arched, her fingers digging into my shoulders.

I swept my hands down her body, bending slightly so I could reach her ass. She gasped with surprise as I lifted her easily, bringing her mouth level with mine. Her arms looped around my neck as her legs wrapped around my waist, her ankles locking neatly behind me.

She kissed me like she was starving for it—like she had to take every second of it just in case I changed my mind. The kiss moved from sinful and sexy to carnal as hell as I fucked her mouth with my tongue the way my cock ached to take her fully.

I turned toward the wall and anchored her against the smooth stone. She didn't blink at the change in position, merely used the wall as leverage to push harder against me, rolling her hips so the head of my cock brushed over the wet lace of her thong.

"Fuck," I groaned, shifting so one of my hands stroked over that same patch of lace from the cleft of her ass to the peak of her sex.

"Cannon!" She threaded her hands through my hair and held me still while she took her turn with *my* mouth, darting that little pink tongue against my teeth, the roof of my mouth, and my tongue.

I slid my fingers under her thong and found her soaked, wet with more than just the shower. She was slippery and swollen with need, with want for me. She made me feel powerful and weak, all in the same heartbeat.

"Please," she murmured against my lips when I hesitated.

Her plea broke me in a way nothing else could, and I sank two fingers inside her pussy slowly. Fuck, the woman was soft, wet, silken fire.

She cried out, then tightened her thighs around me and lifted slightly, only to fall back on my fingers, riding me.

I was going to fucking lose it right here and now if I didn't get away from her. This was it—the breaking point I'd tried so hard to keep from finding. My body rebelled at the thought of leaving hers, but my head knew it was the only way to keep her safe.

"We have to stop." I barely recognized my own voice for the deep, sandpaper-rough way it came out.

She rose and fell again, moaning sweetly as she took my fingers to the hilt. Fuck, she was so god damned tight. When she rode up again, I thrust harder, then dragged my fingers along her inner wall as I retreated, only to push back in again and again.

"Fuck. I mean it. Persephone, you have to stop. We have to stop." I pulled my fingers from the heat of her body and carried her from the shower while she protested.

"No, we don't. Please, Cannon." She looked at me with such stark need in her eyes that I nearly came undone. Instead, I set her on the counter and grabbed a soft, fluffy towel from the cabinet and wrapped her in it. Then I backed away, grabbing my own towel and wrapping it at my waist, which did nothing to disguise my erection.

"It's for your own good." My heartrate spiked at the effort it took to keep the five feet between us.

"My own good?" She hopped down from the counter, then dropped the towel.

I was stronger than this. I wasn't some horny teenage boy. I was a fully grown man with a man's appetite, and man's ability to walk the fuck away.

Then she held my stare and pulled off her thong, stepping free of the lace and throwing the lace toward the hamper. I didn't look to see if her aim was true.

I was too busy nearly swallowing my tongue.

She was all dips and curves that lead to thin strip of pale blond hair just above her sex. My mouth fucking *watered*.

"I'm a big girl, Cannon. I'm capable of deciding what my *own good* is." Her chin rose.

"You're tiny, Persephone. And I'm not sure if you've noticed, but I'm pretty fucking *huge*."

Her gaze dropped to my towel. "Oh, I've noticed."

"That's not what I mean," I snapped. "Do you know how easily I could hurt you?"

Those blue eyes flared in understanding, and her lips parted. "Cannon, you'd never hurt me. Not in a million years. If you don't trust yourself, then trust *me*, because I know that I'm always safe when I'm with you."

I felt the countdown start. My cock pulsed, protesting the pressure of the towel. My breath hitched. My mind started mapping her body and planning my assault.

Three.

"You deserve someone far more gentle than I am to be your first," I protested.

"I deserve *you*. I feel like I've been waiting my whole life for this—for you. I don't want anyone else. I never have. Just you." Her breasts rose with every breath. I'd start there first, maybe.

Two.

"You can't take this back," I tried again. "This isn't something you can do over."

She smirked. "Oh, I'm planning on doing it over and over again. With you. But I'm done chasing you." She licked her lips. "So, I'll make myself as clear as possible. I want you, Cannon. I want your body on top of mine, hot and insistent. I want to know how you feel inside of me. I want you to make love to me, and if that's too gentle for you, then I want you to fuck me however you want."

One.

"But you're going to have to come to me this time."

I snapped.

She was in my arms in a heartbeat, her mouth on mine, her legs around my waist as I carried her to my bedroom—our bedroom. I was going to worship her until she was so limp with pleasure that she'd have to crawl out of this bed.

I laid her down in the center of the bed, made sure she was comfortable, then I spread her knees, slid down the bed, and set my mouth on her.

She arched, crying out loudly as I licked her from pussy to clit, groaning at the sweet, heady taste of her. I teased her mercilessly, swirling my tongue around her, but never getting her there until her head writhed on the pillows above me.

"Cannon!" she demanded, her fingers sinking into my hair.

I sank my tongue inside her.

She groaned, rocking against my face as I filled her again and again. Her sensuality and open acknowledgment of her need took mine up to a painful level. I needed to be inside her. Needed to feel her come around me.

I licked back up to her clit, flicking and lashing the small bud, and when her moans turned to high-pitched, keening cries, I pressed against her with the flat of my tongue and rubbed over her with slow, steady pressure.

She came with a scream, her hips bucking sharply. I gripped her hips and held her still, pulling every wave of pleasure from her body, then working her up again, refusing to let the need ebb. I tested her with my fingers and found her drenched. Good.

"Cannon," she pled, rocking against my tongue. "God. What are you doing to me?"

"Getting you ready." I licked and sucked at her until her moans came in time with her breaths.

"Ready for what? Death? God, you feel so good!" Her hands twisted in the covers.

When her thighs started to tighten around my head, I rose over her and took in every detail of the moment. The flush that ran from her cheeks to her breasts. The quick pulse in her neck. The taste of her on my tongue and the sweet scent of apple blossoms filling my head.

I rolled to the side, reaching into my nightstand for a condom. I never fucked women here. This was my haven, but thank God I'd kept my stock there anyway.

"No," she shook her head when I rose above her again.

"What?" I froze. "Did you change your mind?" My balls were going to be as blue as her fucking eyes, but I wasn't going to take—

"No!" she startled, her hands cupping my face. "I want you. I just don't want a condom."

I blinked. "I'm sorry?" I'd never taken a woman without the thin barrier of rubber.

She tugged her lip between her teeth and shifted her legs on either side of my hips. "I don't want this halfway. I want to feel your skin against mine. I want you to feel *me*."

Holy shit, did I want that. My cock throbbed in agreement. Nothing but soft, wet, Persephone. "Princess, I'm not sure you want everything that comes with that."

She nodded. "I do. I'm on the pill."

Her pills were on the bathroom counter, where she'd taken them every night as we got ready for bed.

"Okay, but—"

"I'm clean," she promised like I didn't already fucking know that.

"Of course you are." Fuck, I couldn't think when I was close enough to feel the heat of her pussy with the tip of my dick.

"And you are, too," she assured me.

"I am?" Why the fuck did that come out as a question?

"You are. First, because you told me you *always* use those," she motioned at the condom in my hand. "And second, because if you weren't, you never would have touched me. You wouldn't put me in danger like that."

My chest swelled with a sweet kind of ache. She was incredible. She was *mine.*

"You're right," I assured her.

She plucked the condom out of my hand and threw it.

Guess that settled it.

The head of my cock nudged her entrance as I settled between her thighs, careful to brace my weight on my elbows as I kissed her deep and hard.

"You're sure?" I asked, my hips flexing instinctively and seating my cock flush against her. One push, one thrust, and I'd be inside her.

"I'm so sure," she said with a bright smile and hazy eyes.

"Tell me if it hurts too much. You understand?" Sweat beaded on my skin, and my muscles trembled with restraint.

"I understand." She kissed me, wrapping her arms around my neck as I pushed forward gently.

Her pussy strangled the head of my dick with exquisite pressure, and I groaned as I took that first inch. Her muscles protested, clamping down and nearly pushing me back out. I would have laughed if I hadn't been so fucking turned on that I couldn't see straight.

"You have to relax, Princess," I whispered against her mouth.

"I'm trying," she promised with a little nod. "God, you feel massive."

This time the laugh slipped free, and I reveled in the simple joy of having this woman beneath me, even as she looked as frustrated as I felt.

"Hold on to me," I told her as I held her tight and rolled. With her ass in my hands, I sat up and leaned back against our headboard, leaving my cock at her entrance as she kneeled above me, one knee on either side of my hips.

"What are we doing?" She rocked, sending a warm rush of heat over my dick.

"This way, you control it," I told her. "Now, give me your mouth and lower yourself at your own pace." I gripped the back of her neck with one hand, held her hip with the other, and kissed her senseless.

She panted through the kiss, rocking back and forth over my cock, taking me inch, by inch, by inch, until she took my entire length inside her.

Pleasure ripped through me, stripping my defenses. She owned me in every single way that I owned her. Totally, completely, and without reservation.

"Oh my God," she groaned against my lips. "You feel so damned good, Cannon."

"You feel like heaven," I whispered, lowering my hips slightly and pushing back up into her with a tight, smooth glide. "Fucking flawless."

She cried out when I stroked her again. Then she picked up the rhythm, rising and falling above me with slow, deep strokes that made me see stars. I pulled the cloth band from her hair, and it fell in a cascade of silk over my thighs as she threw her head back and rode me.

I was so fucking lost in her. The feel of her was beyond anything I'd ever known, and I clenched my teeth to hold back. When she leaned forward slightly, I took her breast in my mouth, sucking and licking at the peak while my hand shifted from her hip to her cleft so my thumb could stroke her clit.

"Cannon," she began chanting, her movements growing jerky and slow above me as her thighs clenched my hips.

"That's it, Princess," I praised her as she gave in to the pleasure and fell over the peak, coming around me in waves that gripped my cock in a velvet vise. At that first squeeze, I flipped us so she was under me, rippling with her orgasm.

Then I pumped into her with deep, hard, steady thrusts, prolonging her orgasm as I chased my own, both seeking it and holding it off as long as possible. I wanted to live here, inside her, in this moment.

When she screamed my name again, clutching at my shoulders with those sharp little nails, my orgasm hit me like a freight train ripping me from my body with its intensity. I fell into her arms as I emptied myself inside her in three long thrusts.

We both shuddered, and I rolled us to my side so she could breathe. I cradled her head with one arm, and stroked down her back with long, sweeping motions with the other. That hadn't been sex. It was something far beyond it. Something that transcended all the definitions in the world. It was beyond anything I'd ever experienced or read about in my entire life.

"You know what I'm thinking?" She asked with a sleepy laugh, tilting her head back so I could see her eyes.

"What?" Fuck, she was so beautiful.

Her grin stopped my heart. "At least I waited for marriage, right?"

I laughed. "You sure did."

Then I cleaned us both up and started all over again. I was never going to get enough of her, and since I was never going to be allowed to keep her, I'd better savor it while it lasted.

It lasted all night.

10

PERSEPHONE

Early morning light filtered through the blinds, casting the bed in a soft glow. I couldn't stop the smile that shaped my lips as I stretched in the bed, my mind waking up.

Cannon's tongue working me into a tangled fury of nerves.

Cannon's muscled arms, encasing me, guiding me, showing me.

Cannon's lips on my skin, his kiss like a brand.

The massive size of him and the way he'd been gentle, caring, as he made love to me for the first time.

Then the way he'd let me take control again and again throughout the night.

Memories and sensations hit me in hot waves of need, so much I had to shift my legs to ease the ache. The soreness between my thighs was not at all unpleasant, and the thought of exploring *more* with Cannon had my heart racing.

Then my arm reached the other side of the bed, and the breath rushed my lungs.

Empty.

Too early for a morning skate.

I bolted upright, cradling the sheet around my naked breasts.

I heard the shower shut off, and soon after, Cannon walked out with nothing but a towel around his hips.

Relief uncoiled within me, my blinding panic at his absence after the night we'd had—

"Good morning," I drawled...To his back?

He headed straight to his closet and disappeared.

The icy panic returned as he came back out fully clothed.

Suddenly, I felt more naked than I actually was.

"Cannon?" I wrapped the sheet around me and waddled over to him, putting myself in his path. "Cannon, look at me," I demanded when he seemed hell-bent not to.

"What happened last night," he said, the wall back over his eyes as he appraised me from head to toe. "It can't happen again," his words were clipped, icy.

I swallowed hard, something cold and oily snaking through my veins. My eyes found the floor. "Was I not...I mean, I don't have the experience you're used to—"

His fingers on my chin stopped my words, and he gently forced me to meet his eyes. "Last night..." A muscle in his jaw flexed as he silently debated something. "Was the best night of my life." The words were a struggle for him to get out like he had to fight some inner demon to free them.

Warmth melted the freezing rejection in my blood. "Really?"

He nodded.

"Then why can't we do it again?" I grinned at him, reaching my free hand toward his face.

He backed away a step.

Then another.

"Persephone," he said, and I knew the use of my real name meant business. "The closer we get, the harder it will be when this all ends." He motioned between us.

"Why not enjoy the time we have together?" I asked, completely ignoring the pain at the mention of our end-date. I knew it would come. We'd known it when we'd struck this bargain, but it didn't mean I had to think about it just now.

He shook his head, true pain and conflict flashing in his dark eyes.

I took a step toward him.

He retreated.

Fine.

He needed a little push, I'd push him.

I advanced slowly, never taking my eyes off of him until his spine hit the wall near the bathroom door.

The most terrifying man in the NHL had been backed into a corner by little old me. Power and hunger and pure *want* sizzled through my veins. "Look at me, Cannon," I said, and boldly let the sheet covering my body drop to the floor.

That muscle in his jaw ticked as a growl radiated from his chest. His eyes feasted on my naked body, trailing along every curve and dip until he met my eyes once more.

"I didn't break," I said, spinning slowly so he could see me entirely. I'd never been so bare, so vulnerable in my life—but I didn't feel fear. No, I trusted this man. With *everything*, and perhaps in that, I should be a little afraid.

A hint of a smile on his lips.

"I'm stronger than you think," I continued. "And it was hard to keep my hands off you *before*. Now?" I shook my head, running my hands over the Reaper T-shirt he wore, digging my fingertips into his strong chest. "Now that I know what you feel like inside me? Taste like?" I sucked my teeth. "I want *more*."

Another growl, this one bordering on frustration.

"Unless you don't want me," I said and took a step back, wanting to be absolutely fair to him. I'd never force something he didn't actually want, but from the way he'd touched me last night...

I reached toward the sheet on the floor, ready to cover myself again.

Cannon stopped me with a gentle hand on my wrist. "You know that isn't true," he said, his voice low, raspy. He guided my hand to his athletic pants and situated it over his very hard, very large cock. The feel of it, even beneath the fabric, sent a pool of heat between my thighs. "Clearly, I want you. That's never been the problem."

I looked up at him, my eyes hooded, needy. "Then what is the problem?" I squeezed him gently, and the hiss he gave me sent chills along my bare skin.

"The problem," he said, taking my hand and putting it back on his chest. "Is that we have an expiration date. And I don't want to get hooked on you only to have you ripped away."

The truth, for both of us.

"Too late," I practically purred. Another truth. I had a Cannon craving I wasn't sure any amount of time with him would ever satisfy.

Another, wider smile.

"Why think about the future?" I asked. "When the present is so much more appealing?"

He leaned his head back against the wall, banging it slightly over and over again. "I need to think about it," he said. "For both our sakes."

I knew that. I had anticipated that. Cannon thought everything through, usually for other people's benefit. Not that he'd ever tell anyone that. But I knew him. Just like I knew if he were a selfish man, he'd take and take what I offered with no regard for the state of my heart when this did eventually end. But he wasn't doing that. Wasn't taking what I so freely offered. He wouldn't, not without a proper think on all the pros and cons and what-ifs.

So, knowing that, knowing *him*, I smiled up at him and nodded. "You do that," I said. "And I'll just be in the shower *thinking* about it." I let my fingers graze down the center of my breasts, showing him exactly where my mind was. Thanks to *him*.

I brushed past him, leaving the door to the bathroom wide open as I turned on the shower.

He didn't follow me in, but I heard him grumble, *impossible woman*, before I stepped into the water.

* * *

"Are you sure you want to take another shot?" Harper asked from her seat to my left. "You know what happened the last time you were this drunk," she teased.

Langley laughed from my right, Delaney on her opposite side, and Echo hiss-chuckled from behind the bar. Annabelle and Faith were on the other side of Harper, sipping their own drinks.

"One," I said, holding up said shot. "I wasn't drunk when I married my own personal Hades." A warm flutter shuddered through me at the thought of him. "Two," I continued, throwing back the shot. "You'd be so lucky if we ended up married tonight." I nudged Harper's shoulder playfully.

"Touché." Harper held up her shot, as did Langley, and threw them back at the same time.

"Like this one is ever going to set a date," Faith joked, her hand covering Harper's engagement ring.

"Nothing wrong with a long engagement!" Harper fired back.

"I agree," Annabelle said, eying her own ring.

"It's been too long," I said, lightly smacking the bar. "I needed this girls' night."

Langley grinned. "Well, we hadn't officially gotten to initiate you into the Queens of Reaper Village club yet. You've been married over two months! It was high time."

Two months?

Had it really been that long? The time with Cannon had been a blur—one big blissful blur and after last night? God, I wasn't sure I ever wanted it to end.

A sizzling chill zinged down the center of me, and I had to shift myself on the barstool to relieve the pressure. It didn't work, and I knew there was only one thing that could satisfy this driving need.

Cannon.

That is *if* he ever decided to touch me again.

"Another shot!" I waved to Echo. "Please," I added with my best smile.

Echo laughed. "You're a mess," she said, but poured the shot. "What's going on up there?" She pointed to my forehead.

"Nope," I said, shaking my head. "Don't use your super-cool-understanding-bartender-voodoo on me. Not tonight. Tonight is about *fun*. About spending time with you girls." I sighed. "You're all just so damn wonderful, and I'm happy you've accepted me into your tight-knit circle."

My statement was met with a collective *aww* and followed by a massive girl-group-hug that had me feeling the love so much it hurt. There was something about having a proper group of girlfriends—women who wanted nothing more than to build you up, have your back when shit went down, and smack some sense into you when you needed it. I'd never known true girl-friendship until I'd met these wonderful women. My girlfriends prior were all social climbers, more using my status and name to advance themselves than to be my actual friend. They never had my best interests at heart, not like these women.

Once the love-fest retreated back to a drink-fest, we drank and laughed and swapped stories for an hour—or was it two? Delaney was as new to the hockey love as I was, so we both hung on the words of veterans like Faith, Harper, and Langley. In the end, though, it all came down to love. Pure, unfiltered, complicated, chaotic, beautiful love.

And something pulsed in my heart, deep in a locked box I wouldn't dare touch. Something I understood with a clarity that shouldn't be possible after this many drinks. I ignored the sensation and focused on the fun—the whole reason for this night in the first place.

Slowly, Reaper men filed into *Scythe* to collect their inebriated wives, fiancées, or girlfriends, but not before having a drink at their table across the way. Mine, of course, had yet to show.

"Come on!" Harper teased. "You *have* to tell us."

I laughed so hard my sides split.

"Yes, we've told you," Faith chimed in.

"Is he *truly* terrifying in *every* aspect?" Harper asked again, waggling her eyebrows. "Or is it a *good* sort of terror?"

I shook my head. "He's never scared me."

Another round of *awws*.

I motioned to Langley. "I mean *her's* on the other hand…"

Langley rolled her eyes. "Axel is nothing but a giant teddy bear."

"Giant being the optimum word," I teased.

"Can't argue that," Langley said, raising her glass.

"I think it's safe to say all our men are large and terrifying in their own way," Delaney said. "I mean, they're like sharks on the ice for god's sake. Watching them? And the fights sometimes?" She shuddered.

I swallowed hard, knowing my husband was the most

frequent of the fighters—that short fuse of his was twice as short on the ice. Something I was closer to understanding because of the surprise visit by that vile man who was his biological father, but I didn't have the full picture yet.

My heart expanded and broke at the same time remembering the shower—his explanation of some of the scars and the tattoos that covered them up. He'd let me in a little, but not all the way.

I have time.

But not much. The cold fact of that made something heavy sink on my chest. I wanted to know Cannon, inside and out. It went beyond the insatiable craving, the primal need—I wanted to uncover what he kept hidden in that soul that made him feel so damn unworthy all the time. I wanted to know him fully, so I could show him how incredible he was and have him actually believe it.

"You know what?" I scooted off my barstool, standing—if not a bit wobbly on my pumps—as I raised my last shot. "I'm so damn lucky!" I said, slightly louder than necessary. "To have you," I said, eyeing the women surrounding me. "And to have Cannon." I closed my eyes, my smile unstoppable as I breathed deep. "He's the best man I've ever known. And I truly don't know what I did to deserve him." I opened my eyes, which were covered in water. "Thank you, Reapers!" I tossed back the shot, the sweet liquor burning all the way down. The girls mimicked my last statement and did the same with their drinks.

"Now look who's making a scene." Cannon's voice vibrated along my skin, his lips at my ear, the heat of his body at my back.

I spun to face him and tilted slightly, but Cannon steadied me with a gentle hand on my hip.

"You're here," I said, my words slightly slurred. Then I

remembered my speech and cringed. "*How* long have you been here?"

The smile he reserved for me and me alone played along his lips. "Long enough to know you're wasted."

I stomped my pump against the hardwood floor. "I am no such thing!" I grinned. "Persephone VanDoren doesn't get *wasted*," I said. "I'm merely, *slightly* inebriated."

"Mmmhmm," Cannon said, placing his other hand on my hip.

"Take me home?" I asked, my head spinning.

Cannon nodded, waving to Connell and Logan and Lukas and Axel, who had joined their girls at the bar.

I said my goodbyes and thankyous and allowed Cannon to guide me out of the bar, only to pause when the cool summer night air hit me. I breathed deep, glancing up at the clear night sky. "Beautiful," I sighed.

"Yes," Cannon agreed.

I glanced at him, only to find his eyes solely on me. I smiled at him, then crooked my finger. "Come here."

He eyed me, but came closer.

"Closer," I said, and he bent until I could reach his neck. I gauged his reaction, but for once, that wall was gone, and nothing but admiration and respect laid in those dark eyes.

So I pressed my lips against his, gently at first, then with more hunger as he snaked his arms around my back, holding me to him.

"Princess," he growled between my lips.

"*Hades*," I teased back, lightly nipping at his bottom lip.

His fingers dug into my rear, lifting me slightly as he guided us to the wall. I slid my tongue along the seam of his lips, demanding entry, and he opened for me. Met me stroke for stroke.

"God, you kiss like a dream," I moaned against his mouth.

"Not a nightmare?" he teased, flicking his tongue along the edges of my teeth.

I pulled back, took his face in both my hands to steady him—the damn spinning making it hard to focus on his dark eyes.

"Never," I said. "You're the dream, Cannon. Can't you see that? The absolute *dream*."

He smiled, free and unburdened. "And you're drunk," he said. "Likely won't remember any of this."

I glared at him. "I remember everything," I said and darted my tongue out to graze his lips. He groaned and pressed me harder into the wall, eliciting a moan from my lips. "And I want you, Cannon. On every level a person can want another. *You*," I clarified, running my hands over his chest and stopping over the dead center of it. "Not your body. Not your glorious, delicious body."

He eyed me.

"Okay, not *only* your body." I giggled. "I want what's inside." I patted the center of his chest. "I want *you*."

Something more serious flashed in his eyes, but he quickly replaced it with a wicked smirk. He planted a gentle kiss along my lips, backing us away from the wall. "Tell me something else you want, Princess."

He guided us back and back until he merely tucked me into his side, and he walked us toward his car. Once he had me properly situated and buckled inside, I rested my head against the seat and smiled at him.

"Tacos," I answered.

A hoarse, beautiful laugh as he nodded from behind the wheel. "I *knew* it."

We laughed some more, and as he drove, I never once took my eyes off him.

11

CANNON

Ten. I crossed another day off in my mental calendar as I entered my kitchen. *Our kitchen.* I'd made it ten days without putting my hands on Persephone again, without falling into the shelter of her body and the bliss of the oblivion only she brought me.

Ten days.

Who cared that I walked around in a permanent state of arousal? As long as I wasn't getting off, I wasn't getting any closer to her, right? I wasn't growing accustomed to the little make-up bag on my counter, or the junk food in my refrigerator. I sure as hell wasn't making a habit out of reading with her at night, or cooking her breakfast in the morning. That was all just…well, circumstance.

This was all just fucking circumstance, and it would be over before we knew it.

But we were the only ones that knew it.

"Good morning," Persephone said cheerfully as she came into the kitchen. Fuck me, she was wearing one of those little silk slip nightgowns she liked to torture me with, and her hair was up in that bun she slept in, but softer, now. She looked delectable and ready to be taken right back to the bed I'd tried to sneak out of.

"Hey," I replied gruffly, grabbing a water out of the fridge and trying to look anywhere but at her fucking *legs*. The memory of having those wrapped around me, her soft thighs cradling my hips as I drove into her, hit me with the force of a tsunami.

"Where are you headed?" She rose on her tiptoes for a mug.

"Last informal pick-up game before preseason starts," I answered, reaching over her head and grabbing the pale purple mug she favored.

"Thank you," she said softly as I handed it to her.

"No problem." I needed to move the mugs a shelf lower to accommodate her height, but doing that felt permanent like I was making room for her in a life that she really didn't want. Room that would hollow out the moment she left. "What are your plans this morning?"

"I thought I'd bake a little. Mom isn't feeling well, so I might run her over some chocolate chip cookies." She leaned into the frig to get her coffee creamer, sending her slip riding up the back of her thighs.

I clenched the counter, wishing it was her hips in my hands, that I had her bent over this very counter, her feet dangling, utterly powerless to do anything but accept every thrust I wanted to give her.

"You like chocolate chip, right?" she asked, glancing over her shoulder.

"Peanut butter," I replied, then cleared my throat. "Were you planning on getting dressed today?"

She shut the fridge and grinned. "What? You don't like the color?" She trailed a hand from her ribs to her waist, then over her hip to play with the hem.

That little hellion knew exactly what she was doing to

me. "I'm a fan of pink," I admitted, stalking over to where she leaned against the counter. I caged her between my arms and stared at the contrast between my overwhelming ink and her bare, creamy skin. "I like the blue one better. Looks like pure fucking heaven with your eyes."

Her lips parted.

Then I reached around her and grabbed a banana from the fruit basket. "I'll see you later, Princess." Then I pressed a kiss to her forehead because I had to. Those tiny touches were what kept me from losing my fucking mind around her.

"Bye, Cannon," she whispered.

As I grabbed my gear bag from the mudroom, I turned, popping my head back into the kitchen, where she still stood, stirring sugar into her coffee. "By the way, I picked you up a little something at the store." I motioned toward the fruit basket and headed toward the door.

"Oh my God. Cannon! Is this a freaking pomegranate!" she shouted at me.

"Well, I mean, you did call me *Hades* the other night," I teased, my hand on the doorknob.

"Ugh!" She moaned loudly. "You swore you wouldn't hold my drunken words against me!"

I couldn't help it, I turned around and leaned into the kitchen again. "Yeah. Well. I guess I lied." I grinned. "Now seriously, you have to change before I get back. You're killing me in that."

Her smile spread slowly as she gripped the hem of her slip, then pulled the damn thing completely off, leaving her in only a pair of white panties. "There, now it's off."

I looked my fill, taking in her high breasts, narrow waist, and the curve of her hips. "You know, people think I'm the devil in this relationship, but compared to you, I have a fucking halo over my head."

"Want to see just how bad I can be?"

Yes.

"Nope. Gotta go. Enjoy your baking!" I fucking ran out of there before she learned exactly how reckless with her body I could be.

Three hours later, I sat on the bench in front of my locker, freshly showered, and tying my shoes.

"I think you might be even faster than last year," Connell grumbled as he sat across from me. "I was kind of hoping I'd catch you."

I lifted an eyebrow but didn't respond. I'd been running and skating my ass off since I married Persephone, channeling that sexual frustration in any way that might help relieve the pressure. Nothing worked in that department, but I'd never been in better shape.

"Cannon," Sterling asked from the corner of the locker room as he pinned something to the bulletin board. "Settle an argument for me."

"What?" I finished tying my other shoe and sat up.

"You see, I think I'm your best man, but Briggs over there thinks he is." He motioned to the new defenseman we'd just gotten on trade from Calgary. Rumor was the guy fucked the wrong woman and ended up losing his jersey, but their loss was our gain. Briggs had puck-handling skills that even I envied.

Briggs shook his head, rolling his eyes at Sterling.

"Logan is my best man." I nodded to where Ward sat at my right.

"What? I was *there*. I drove you to the chapel!" Sterling's jaw dropped. "Where is the love?"

"Right, and if Logan had been there..." I cut myself off before I finished that sentence. Logan wouldn't have taken me to the chapel. He would have handcuffed me to a fucking radiator before he would have let me marry Persephone while we were both delirious.

Logan shot me a look that said he'd followed my line of thinking. "Right, and if I'd been there, I would have gotten way better camera footage." He grinned at Sterling.

"So it's official? You guys are making this thing real?" Axel asked from where he stood next to Lukas.

"Yep. Fancy ass venue and everything," I answered.

Logan was the only person who knew the *why* of it. Well, and Delaney of course. He'd learned his lessons about keeping secrets from his woman. That had been a promise I'd given Persephone. To the rest of the world, especially her mother, this looked legit.

Problem was, it was starting to *feel* legit.

"Good! I'm happy for you!" Our captain gave me the nod of approval.

"Have to admit, you're pretty cute together," Lukas agreed.

"Cute?" I challenged.

"Well, it seemed better than total-opposites-who-are-hot-for-each-other, so I went with it." He shrugged.

"You should have seen the douchebag crowd she used to run with," Sawyer interjected. "That woman is way better off with you than turning into a Charleston Stepford Wife."

"She still runs with that crowd, so let's keep the douchebag comments to a minimum," Logan reminded him.

That was true. She still had her lunches. Still met up with her friends to shop every few weeks. Still sat on the board for two of her mother's charities, which included meetings with the same people who had been at our engagement party. She might be stepping into my life, but she still had a foot firmly planted in hers.

Good. That was good, right? It would be easier for her when this all went to shit. Her snotty ass friends would forgive her *indiscretion*, and she'd fall right back in where she belonged, in that untouchable sphere of manners and money…and Michael.

My stomach twisted at the thought of him ever touching her. At anyone touching her.

Coach broke up the conversation, walking into the locker room with a clipboard. "Okay, Reapers. We're about a week out from preseason training, which means these little meetups won't just be for fun, they'll be for your salary." He crossed the locker room toward the bulletin board. "You'll see the schedule right—who the fuck put this here?" He unpinned whatever Sterling had stuck there. "Seriously. Cannon, you know we're all happy for you and Miss VanDoren—"

"Mrs. Price," Sterling corrected him with a shit-eating grin.

"Right. Whatever. But do you really need to pin your wedding invitation to the goddamned board? It's not like you don't already have the front page of the society section."

My eyes narrowed on Sterling. "Really?"

"Just wanted to show off that I got mine first. See, that's why I should be the best man." He raised his arms, palms out.

"You got yours first because you showed up at my house last night and begged Persephone for one," I snapped.

"Still. Got mine first. Suck it, Ward." He shot Logan a look and sat back down.

Coach chucked the invite at him. "Right. If you're all done gossiping like girls, maybe you'd like to see the schedule."

"Best man, huh?" Logan asked as we walked to the parking lot ten minutes later.

"I probably should have asked you first."

"You never have to ask. I'll be there."

"Thanks." I hit the unlock button on my car, my eyes scanning to see if my father had somehow sneaked his way into the player's lot. He was probably long gone by now, but it never failed to shake me for a few weeks after he'd randomly show up and ask for money.

"You doing okay with this thing?" Logan asked as I tossed my bag into the back of the Hummer. "The fake marriage thing," he clarified in a whisper.

"I know what you meant." I shut the hatch and turned to my best friend. "Honestly? I'm torn between keeping my distance from her and just living in the moment." It was the closest I'd ever gotten to admitting how badly I wanted her.

He watched me carefully, then sighed. "Shit. If this ends—"

"When this ends," I corrected.

"Fine. *When* this ends, it's going to fuck you up. It's going to fuck you both up."

"Well aware. That's why keeping my distance is the smart move." I folded my arms across my chest.

"You falling for her?"

That ache was back in my chest, demanding to be acknowledged. "It doesn't matter what I do or do not feel for Persephone. This is doomed for every obvious reason. I can't stand her fucking friends. They look down on her for marrying me. Her father hates me. Her mother is dying. She's the purest, kindest woman I've ever known, and she deserves someone way better than I am."

Logan narrowed his eyes. "Right. I mean, why settle for the most driven, tenacious, protective asshole I know when you can run right back to the simpering, weak little banker who got everything from his daddy and doesn't know his Sartre from his Nietzsche?" He rolled his eyes in mock indignation.

"You're not helping." My jaw clenched.

"You're not seeing what's right in front of you," he countered.

The leash on my temper slipped a few inches. "In what

fucking world do things like this," I gestured to my torso, "work out when it comes to a woman like her? I'm the guy you fuck for fun, not the guy you marry."

Which was what she wanted. Sure, she said she wanted me, but how the hell could she want someone as scarred and fucked up as I was when she could have her literal pick of any man on the planet?

"She didn't ask you for the annulment. She asked you to marry her for real," he reminded me.

"To make her mom happy!"

"Or maybe to make herself happy!" he hissed. "Jesus, she bought you at that auction. She watches you when you're not looking, and it's been going on for almost two years. That woman is so far gone for you that she might as well tattoo that ring on her finger. If you want to run away from this because you're scared, I get it. I do. It's fucking terrifying to give yourself over to someone completely. To give a woman the power to destroy you. But you're fooling yourself if you don't see that she already has that fucking power in those hands of hers. I've seen it every time you've put yourself in front of her against a threat, and every time you have to rip your eyes away from her."

"What the fuck are you trying to say?" I ripped my hand over my still-damp hair.

He shook his head, obviously searching for words. "I'm saying that if you're torn between keeping your distance and living in the moment, then my suggestion as your friend is that you live in the moment."

"You were the one who told me to run," I reminded him.

"For fuck's sake. I told you if you were going to use your damage as an excuse to run, that you do it back then. Months ago. That was then. This is now. And you might not see it, but you are in this so fucking deep, my man. So if there's even the slightest chance you think it could work

—and I mean like a one in a billion shot—then you take it. Because the pain is coming for you either way at this point."

"I'll hurt her. My temper—"

"You haven't really lost your shit in almost two years, Cannon. You're not the same guy you were before you came here. Before you met her. But maybe the truth is that you're not scared of hurting her. Maybe you're scared of her hurting *you*."

My eyes flared, and my stomach tensed.

"Yeah, that's what I thought," he said softly. "Look. We don't get a lot of chances to be happy in life. If you have a chance to be happy, even if it's just for a few months, then be happy. It's better to have loved and lost, right?"

"Alfred Lord Tennyson was a fucking idiot." I turned and walked toward the car door.

"Think about it!" Logan called from his car in the next spot.

"You're no longer my best man!" I snapped, but didn't mean a single word of it.

"Whatever. I'm planning the best bachelor party ever, you surly bastard."

"I'm already married!" I got in the car.

"No shit! Now act like it!"

I contemplated his words as I drove home. Maybe he was right, and I should enjoy every second I had with Persephone while I had it. But it would only hurt that much more when shit went south, and I was fooling myself to think she'd be the only one hurt.

I wanted her with a ferocity that bordered on insanity. Not just her body, but her heart, and her mind, and her inherent goodness. I wanted to be the man she thought I was. I wanted to prove myself worthy of her…but was that even possible? What if all she really wanted was what she'd said—

to make her mother happy. Oh, and sex. She was pretty clear that she wanted that.

But what if I lost myself a little more every time I took her? What the fuck would be left of me when this all fell apart? When she laughingly walked away and returned to the country club crowd?

My thoughts raced as I pulled into the garage and then hauled my gear inside, dropping my bag in the mudroom.

Holy shit, it smelled delicious in here.

I hung my keys and headed into the kitchen, then leaned against the doorframe and watched my wife's ass—the only visible part of her thanks to the door—wiggle as she got something out of the pantry. The Beatles were on full blast, singing about holding someone's hand.

Her shorts were impossibly small, ending just beneath the curve of her ass, and I had the sudden urge to bite that little strip of flesh beneath the hemline.

"Honey, I'm home," I called out.

"Ooh!" she shrieked. "I didn't hear the door open. I must have been lost in my own thoughts."

I pivoted toward the speaker, turning off the tunes. "Or it could have been the music up on decibel four trillion. What is that incredible smell?"

Her head popped out of the pantry. "Peanut butter cookies."

I blinked, then followed where she pointed to see a cooling rack full of my favorites. Shit, that ache was screaming in my chest. "I thought you were making chocolate chip cookies?"

"I already did. And ran them over to my mama. Then I got home and decided to make you a little treat." She walked out of the pantry with a tub of peanut butter. "I ran out with the first batch, and this sucker was on the highest shelf."

She set the jar on the counter and I grinned. She was

wearing a Reaper jersey, tied at the side and rolled at the sleeves.

Walking forward, she plucked a cookie off the cooling rack and then held it to my lips. "I promise it won't kill you. And I promise I won't bake again until after the playoffs."

If she was still here.

I opened for her and took a bite of the cookie, letting my tongue drag over her fingertips. It was still warm and soft and tasted like Saturday afternoons, which ironically, this was. "That's amazing," I praised.

She smiled wide, stopping my heart. "I'm glad you like it."

She handed me the rest of the cookie, and I devoured it as she turned to walk around the island.

Holy. Fucking. Shit.

She wasn't just wearing a Reaper jersey. She was wearing one of *my* Reaper jerseys. Not the ones the fans could buy on websites or even the store in the arena. It was one of my game jerseys. That's why she had the sleeves rolled and the waist tied. That thing had to have come to her fucking knees.

"Cannon? Are you okay?" Her brow puckered as she stood over the mixing bowl, watching me.

"You're wearing my jersey." She had my name on her back. A wave of primal possession washed over me.

She glanced down and laughed softly. "Oh. Right. Sorry, I got peanut butter all over my shirt, and this was hanging in the mudroom closet. Wait. Are you mad?"

The way her southern accent curved around the words was sweeter music than anything she could have been playing through the speaker.

"No." My tone was gruff.

"Okay, then. Good," she said with a bright smile. "What were you thinking about for dinner?" she asked as she turned around to grab a cookie sheet, flashing my name and number over her back again.

If you have a chance to be happy, even if it's just for a few months, then be happy.

Logan's words echoed through my brain.

Then the only sound in my head was my own voice chanting, *mine. Mine. Mine.*

I stalked across the hardwood floor, rounding the corner of the island when she looked up. She must have seen something in my eyes because the cookie sheet rattled against the counter as she dropped it.

"Cannon?"

"Persephone," I growled her name like the curse and the prayer it was, then gripped the nape of her neck and kissed her.

She gasped, and I filled her mouth with my tongue, stroking it against hers, demanding her response. She gave it, gripping my arms and rising against me, kissing me back without reservation.

I grabbed her ass with both hands and lifted her, and she wrapped her legs around my waist just like I knew she would. The kiss was ravenous and consuming, neither of us giving quarter as I sat her on the edge of the island.

Her fingers tunneled into my hair, and she pulled slightly, holding me to her kiss with the sweetest bite of pain as she licked the roof of my mouth. "I love kissing you," she whispered against my mouth.

"Good." Because she wasn't kissing anyone else. This mouth was mine. This body was mine. She was *mine*. I tilted her head and kissed her deeper as my dick surged against the cabinetry. Would there ever be a time when this woman didn't get me hard as the fucking granite with a single kiss? I doubted it. "Tell me you still want this—you want me."

Her pupils dilated as she tugged my hair again lightly. "I want you."

"I'm not a gentle man. What you saw—and felt—the first

time we were together was me being exceptionally careful," I warned her, knowing that if all she wanted was gentle and sweet, then I'd give her exactly that.

"And it was delicious." Her voice lilted in a way that sounded like she was thanking me for dessert. "But I want whatever it was you were holding back. I want all of you, Cannon. You won't break me. Let me prove that I'm strong enough for you." She feathered her thumb over my lips, and I nipped at it.

"You have nothing to prove to me."

She responded by jerking my shirt over my head. It landed in the mixing bowl, but I didn't give a fuck. Not when her lips were at my neck, my throat, my chest. Her kisses were little flicks of fire to my nervous system that gathered in my cock.

Her hands skimmed my sides, feathered over my abs where they lingered when her touch made the muscles tense. "You are pure fantasy. It's like you stepped out of my hottest dreams. You know that, right?"

"Then we must have the same damned dream because you sure as hell have starred in mine," I growled, bringing her mouth back to mine. I kissed her with reckless abandon, not slowing to seduce her or gentling when she whimpered. Her hands reached for the waistband of my athletic shorts, and she tugged.

The fabric protested over the head of my dick for a second, then fell to the floor. I kicked off my shoes and peeled off my socks quickly.

Our mouths never parted as I flicked open the button of her shorts and yanked down her zipper. She lifted her hips, and I peeled her shorts off her ass, taking her panties with them down her thighs and past her knees, stepping back only long enough for her shorts to join mine.

My jersey and her bra went next, leaving her naked and

hungry for me. Her fingers found my boxer briefs, and then she squeezed the length of my cock through the fabric.

"Fuck," I hissed, leaning into her.

"Harder? Faster?" she asked as her hand slid up and down slowly.

"Goddamn, Persephone," I growled.

"Teach me." She ran her thumb over the exposed head where I rose above my waistband, then brought her thumb to her mouth and licked off a drop of pre-cum before reaching for my cock again.

I managed to grab her wrist, stopping her. "Not today."

She blinked, then ran her tongue over her lower lip. "I want to know how to please you. How to make you as wild as you make me."

"You already do," I promised, stroking my thumb over the inside of her wrist. "But you start touching me like that, and I'm going to have to hold back, and I want you too fucking badly for that kind of restraint right now."

"But you'll teach me another time?" she asked, already shifting her thighs.

"I'll teach you whatever you want to know," I promised. I would. She could pull out the Karma Sutra and leave it on the fucking coffee table like a takeout menu if she wanted. We'd do everything she wanted.

I let go of her wrist and ditched my boxer briefs. Then I gripped her hips and pulled her to the very edge of the counter.

Our mouths met in another kiss, and I let myself off the leash. I anchored her at her hip, and took her breast with the other hand, thumbing the already pert nipple. She moaned and leaned into my touch.

Then I tongued that spot on her neck that drove her crazy and was rewarded by a gush of warmth against my cock as she cried out. My fingers found her already wet and slippery, so I moved the head of my dick to her entrance. Fuck, she already felt amazing, and I wasn't even inside her yet.

"Are you taking me upstairs?" she asked as her nails bit into my shoulders.

"No." I grinned, letting every ounce of my intent show.

"But…" She rocked against me, but she didn't have the leverage to bring me inside. "I don't want to wait."

"We're not going to." Hands on her hips, I pinned her and slowly pushed inside of her. I gritted my teeth against the pleasure that assaulted me as I took possession of her inch by inch. She was so fucking tight.

Her breath came in jerky gasps as she stared at me with wide, desire-glazed eyes.

"Put your legs around my waist," I instructed, feeling her give and soften around me as I kept pushing forward.

She did, locking her ankles at the small of my back. "Like this?"

"Just like that. Fuck. You feel so damned good. Are you okay?" I rested my forehead against hers.

"Uh huh." She tried to move, but I wouldn't let her. "I thought you said you weren't holding back."

"Feel how tight you are?" I barely managed the words as I pulled out slightly only to drive back in, taking another inch.

"I feel how massive you are. You're stretching me, and it stings so good." She gripped my hair.

"There's a difference between not holding back and not hurting you." I'd made her come almost twice before I'd taken her that first time, but I'd been too impatient to wait now. I tilted her head with one hand and set my mouth on her neck.

"I can take it." She writhed and rocked against me.

She relaxed, and I took that last fucking inch, seating myself to the hilt as she cried out, but there was only pleasure in her eyes. "You'll never have to take it because I'll never fucking hurt you."

"I'm not weak." She flexed her thighs around me.

"I know that. Now hold on." I couldn't hold still any longer.

She locked her hands behind my neck as I pulled nearly all the way out and drove back in. We both groaned.

"Again," she ordered.

I obeyed, taking her in another long, deep thrust as she called out my name. Then I did it again and again, starting a hard, slow rhythm and keeping it. She met my every thrust, taking and giving all in the same motion as she gripped my cock like a fist.

"Fuck, I'll never get enough of this." I took her over and over, letting my control slip slightly as I lost myself in her. Every stroke was better than the last, every kiss hotter.

"Good." She let go of my neck and laid back on the counter, her arms rising until she gripped the edge of the other side. "Now stop holding back and fuck me."

She looked like a wanton goddess stretched out in front of me, ready to be worshiped, and those words on her lips shredded what was left of my control.

I thrust deep and hard. "Is that what you want?"

"Yes!" she shouted, arching her neck.

I lost it, driving into her faster, harder, taking everything she gave, and giving her back only myself. Pleasure spiraled down my spine, and I felt the approaching orgasm gather.

"You're so fucking beautiful." I used my thumb to tease her swollen clit as I swung my hips like a piston, driving us both closer to the edge.

Her thighs trembled, her stomach tensed, and then she cried my name as she came apart under me. Arching up as her orgasm took her in waves. Her pussy gripped me tight but still I kept driving on, not ready to surrender, for this moment to be over.

"Again," I ordered just like she had, and pressed on her clit as I shifted my angle inside her. Her fading orgasm stuttered, then flared into a second one.

This time she screamed my name as she bucked under me, riding out her pleasure.

She squeezed me tight again, and this time I let go, roaring as the orgasm ripped through me, nearly blacking me out. Fuck, if I came this hard every time we fucked, I wasn't going to survive.

I gathered her against me as we both gasped for breath.

"You okay?" I asked as she wound her arms around my neck.

"Uh huh." She nodded. "You're really, really, really good at that."

I laughed. "I'm kind of your only experience."

She shook her head. "Nope. I've heard stories. Girls talk."

"Does that mean you're going to talk about me?" I kissed her nose.

"Heck no. I don't need anyone trying to steal you away. You're all mine." Her gaze dropped to the mixing bowl as she wiggled her hips. "Sorry about your shirt."

"I don't give a fuck about the shirt. Ruin whatever you want." Fuck, I was already hardening inside her.

"Does this mean we're scratching rule number five?" She arched her brows over those hopeful blue eyes.

"Fuck rule number five."

"Oh really?" Her eyes narrowed. "What changed your mind?"

I debated keeping quiet. It wasn't like the woman needed any more power over me. "It was the jersey. There's something incredibly fucking sexy about seeing my name across your back."

"Ah," she said with a little nod. "Well, actually, it's *my* name."

I laughed, and she grinned up at me, a dangerous twinkle shining there. "What are you thinking, Mrs. Price?"

"I'm wondering exactly how many jerseys I can order. I mean, if wearing one gets you to fuck me like that—"

I kissed her quiet, then lifted her in my arms and carried her toward our bedroom. "You have no idea how many ways I can fuck you, Persephone. But I'm going to show you every single one."

She bit her lip and then nodded. "Yes, please."

"So polite."

"Manners are everything."

"You're everything." I walked us straight into the shower and started all over again.

12

PERSEPHONE

"This is one of the best-kept secrets in Charleston," Echo said, holding open the door to the boutique for my father, mother, and myself. "I know the owner." She winked as she followed us inside.

"Of course you do," I teased. "I swear you have just as many connections as we do."

Echo smiled and shrugged. "Comes with running one of the most sought-after bars in the city."

"It comes from hard work and compassion," my father said, grinning at Echo. "Don't brush off your success. Own it. You've worked hard for it." He patted her on the shoulder, and Echo swallowed hard.

"Thank you, sir," she said.

"Oh, sugar, look at these!" my mother squealed from a corner in the back of the store. "They're marvelous!"

I hurried over to her, leaving my father and Echo chatting behind me. Both my parents had loved her, naturally, but my father had taken a true liking to her. I wish he'd extend that same kindness to Cannon, but, one thing at a time.

"Look at this beadwork along the neckline," Mom said, holding out a beautiful silk gown with delicate pearl beads along the deep V of the dress. "It's divine."

I gasped, fingering the intricate design. "It is," I said, and fiddled with the material in search of a label. "Who is it by?"

"Me," a female voice said from behind us. I spun to see a tall woman with gorgeous red hair and blue eyes standing behind us. She pointed to the sign above the section. "Luna," she said, pointing from the sign to herself. Then she indicated the shop around her. "This is my boutique. Most of the items I painstakingly harvest from vintage shops, but this section here is all mine."

"You're incredibly talented," Mom said, and I agreed.

"Yep!" Echo popped up beside us, my dad in tow, and grinned at Luna. "Told you," Echo beamed.

"It's about time you visit me!" Luna said, wrapping Echo in a quick hug. "It's been months."

"That door swings both ways, Luna," Echo said, giving her a faux glare. Both the women giggled before Echo jolted and fished out her phone. "Not the babysitter," she clarified, more to herself than anyone else. "Notification." She glanced at me. "We're up." Her eyebrows rose. "Aw, they have Sterling in goal."

"We must be *way* up then," I said, hating that we were missing the game. But I *had* to find a dress. "If they took Sawyer out."

Echo nodded. "Sterling is talented. Good kid, too. Sawyer has taken him under his wing. It's good he's getting in-game time."

I smiled, absorbing the knowledge and letting it sink into me. It had been a whirlwind month since our last girl's night at the bar—the same night I'd made a fool of myself spouting poetry about my husband.

My husband. The man I'd marry, *again*, and was shopping for the dress now.

We'd fallen into a wonderful rhythm, not even missing a beat once the season started. I went to as many games as I could—both home and away—all while working with Silas on the new charity as well as planning this wedding with my mother.

A beautiful, steady stream of delightful chaos. That's what my life had become since marrying Cannon that fateful night in Vegas, and I honestly didn't regret it for one second.

Seeing Mom like this? Out and about and so damn happy? A much-added bonus.

Though, a prick of cold pinched me when I thought about the truth—that my mother was Cannon's sole motivation for re-marrying me and staying married for a time. To bring her joy—as a gift to me—before her final days. The kidney donor list was lengthy, and it didn't matter how much money we had—Mama would never use her status, power, or wealth to try and hop the line.

"May I try this one on, please?" I asked Luna, needing the task to distract me from the thoughts I tried to keep locked away.

"Absolutely," she said, taking the gown.

"And this one too," Mom added, handing her another. "You want to see your options."

I nodded. We'd already been to four other dress shops. I was beyond exhausted, but I hadn't *clicked* with one yet.

"I'll go get these set up in a room for you," Luna said, and Mom followed her.

Echo's phone rang, and she jolted again, eying us. "This *is* the babysitter! I'll be right back!" She hurried out to take the call, and I smiled. Motherhood was so beautiful on her.

"I like her," Father said as he followed me to the dressing room where Mom and Luna chatted.

"I'm glad," I said, pausing. "She's wonderful."

"But?" Father urged, reading my hesitance easily.

"I wonder why you can't extend the same attitude to Cannon?" Echo had just as many tattoos as him, and even more piercings. Her style and demeanor was close to his—despite their stories being totally different.

"Echo isn't marrying my daughter," he grumbled.

"Try *married*."

"*Trying* to forget it."

I sighed.

"Echo has a plan," he continued. "Cannon doesn't."

"How would you know?" I countered. "You've barely spoken to him!"

"What happens when he slows down? Huh? What happens when he gets hurt? How will he take care of you then?"

I arched a brow at him. "Father, I haven't needed a man to take care of me in quite some time."

"I understand that, Sephie," he said, his voice softening. "I love you. I've loved you and cared for you and worried about you since the day you took your first breath." He swallowed hard. "I want you to have the best life possible. And, I'm sorry, sugar, but I don't know if Cannon can give you that."

Something like a blow hit me in the chest. "Why?"

"His history is bloody. Violent. Darkness you shouldn't have to deal with."

I shook my head, my shoulders sinking. "You should know that those aren't the only pieces of him. You should trust *me* and *my* choices."

He opened and closed his mouth a few times, but I didn't wait for his response. I hurried into the dressing room where Mom waited anxiously perched on the cushioned bench next to the mirror.

"You want to talk about it?" she asked softly as I unbuttoned my sundress.

"Not really," I admitted. There was no point. Father would learn to accept Cannon, or he wouldn't. Especially since he'd leave once…well, once all was said and done.

Then why are you fighting so hard to defend him.

Good question. Yet another I filed away.

"Your sister came by the house yesterday," Mom said.

I hissed. "And?"

"She apologized to us. And to Gerald."

"Funny, I never got an apology."

"I think she's afraid to speak to you. She's so ashamed."

"As she should be," I said, stripping down to nothing but my undergarments. I stepped lightly into the first gown, and Mom hopped up to help me zip the back.

I looked in the mirror, eying it. Pretty, but…

"Not the one," she said and unzipped it again.

I stepped out of it, smiling at her. I loved that we were both on the same page. Loved that she could tell what I loved and what I didn't.

"Anne will come around," Mom said as I grabbed the other dress. "She needs to be loved harder. I'm not sure why, but she does. We have to do our best to not give up on her. Time goes so fast, and there isn't much left and—"

I cut her off with a hug. "Mom," I said, needing her to stop. "I will forgive her, I promise." I could tell she was worried her daughters would still not be speaking, and she'd leave this earth with unfinished business—because she took our fights on as her own, being our Mama.

Mom straightened and nodded. "Enough about that. Let's get this one on. I have a good feeling about it."

I sucked in a deep breath and let go of the grief I could feel building despite my mother still being here. Let go of the hurt from the pain my sister had caused. Let go of my father's disapproval of Cannon, and slipped into the gown.

Mom buttoned the back, and as she fastened the last one and stepped out of the mirror's view, I gasped. The sleeveless cream silk hugged my curves and pooled around my feet, the deep V showing a little of my skin, the delicate beadwork glistening under the light almost making me look like I had some inner glow.

This is the one.

The gown I'd wear down the aisle, Cannon at the end of it.

The picture was so clear in my mind like a movie I'd already seen. Him standing there in a tux, those sinfully dark eyes tracking my every step toward him, toward our future together. My heart swelled, each beat thudding with one singular truth.

I *wanted* to walk down that aisle toward Cannon.

I *wanted* to marry him, and no one else.

Till death do us part—not some agreed upon expiration date.

Forever.

Tears coated my eyes—not of fear or sadness, but of joy.

"That's the one," my mom said behind me, coming up to hug my shoulders.

I nodded, choking back the tears. Tears my mother thought were for the dress but were really for the realization snapping through my soul like a lightning strike.

Cannon Price was my forever.

* * *

Asher Silas: Just got verbal confirmation from Weston Rutherford for a sizable donation for the new charitable focus.

I excitedly read the text twice to make sure I'd read it correctly. Having a donation and support from the owner of the Raleigh Raptors—the NFL team Nathan Noble's twin brother, Nixon played for—would be invaluable.

Me: That's wonderful! Thank you! Are you at your monthly poker game now?

Asher Silas: Yes. Weston is having some drama with his QB but he'll get confirmation on celebrity appearances as well soon.

I bit my bottom lip, not wanting to cross the line between friendship and business too much, but ultimately decided I couldn't *not* ask.

Me: Is Nixon all right?

Asher Silas: Physically he's in peak shape. It's a media issue. Nothing too terrible.

Relief hit me upon hearing he was physically fine. Funny how being accepted into this Reaper family also afforded me an extended family as well. Sure, I didn't know Nixon Noble as well as his brother Nathan, but that didn't mean I didn't care about him.

Me: Glad to hear it. You think you can rope Ethan Berkley in on this too?

I unabashedly sent the text—having the owner of the Charleston Hurricane's support would be just as invaluable. Plus, Hudson Porter's little brother played for the MLB team, so the connection had a family tie as well.

Asher Silas: I'm already working on him. I don't see an issue. Simply hard to get much business done between the gossip and cards.

Me: LOL. Have fun. Leave them some money to donate!

Asher Silas: I'll do my best.

I blew out a breath and settled into the plush chair situated in Cannon's library. I had decided to wrap up a little work from here after dress shopping, and he was due home any minute. I had one phone call left to make, and I'd been putting it off for a good while.

Time to put my big-girl panties on.

I swallowed the nerves twisting my stomach, and dialed the number.

"Hello?" Lillian answered after a couple of rings. I could hear her son giggling in the background.

"Hello, Lillian, it's Persephone." My voice cracked slightly.

"Everything all right?"

"Yes, of course," I hurried to answer. "Why wouldn't it be?"

"You sound kind of nervous. Just wanted to make sure."

"Well, I'm sorry to bother you, but I was hoping to ask you something." I took a deep breath. "There is absolutely no pressure at all, and I will totally understand if you don't feel comfortable…I know we don't know each other that well. But, you see, I'd be so honored if you'd stand with me at the altar when I re-marry your brother." The words came out in one long stream of consciousness. Normally I had the grace and poise strong and smooth enough to wrangle billionaires and their contributions, but speaking to Cannon's sister? The most important person in his life? Not so much.

"Oh, wow," she said. "Is that all? I'd love to."

A breath rushed from my lungs. "Thank you. And, if it's not too much trouble, we'd love Owen to be the ring bearer."

"I'm sure we can handle that," she said, but there was a hesitance in her tone that gave me pause.

"If you're not comfortable with him in the wedding, it's absolutely fine," I said.

"That's not it at all," she said. "It's just…"

I waited a few heartbeats, but she didn't continue. "What is it, Lillian?"

"Well, you know I have to give you the sister speech now, right?"

My stomach tightened, but I nodded like she could see me. "Hit me with it," I finally said.

"Don't hurt my brother," she said, her tone switching from friendly to fierce in the span of a breath. "All those tattoos aren't armor. He may seem like the strongest, toughest asshole in the world, but he isn't." She sighed. "I'm not sure how much you know about our history, I'm assuming a great deal since you're…well, whatever you are… but Cannon is a self-sacrificer to a *fault*. He took on the brunt of everything to protect me. And it's my turn to protect him."

I held my breath, my heart aching. I knew this about Cannon, but I didn't know him like she did, and I wanted to so badly. I wanted him to let me in. To help shoulder some of his past burdens. Sure, he'd let me in physically—our time spent between, above, and beyond the sheets kept a permanent and pleasurable ache between my thighs. But emotionally? Just pieces. I wanted all of him.

"Be patient with him," she continued. "He's never truly dealt with some of the issues from our past, and to some, that makes him this closed-off jerk, but truly? He's the most kind, compassionate person I know."

"I see him," I said, my voice clogged with emotion. "I'm trying, but he still keeps me at a distance in some things. I promise you, Lillian, I have no intention of hurting him. Ever. I want to be there for him in the way he's been there for others."

"Good," she said, back to friendly. "It's about time he let someone help him for a change. I just hope he doesn't scare you off."

"Not going to happen."

"I like you, Sephie," she said. "And I can't wait to stand up there with you."

"That means the world to me," I said, and I heard the

front door open and close. "I'll send you all the details. I just heard your brother walk in, have to run!"

"Take care of him," she said before hanging up.

And I silently vowed to her that I would do my best.

I left my phone on the desk, needing to disconnect for the night, and hurried down the hallway. I found Cannon in the kitchen, shirtless near the sink and holding a paper towel over his right pec. The center soaked in red.

"Cannon!" I hurried over to him, and my sudden presence made him flinch.

"*Jesus*," he said. "You scared the hell out of me." He eyed my bare feet. "It's impossible to hear you without your heels on."

I rolled my eyes and reached for his hand. "What happened?"

He backed away from my touch. "Got into a knife fight."

I gaped at him, and he laughed.

"Cannon Price."

He sighed. "Wasn't watching where I was going. Ran into Logan's skate in the locker room, which he had over his shoulder. Not a big deal," he said, but he winced when he removed the paper towel.

I shook my head at the poor use of the towel. "Follow me. Now." I didn't bother looking behind me as I made my way to our room and into the bathroom. "Sit." I snapped my fingers at the edge of his giant, marble encased tub, and bit back a smile when he obeyed.

I bent over, rummaging through the cabinets until I'd found the first aid kit.

"This isn't necessary," he grumbled. "It's a scratch. I don't need to be fawned over."

"Like that would be so bad," I said. "To have someone heal *you* for a change."

I fingered through the products until I'd found the

alcohol and gauze and bandages. I carried everything over to him, sitting it all down next to him on the marble. I reached for the paper towel he held over the wound, and he flinched away, *again.*

My heart ached, the earlier conversation with his sister coming back to the forefront of my mind. How many times had he had to clean up wounds on his own? And then hide them? Bury the source of the pain?

"Cannon," I pled, sinking to my knees before him. "Please, let me help you."

His eyes shuttered—at the sight of me or at the desperation in my tone, I didn't know—but he dropped his hand, exposing the small cut over his pec. The blood welled once he dropped it, the red marring the beautiful whorls of black decorated there, but it was small. I dabbed a cotton ball with the alcohol and eyed him as I held it toward the cut.

"I'm fine," he said.

I wiped the wound clean. He barely hissed. Then I took extra care in pressing a small square of gauze over the cut, using clear surgical tape to secure it. He'd rarely let me this close to his bare chest—not unless we were in the throes of passion—like that one time in the shower when he'd let me wash him, and he'd explained some of the scars—but since then, he'd always taken the reins on what I could and couldn't touch. Which was absolutely his right, I just wanted him to trust me enough to help him.

My fingers traced the edges of the tape, double-checking the tightness, and then lower.

I felt him tense beneath my touch as I ran my fingertips over the patterns of ink, over his strong abdomen, and then I paused at some puckered flesh now invisible due to the ink. Some old scar.

His hand tightened around my wrist, stopping me from moving.

I flicked my gaze up to his, my heart breaking at the fear in his eyes, the shame.

"Cannon—"

"Don't," he said, his normal response, and one I would respect. I didn't try to move or break his grasp, but he didn't push me away either. I took that as a small crack in the door Cannon kept parts of himself locked inside.

"This doesn't scare me," I whispered, my hand still in his brushing against the scar. "You *know* it doesn't."

He sighed, his muscles relaxing underneath my touch, his grip loosening enough that my hand fell.

"You're beautiful," I said, running my fingers freely over his body, catching on all the hard pieces of old scars. "Every." I kissed one scar. "Single." Then another. "Inch."

"Persephone." My name was a broken whisper.

I tucked my fingers into his athletic pants, tugging them free of his feet and tossing them behind me. Leaving him in nothing but his boxer-briefs.

"Let me in," I said. "Please, let me help *heal* you." He knew I meant so much more than the cut I'd just tended to.

I continued my exploration of his skin, stopping on a four-inch-long piece of hardened skin, my gaze on his, questioning, open. Just like we'd done that day in the shower. All he had to do was make the choice to walk through the door and come to me.

"Razorblade," he said, his voice rough. "Dad had come home drunk. Lillian had left her toy car—my old one—near the dining room table." He shrugged. "She was three."

I swallowed hard, that would only make him four.

I kissed that scar and moved on to another.

"Broken arm," he said. "Thrown down the stairs."

Tears burned the backs of my eyes, but I kissed that one and moved to the next, a peppering of raised slashes.

"Kitchen knife," he explained. "To prevent Mom from ever trying to leave again."

I kissed each one, tasting salt from the warm tears I couldn't hold back that splashed upon his skin. He'd told me before about the stove burner and the cigarette burns…but, God, there were so many stories here. So many dark pieces of his past.

Over and over again, I worshiped his body, kissing and caressing those broken pieces of himself hidden beneath the ink, giving those jagged edges more time and care. Silently listening to his story, my heart shattering with each reason behind every scar.

And after what felt like an eternity, a slow-torturous journey through Cannon's dark past, I kissed my way up to his lips and cradled his face in my hands.

"I see you, Cannon," I said, not bothering to wipe the tears from my eyes. "And you're not only the most beautiful man I've ever seen but the *best* man I've ever known."

Something dark and broken shuttered in his eyes before he clenched them shut and pressed his forehead against mine. His arms came around my back, clutching me to him, holding me as he trembled, as those raw, exposed moments from his past lay open and bare between us. And I clung to him, held him silently, pouring every ounce of light and love I had into him until I couldn't take the small distance one second longer. Until I knew I needed to give him something else entirely.

My heart.

My soul.

I fingered his hair, gripping the strands a bit tighter and tugging until his face was level with mine. I held his dark gaze for a few heartbeats before gently kissing him. He opened for me, and I claimed his mouth, giving and taking and relishing in the taste of him. His hands clenched on my hips as he hefted me up to straddle his lap without breaking our kiss. But I didn't stay there for long—no, we'd had passionate, wild sex in many places in this house. Now wasn't the time for that.

I stepped off of him and reached for his hand. He looked up at me questioningly but took my hand. I led him out of the bathroom and to the bed where I gently nudged him until he lay on his back. Slowly, I peeled off my clothes, and his remaining underwear until we were bare before each other. My blood thrumming and thrashing, begging me to go hard and fast with this man. Just like he liked, how *I* liked. But I hushed the consuming need. Tonight was about Cannon, about *him* letting me in.

Tonight, he needed to learn what it felt like to be worshipped.

To be adored.

To be the sole focus of another person. Someone he could trust to take care of him.

So, I crawled on the bed, hovering over him, and continued my slow, sizzling kisses over his scars. So many damn scars. I kissed the ones on his thighs while I gripped his hard length in my hand, pumping and stroking the silken heat.

A low growl and he reached for me, his fingers hurried, needy, but I flashed my eyes up to his.

"Let me take care of you, Cannon," I said, my warm breath hitting his cock in my hand. "Just, tell me if I do something wrong, okay?" He'd taught me so much, but there was a ton I didn't know.

"You could never do anything wrong," he hissed as I teased him, but his hands relaxed at his sides. His hips jutted upward as I set my mouth on him, taking him inside me in a slow, tortuous sweep of my mouth. Up and down, I sucked and pumped and hummed around his cock until his entire body was coiled with need, and he growled my name.

I smiled around his flesh, pulling him out of my mouth with a satisfying popping sound. Then I settled myself atop him, taking him in and in, his heat sliding inside me, filling me until I could barely breathe. I threaded our fingers and pulled him upward until we were chest to chest, eye to eye.

And then I moved on him.

Slow, so agonizingly slow.

Each roll of my hips a tortuous raking of internal heat that thrashed and shuttered and pleaded.

An ache so deep I didn't think I could ever soothe it.

"Goddamn," Cannon hissed, his lips brushing mine. "You're gorgeous," he said as he watched me move on him, as his hands explored my skin with electric caresses.

I cupped his cheeks, keeping pace as I trembled around him, and kissed him. Drank in his sounds as if they could fill that spot in my soul he'd claimed. I kissed him deep and long, in time to the rhythm I'd adapted, riding him in long waves of heat and need and hunger. Dragging out the moment as long as either of us could physically take, drawing us right to that sweet, sharp edge, only to pull us back again.

And just as I felt Cannon harden more inside me, just as my own rising orgasm built and coiled and tightened, just as he clenched his eyes shut and threw his head back, I gripped his hair and drew back his focus.

Caught that dark gaze as I upped my pace, as I sank harder atop him, taking him fast and deep.

"Stay with me," I pled, needing his eyes on me. Needing him to come with me. Needing *him*, all of him.

"Always," he whispered against my lips as I sank atop him again, rolling my hips until I couldn't hold myself together one second longer.

Cannon gripped me tighter against him as I shattered

into a million tiny pieces. He devoured my moans, drinking them in as he found his own release inside me.

And I didn't stop kissing him.

Didn't stop breathing him in.

Not until we were forced to pull apart to catch our breath.

And even then, I wanted *more*.

13

CANNON

"Three, two, one!" The crowd counted down my penalty. Two minutes for roughing had been worth it. Then again, since we were up four to one against Detroit with only three minutes left in the third period, it was fair to note that it hadn't been my first time in the box tonight.

I flew out onto the ice and positioned myself near the blue line as Briggs and Noble fought to get the puck out of our zone.

One of the Red Wings rubbed a little close on me as I maneuvered forward, so I gave him a little bump. The guy lost his balance and ran into the boards. Whoops.

Briggs drove through two of the forwards, moving the puck so quickly I had to focus, then shot it my direction when the Red Wings' center took him on. I caught the puck and sent it flying toward Axel, then took off, careful not to pass the blue line until he brought the puck over it.

They backchecked, naturally, but Axel fired the puck at me just before they caught him. I caught the puck and took off toward the goal, beating the first defenseman with pure speed and faking out the second with a quick stop and change of direction. My heart pounded, and the roar of the crowd faded as I honed in on the goalie.

I'd played with this asshole for years, which meant I knew his moves, but it also meant that he knew mine. I drove glove-side, knowing his upper right pocket was his most vulnerable spot. When he moved to cover, I flipped to backhand and shot the puck stick-side.

It sailed just under his arm and hit the back of the net.

The lamp lit, the crowd thundered, and I shouted in victory as Axel pounded on my back in congratulations.

"Nice goal!" he shouted.

"Nice assist!" I countered.

I skated toward the family seats and noted with a grin that Persephone sat in the front row, not up in the box seats some of the others favorited. My girl liked to be close to the action. I pointed straight at her, and she smiled, shaking her head and clapping for me.

She looked every bit the part of an NHL wife, from her designer jeans to her tailored Reapers Jersey that fit her like a fucking glove. Her hair was down, framing her incredible breasts, but I knew the best part was the fact that my name was on the back of the jersey. I hadn't even seen it before I left for the game this afternoon, but I would have bet my bonus on it.

I halted just in front of her and twirled my finger with a smirk.

She cocked an eyebrow at me, but turned around, no doubt thinking about how much it turned me on to see Price on her back.

But it was her turn to surprise *me*. She'd had it custom made with my number, but it read, "Mrs. Price." She turned back around and threw my own smirk back at me.

"So fucking hot," I said toward the glass, knowing she would read my lips.

Her grin was heart-stopping, and I pounded at my chest to let her know it.

"For fuck's sake, Price!" Coach yelled from the bench, and I took off for fear that we'd get a penalty for too many men on the ice if I stalled much longer.

"Sorry, Coach."

He smacked my helmet. "Make googly eyes at your wife on your own time, Price. Not mine. That being said, it was a damn fine goal."

We finished the game five to one, and I left the ice feeling like I hadn't just secured a victory against the team that had traded me when my PR issues were too much for them to handle—I'd won against the Cannon I'd *used* to be back then, too.

I returned a text from Lillian, showered, and went through the post-game nonsense. I answered a few questions from the reporters brave enough to walk over and ask them, but I left most of that spotlight shit to Axel as our captain, and the guys who liked the attention.

Throwing my bag over my shoulder, I walked out of the locker room with Sterling.

"You did really well tonight," I told the kid as we made our way through the small crowd of reporters, staff, and really fucking bold puck-bunnies.

"I let that one in," he argued, shaking his head, as we cleared the crowd.

"Look, I played with Brian for *years*. The guy leads that team in scoring for a reason. It says a lot about Coach McPherson's confidence in you that he let you out there tonight. Don't beat yourself...holy shit." I paused mid-sentence at the sight of the middle-aged man headed our direction.

The guy was a living, breathing legend. Sergei Zolotov was one of the best goalies the game had ever seen. Even though he'd been retired, the guy still held a shit ton of records.

"Fuck," Sterling muttered, adjusting his bag on his shoulder.

"No, shit, right? What the fuck is he doing here?" Not just here, but walking straight for us, his eyes narrowing on Sterling.

"Making my life miserable," Sterling answered, clenching his jaw in a way I'd never seen.

Zolotov barely glanced my way as he pinned Sterling down with his stare. "It was easy to see that he'd take you glove-side. You're weak glove side. You don't anticipate or react fast enough."

What the fuck?

"You fly all the way out here to tell me that?" Sterling fired back.

"I flew all the way out here to see if the rumors were true, that you would be the one to watch in the coming seasons, but I see the reports were mistaken. You carry the same flaws you did in college, but on this stage, they're even more obvious." He crossed his arms over his chest, straining his suit fabric.

My gaze darted between the two. Same height. Same posture. Holy shit, they even had the same exact eyes.

"Well, you can head on home to the wife and kids, just as disappointed as always," Sterling snapped.

"Don't be an ass, Jansen."

"Don't act like you're my dad, *Father*."

Whoa. I'd stumbled into the motherload of family drama. I so wasn't qualified to help him handle this shit. Where the fuck was Logan? Or Axel? Those two were way better on the emotional stability charts.

"Don't call me that in public," Zolotov sneered.

"Then don't show up at my games. Easy." Sterling shrugged.

Zolotov's shoulders sagged slightly. "Jansen."

"Just leave me the fuck alone, would you? It was easy enough for the first twenty-two years of my life to ignore my existence. Don't come around just because I made it to the NHL, because I did that shit *without* your help." Sterling pushed past his father and headed deeper into the arena, farther from the crowd.

"He's difficult," Zolotov muttered.

"He's my friend, so go to hell." I followed Sterling, catching him before the hall curved.

"Fuck. I'm sorry you saw that," he growled, looking more serious than I'd ever seen him.

"Look, I'm the last person to lecture you about family shit."

"He never came around when I was a kid. And I get it. He's been married to the same perfect Russian woman for the last twenty-six years, and has three, perfect, Russian kids." His jaw ticked. "But the only thing I'm grateful to that asshole for is that he paid my mother child support. He might have paid for my ice time, but he sure as fuck didn't coach me up like he did for his real kids."

"Shit. Maxim Zolotov was a rookie last year, too."

"Yep." He paused, and I turned when I realized he wasn't walking. "Look. Can you not tell everyone else? I got here on my own, and I don't need his fucking legacy hanging over me."

"No problem."

"Cool." He took a deep breath, and when he looked up, it was as if the last five minutes hadn't happened. "So, I've decided I'm going to wear a blue leisure suit to your wedding."

The abrupt change would have caught me off-guard if I didn't have an intimate understanding of hiding family dynamics.

"And that right there is the reason you will *never* be my best man." We came around the corner and found a group of women standing in front of the elevator. The elevator I needed to get on so I could meet Persephone in her office.

"Oh my God, if it isn't Cannon Price," one of the women said, looking me up and down with a wide smile.

These were Detroit girls. I scanned over their faces, noting a few wives of the Red Wings players, and more than a few bunnies that must have elevated themselves if they were traveling with the team.

I gave them a nod and grimaced as a tall brunette swayed her way over to me. Her arms were covered in colorful tats, and her nose was pierced with a single stud. I knew her, but couldn't remember how. Fuck. Tiffany? Taylor? Tina? What was her name? Thank God I'd never fucked her because I wasn't inviting that drama into my life.

"I came all the way to see you," she purred, staring at me like I was lunch.

"Then I hope you enjoyed the game."

The elevator dinged, but I couldn't see past the Red Wings women.

"Oh come on, Cannon. You said you'd never be interested while I was dating Ambrose, and now I'm not." She held out her hands like she was serving something…serving herself. "So when my friends demanded a girls' trip, I figured you'd be my reward."

Tanya. That was her name. She'd been the on-again, off-again girlfriend of one of the guys who'd been called up from the minors, and from what I'd read, he'd gone right back down at the end of last season.

"Sorry. Not interested."

Her face fell. "I'm sorry?"

"Not sure if you've heard, but Cannon here got married," Sterling thumbed my direction. "I, however, am single and absolutely available to reward you."

Had to give it to the kid. He had balls.

Tanya glanced him over, then arched a sculpted brow at me. "No fucking way are you married. I've never seen you with the same woman twice."

"Then you haven't seen him lately," Sterling chimed in.

I held up my left hand, and her eyes fell to the ring, widening as she took it in.

The crowd of women parted slightly, and Persephone emerged. Her little kitten heels did jack and shit for her height, but she still turned every woman's head as she came my way.

"There you are!" she said with a grin. "You were amazing!"

She flew into my arms, and I caught her easily, lifting her against me as my hand splayed over the number on her back. I squeezed my eyes shut and breathed in her apple blossom scent, feeling that ache in my chest transform into a fucking glow as she kissed me quickly.

I opened my eyes to see Tanya staring at Persephone's back. I lowered my wife carefully, and she tucked into my side, turning a ready, kind smile on Tanya.

"Oh, hello! I'm so sorry, was I interrupting something?" She glanced between us.

"Persephone, this is Tanya. She dated one of the players when I was with Detroit." I kept my arm comfortably locked around Persephone's waist, careful not to let my bag fall on her. "Tanya, this is my wife, Persephone."

"It's lovely to meet you." Persephone offered her hand, and Tanya took it, shaking it awkwardly.

"You're…his wife?" She stared openly at Persephone.

"Yep!"

"But…you're not his type." Her brow furrowed.

Rage simmered in my blood, but Persephone patted my chest. "To tell you the truth, he's not mine, either, but the man literally swept me off my feet a couple of years ago, and the rest is history!"

I stifled a laugh at how she'd twisted our first encounter, and managed a nod. "True. And once she fell for me, I couldn't resist her."

Tanya's jaw dropped. "You're really, honestly married. The two of you." She glanced between us.

"They are. I was there," Sterling assured her. "It was a beautiful, impulsive, almost drunk-on-joy ceremony, and I was the best man."

I turned my head slowly to raise my eyebrows at him. "You are not the best man."

"I feel like there's room for negotiation."

"A nice little girl like you ended up with…Cannon Price. Oh honey, do you know what you've gotten yourself into?" Tanya's voice dripped with fake sympathy.

If Persephone was right, and women gossiped about the bedroom habits of men, then I had no doubt she'd heard some of those stories back in Detroit, when I hadn't been selective about the women I'd taken to bed.

"Oh, I know exactly what I've gotten myself into. Don't you worry." Persephone scrunched her nose in a way that told me she was geared up for battle, southern belle style.

"Was it the money?" Tanya questioned. "Or the sex?"

My eyes narrowed.

"Absolutely not! I have more money than I'll ever be able to spend in a lifetime, bless your little heart." Persephone smiled at Tanya and rested her hand just above her breasts. "I honestly can't tell you why I decided to marry him. That's all a blur, really. But my God, did I win the husband jackpot or what? I mean, I absolutely adore everything about the man, and he's just the most loyal, protective, sweetest, most attentive husband a girl could ask for, but I have to admit, that dick sure is a great bonus!"

Tanya's jaw dropped.

Sterling sputtered.

I flat-out laughed. "And on that note, I'm afraid we have to be going." I scooped up Persephone and hoisted her over the shoulder that wasn't carrying my bag, then splayed my hand over her ass to steady her as I turned around to head back down the hall.

"I hope you have a lovely trip!" Persephone called back at Tanya.

"I should spank you," I muttered up at my wife, still grinning from ear to ear.

"Mmmm….yes, please." A passing mirror showed that she was wiggling her fingers in goodbye at Tanya as we walked away.

My little kitten had out her tigress claws.

"You are so fucking hardcore," Sterling said up at my wife.

"A girl's gotta mark her territory," she answered. "Now, you might have to move a little faster, Cannon, or we'll miss our dinner reservations."

"We have dinner reservations?" I cringed. All I wanted to do was get my wife alone.

"At the most exclusive spot in town," she assured me.

"Sounds perfect," I lied.

An hour later, I pulled onto a stretch of road that had been marked as private property, following the directions of my wife.

"Turn here," she instructed as the grass became taller and the terrain unmistakably sandy. I did as she instructed, then parked where the pavement ended. We met in front of the Hummer, and she took my hand, a gesture that had become so normal I'd almost forgotten what it was like to *not* hold her hand.

She led me down a sandy path, and I was glad I'd ditched my suit coat in the car since she still wore her jeans and jersey. Where the fuck was this restaurant?

We crested the small dune, and the Atlantic appeared before us in all her evening glory. On the stretch of beach in front of us, there was a small gazebo with a table and chairs.

"What did you do?" I asked Persephone softly.

She gave me an impish smile. "Follow me."

We made our way down the dune and across the sand as a woman emerged from the gazebo.

"It's all as you requested, Miss Van—" She shook her head. "Mrs. Price."

"Thank you so very much, Patricia. I've got it from here."

"Of course. You two enjoy your evening." The woman headed up the beach, leaving us alone as we walked up the wooden steps.

"Okay, so what is all this, and where is she going?" I asked.

"My family owns a beach house up that way. Don't stress," Persephone assured me.

I took in the table, the silver covers over the dishes, the iced bottle that sat perched near the edge of the table, and the small chocolate cake that rested between the plates.

"Persephone," I whispered, utterly speechless.

"Happy Birthday, Cannon." She rose on her toes and brushed a kiss across my mouth. "I figured you weren't one for parties if you didn't even mention that today was your birthday, so this seemed a little more your style."

I wrapped my arms around her and pulled her close. "How did you know?"

"Lillian," she answered with a smile. "Do you like it? If not, I'm sure we can call your friends—"

I kissed her soundly, savoring the brush of our tongues, and her soft sigh.

"This is perfect. You're perfect." She knew me so fucking well.

Her nose scrunched, and I immediately got worried. "Well, you might think that right now, but let me give you your present first."

"I don't need a present. I have everything I've ever wanted." I'd never spoken truer words.

"That's not exactly true. Now sit right there." She pointed to my chair.

I sat dutifully as she picked up a picnic basket from the floor and placed it in my lap. "Did you make me more cookies?" I was so down for cookies.

"Nope. Do you remember that night we were curled up reading, and you mentioned that you never stayed in one place long enough for—"

Her story was interrupted as the lid on the basket moved. I flipped it open, and a wet nose emerged, followed by black fur, big brown eyes, and a pair of floppy ears.

"Happy Birthday!" Persephone shouted like her surprise hadn't been hijacked by the puppy who was now climbing from the basket and clawing its way up my tie.

I caught the wiggling, soft, tiny monstrosity and held it under its armpits at a slight distance so I could get a grip. She —he—stared at me and wagged his tail.

"You bought me a dog?" I whispered.

Persephone nodded. "You said you always wanted one, but couldn't have one because your dad couldn't be trusted around small animals, and then you were in so many foster homes, and then the dorms, and now your travel schedule is all over the place."

I dragged my eyes from the puppy to my wife's hopeful but apprehensive face. "You bought me a dog?" I repeated.

"Well, I figured I'm home, right? And maybe it means that I can't make it to every away game, but we can hire a puppy sitter to come stay with him when I do decide to go with you every once in a while." She watched me for any sign of a reaction.

The puppy's tongue emerged, and his entire butt wriggled with his tail. "What type of dog is he?"

"He's a mix. The animal shelter wasn't clear, but they think he's Lab, Shepherd, and something else. All his brothers and sisters got adopted, and this little guy was all alone, and I couldn't leave him there." She pressed her lips in a thin line. "Cannon, if you don't like him, we can find someone to adopt him," she finished quietly.

"What? No. He's awesome! Aren't you?" I asked the little man. He tried to lick my face as his answer.

"You like him?" she asked, reaching out to scratch him behind the ear.

I transferred him to my other arm and tucked him in like a football, then pulled Persephone onto my lap. She wound her arms around my neck.

"I love him. I've never been given a better present in my life. Ever. He's perfect. You're perfect. This is all…" I looked over the dinner she'd set up for us, the secluded setting, and finally, the wriggling little monster under my arm.

"Perfect?" she suggested, her smile widening.

"Yeah. I fucking adore you, Persephone. You're incredible." I kissed her soundly as the puppy tried his best to eat my tie. I didn't care. He could have the fucking tie.

"Happy Birthday," she said again, kissing my cheek softly. "What are you going to name him?"

Keeping her on my knee, I adjusted my grip on the puppy and brought him eye level. Then I looked from him to my petite, goddess of a wife and back again.

Hades. She'd called me her Hades.

"Cerberus," I answered. "He doesn't have three heads, but something tells me he'll guard our little house just fine."

Pure feeling shined through her eyes, and her smile was a little watery as she stroked her hand down Cerberus's back. "Cerberus," said softly. "Guardian of the underworld."

We locked eyes, and that glow in my chest threatened to overtake every inch of my body. Fuck, I felt so much for this woman that I wasn't sure I'd be able to put it to words or contain it. She hadn't just given me a puppy. She'd given me a home.

"I adore you too, you know," she said softly.

"Oh yeah?" I leaned forward to kiss her, my lips just reaching hers—

A sound stopped me dead in my tracks, and then wetness seeped into my shirt. Cerberus had peed all over me.

Persephone laughed so hard she nearly fell off my lap.

"You and I are going to have to set some ground rules, little man."

He had the nerve to wag his tail and lick my face.

Best. Birthday. Ever.

14

PERSEPHONE

I closed the gate on the puppy crate, Cerberus snoring within seconds of stepping inside. I'd taken him for an extra-long walk this evening, a new and surprisingly fun nightly adventure that was quickly becoming a habit. Reaper Village offered the perfect place to raise a puppy, offering not only the safety and comfort of walking the sidewalk paths at night but also having the delightful chance to run into one of *many* friends who lived in the neighboring houses. Echo, Harper, and Faith had already fawned over Cerberus several times. Langley's cats? Not so much.

Seeing that he was happily in puppy snooze town, I kicked off my shoes and headed to the living room where I knew I'd find Cannon. He didn't hear my approach, totally consumed in the hardback he had cracked open before him, so I simply hovered in the entryway like a creeper. I trailed my eyes over the relaxed position—his long, strong legs stretched out before him, his head propped against the back of the plush couch. A simple white T-shirt covering his hard chest, the fabric thin enough to show the ink decorating his skin beneath.

With our puppy snoozing in the next room, a full and satisfying day's work put in earlier, and coming home to him like this now? Happiness filled me so much I wasn't sure how to contain it. Didn't know if I was *capable* of containing it.

Didn't know if I *wanted* to anymore.

"It's considered stalking to silently stare at someone without making yourself known." Cannon hadn't even looked up from his book.

"How did you know I was here?"

Finally, he tore his gaze away from the pages to look over at me. "I can feel you." He waggled his eyebrows, the look so playful it broke the last restraint I possessed.

Fueled by a rush of blissful adrenaline, I hurried over to the couch, gently removing his book from his hands. I marked it before setting it on the coffee table next to the couch and took the liberty to perch atop his lap.

His thumb grazed my lips, light dancing in his eyes. "What's that grin for, huh?"

"You," I answered honestly. The man was responsible for so much of my happiness these days. "Can I tell you something?" My breath caught in my lungs, a slight terror creeping up my spine. Was I about to ruin this for us?

"Anything," he said, his brow furrowing. "You should know that by now."

I nodded, sucking in a sharp breath. Nerves took over, causing a slight tremble to shudder my body.

"Princess," he said, smoothing his hands over my ribs and settling on my hips. "You're shaking."

I huffed a laugh and brushed my long blonde hair out of my face. "That's probably because I can't hold this back anymore," I said. "But I don't want things between us to change." I tightened my thighs on either side of his hips—hey, if he couldn't move, he couldn't run, right?

Cannon tilted his head.

Here goes.

"I'm in love with you, Cannon." The words burst from my lips in one big rush, my body calming at their release.

I pressed my finger against his lips, urging him not to speak.

"I know that breaks another one of your rules. And I know that you *can't* say it back. I fully understand that. You're not there. You may never be there. And I get that. After everything that has happened in your past…it's hard to love people. Especially when you don't know how long they'll be around."

Cannon's dark eyes widened, but he made no move to speak, so I dropped my finger.

"But you needed to know. You deserve to know." I leaned down, brushing my lips over his, my entire body reacting to the small contact. "You deserve to know that you're a man worthy of love. A man *easy* to love. And a man that I'm totally, helplessly in love with."

He swallowed hard, and I saw that internal battle raging in his eyes. His need to parrot the words back to me because that would be the solution to cause me the least harm. But I shook my head. "Don't say it back. Please. That's not why I told you." I smiled at him. "You're an incredible man. You make me so happy. And I just wanted you to know. No expectations. Just truth. Okay?"

Cannon blinked, once, twice, and then nodded.

"Whew," I said and blew out a breath. "Now that the easy part is out of the way," I teased, and reached in my pocket for my cell phone. "I have a very serious question for you."

Cannon visibly swallowed.

I pulled up the Cosmo web browser I had up from earlier

and flipped the screen toward him. "Can you show me how this works?" I asked in my most innocent tone. My skin flushed as I watched his eyes flare as he took in the illustration on my phone.

The seriousness in his eyes shifted to wicked delight and challenge. "I'm not sure, Princess," he said. "I've never done that before."

A thrill shot through me. Another piece of him I'd hold all to myself and hoard like the treasure he was.

"Too challenging for you?" I teased.

He studied the illustration for a few more seconds before he plucked the phone from my hand and set it atop his book. "Never," he growled as he nipped at my neck.

I wiggled above him, laughing from the tickle in his attack.

Then the real game began as Cannon hefted me upward and spun me around until I was flat on my back on the couch. He stood, scanning the room. "Supplies," he said and snapped his fingers. "Get naked."

Every nerve in my body stood at attention at the command in his tone.

"You too," I snapped back, but there was zero bite in my tone. I hurried to strip myself bare as Cannon grabbed a thick pillow from the loveseat across the room. He tossed the pillow at me so quick I barely had enough time to catch it. I giggled as I clutched it to my chest, watching him drop his clothes in a pile around him.

I breathed out, some part of me relieved at the sight of him. Would this ever end? This constant hunger? This primal need to be with him, be as close to him as humanly possible? I sure as hell hoped not.

"You sure?" I asked as Cannon met me on the couch, his lips an inch from mine.

"You don't have to ask every time," he said, a real grin on his lips.

"Yes, I do," I said. "This is my silly need to try new things. You don't have to satisfy them."

He cocked a brow at me. "Princess," he said, flicking his tongue over my lips. "That's exactly what I want to do." He settled on his knees between my legs, motioning his head at me. "Pop those hips up."

Again, that primal command, that deep tenor of demand, set my blood on fire, and damn me if I didn't immediately obey. He tucked the pillow underneath my hips, my spine still flat against the couch, my center now on a raised platform to do with as he pleased. The submission in this simple position made my toes curl.

Cannon sensed the shift in me, spotted the tremble and chills raised along my skin, and he chased them with his fingertips. Everywhere he touched was like the sweetest burn, and I couldn't help but arch into each caress. Then he brought his mouth into the mix, and I became downright incoherent. He palmed my breast, sucking my peaked nipple into his mouth, nipping enough to hurt in the most delicious of ways. I lifted my hips, desperate for him, but he took his time. Kissed his way across my breasts, over the planes of my stomach, and lower.

"Cannon!" I screamed as he wasted no time in sliding his tongue between my heat.

"Mmm," he moaned against me, the vibrations making my body clench around him. "You're already so wet for me," he said against my heat, his lips grazing every spot with a too light touch. "How are you this perfect?" he growled, his tongue lapping and darting in and out of me, feasting on me until I could do nothing but writhe against him. "How do you taste so fucking sweet?" He continued his feasting, and my body tightened like a coiled spring of pure flame.

"Cannon, please," I begged, arching against him, my fingers gripping his hair like a lifeline. "God, *Cannon*."

"Always in such a hurry," he teased, replacing his tongue with his fingers as he raised up enough to look at me with a smirk. He pumped those fingers inside me, teasing that inner edge until I saw stars. "This what you want?" He curled those fingers.

I moaned but shook my head. "You," I panted. "I want *you*."

"You have me." He lowered his face, pumping faster as he sucked that bundle of nerves into his mouth.

"Cannon!" I screamed as my orgasm hit me hard and fast, my body curling against him as the waves crashed over me again and again.

He kissed my sensitive flesh before rising above me. "*Now*, you're ready," he said, his hands gripping the backs of my knees until he'd situated one around his hip. He slid his other hand down my leg until it reached my ankle, and he placed my bare foot against his chest. And without blinking, without catching my breath, the man plunged himself inside me, the elevated angle so deep I moaned and threw my head back.

"Goddamn," Cannon hissed. "You're so fucking tight, perfect," he growled as he controlled the pace with one hand hooked under my knee at his hip, and the other pressed against my knee near his chest.

I couldn't reach him. I was powerless to his will, and I *loved* it. The thrill of it, the submission, the trust. I'd never felt so connected to another person in my entire life. I gripped the edge of the couch with one hand, digging my fingers in as he thrust inside me, over and over again.

"Touch yourself," he growled, and my eyes flared at the command, at the way his eyes churned with desire as he motioned to my free hand. He slowed his pace, taking his thrusts long and deep only to pull out all the way and do it all over again.

I didn't lose his gaze as I reached my hand up, dragging it slowly over my breasts, and lower, loving that flash of flame in his eyes as I found that bundle of nerves his mouth had been on minutes ago.

"Fuck," he hissed as I touched myself in time to his thrusts, never once hiding the pleasure rippling over my face. Never once breaking our gaze.

"Harder," I said, if not demanded.

Cannon smirked. "Where are those southern manners?" he teased, his breath coming out ragged.

"Please," I nearly growled, my back arching off the couch as he sank deeper and deeper inside me.

"There she is," he said, and obliged me, thrusting with the power his immaculate body was capable of, allowing me to *feel* that strength with each time he sank into me to the hilt. I kept up with him, teasing myself as he pumped into me again and again.

Each thrust felt like a promise or a plea.

"Cannon," I moaned, my muscles clenching around the hardness of him.

"Fucking hell, Princess," he groaned, feeling me tightening around him, just as I felt him holding back, felt the leash he kept on himself.

"I can take it," I said, and understanding and question flashed in his eyes. "Take me as you need me, Cannon." My words were breathless, but he caught everyone.

Then he unleashed himself, a fury of hard pumps as he pistoned his hips into me, pressing down on my knee to go deeper, as deep and fast and hard as he possibly could.

Blinding, beautiful pleasure burst from every coiled cell in my body. One orgasm rolling right into the other as I came hard and long. I trembled around him as he found his own release, his thrusts slowing down into a rhythm that eased our heated breaths until he stilled inside me. He shifted between my thighs, dropping one of my legs until he could lay his head against my chest, our bodies slick with sweat.

And as he settled his head in the center of my chest, the words I'd spoken earlier radiated from me. I kept them silent but was certain he could *feel* them.

Cannon propped his chin up, eyes fixated on mine. "What website was that?"

I laughed. "Cosmo," I answered.

He smirked and nodded against me. "What other illustrations did you find?"

So I showed him.

And then he obliged to *show* me.

Two more times.

15

CANNON

"His paws are massive," Nathan noted as we walked down the path from the woods behind Reaper Village. Persephone had a late evening, and when Nathan had seen me taking off on our evening walk, he was quick to jump in. I was happy for the company, but since we'd just gotten home this afternoon from a three-day trip, I really fucking missed my wife.

"Yeah, he's going to be a big guy," I agreed as Cerberus ran out ahead of us in a tangle of legs and tail. He reached the end of the leash and then ran back to us again before repeating it all over again.

"How old is he now?"

"Almost eight weeks." We'd had him for two weeks now, and life had changed drastically.

"So pretty much a baby," Nathan laughed.

"You have no fucking idea. He whines all night unless Persephone lets him into bed with us, pees wherever he wants to, chews on whatever stick he can find lying around, to include the *hockey* ones, and just when you're about to kill him—he curls up and naps on you." And I loved every fucking minute of his idiocy.

"Yep. Exactly like a baby. Without the stick chewing, or so I'm told." We crested a small hill, and our subdivision came into view. "Not that I'm ever going to find out at this rate."

Fuck. I sucked at relationship shit. Even my own marriage was fake. When the fuck had he decided that I was the emotionally stable one?

"Uh…you guys okay?" Hey, I was trying.

"Yeah, yeah," he said quickly. Way too quickly. "It's just seeing all the wedding prep you and Persephone are going through. That's all. I'm not sure Harper will ever actually want to take that step, or if she's happy being permanently engaged. Maybe I'm a little jealous." His speech slowed at the end as if he was just coming to the realization.

"I get that." I had half a mind to tell him not to be jealous. That he might have a gun-shy fiancée, but at least his relationship was real. Mine would end when Persephone's mom was no longer with us, which was so fucked up to think about that I tried not to.

"You guys look happy, though, which is way more than I thought possible when you two stumbled out of that hotel suite in Vegas." He tilted his head and gave me an appraising look. "Love looks good on you, man."

I almost tripped over my own feet. Sure, I adored my wife. Worshipped her. Enjoyed her company and missed her when we weren't together, but love? Fuck that nonsense. Love was for healthy hearts capable of giving their all. Was I infatuated with my wife? Hell yes. Did I love her?

It wasn't possible.

"Persephone mentioned that Nixon was having some PR troubles up there in North Carolina?" I changed the subject as quickly as possible.

"Yeah, it's all over the fucking tabloids," he seethed.

"Neither of us read the tabloids. We're more general fiction or fantasy readers." Every night we curled up in bed and read together. Was it possibly geriatric? Sure, but we enjoyed it, so who the fuck cared.

Noble and I took the path that ran between Sterling and Briggs' yards and came out on the sidewalk. I shortened Cerberus's leash so he didn't run out into traffic. The dog was a hundred percent enthusiasm and zero percent common sense.

"Well, I'm the last person to gossip about my twin, but let's just say that what happened in Vegas didn't exactly stay there."

"Really." My eyebrows shot up as I thought back to Nixon's little brunette charity auction date, Liberty. Guy could do worse, if that was who Noble was hinting at. "Guess that happened a lot on our trip."

Noble snorted. "Right. Except you and Persephone already knew each other, wanted each other—don't even fucking deny it—and you guys woke up married. Nix..." He sighed. "He's a hot fucking mess with a shit ton of trust issues, and waking up married would have been easy compared to what..." He shook his head.

What the hell had happened after we left? Nixon had stayed an extra day with his date, but everything had seemed easy between the two that morning. Then again, I'd had my head so far up the what-the-fuck-did-we-do-last-night mindfuck that I wouldn't have noticed if Liberty had been breathing fire across the table.

"So drama. Got it. Tell your brother I think he's a solid guy, and I hope it works out."

"We'll see. Guy can't seem to get the fuck over himself some days. I mean, just because you had some bad shit happen in your past, it doesn't mean that has to be your future, right?"

I wasn't touching that comment with a ten-foot pole, and I didn't have to, because we'd reached my house. "You good?"

"Yeah. I'm good. Thanks for letting me vent." He gave me the nod and then took off across the street toward his house.

"Women are trouble," I said to Cerberus, who promptly jumped up my leg. "Hey, no. We can't do that. Four on the floor, bud." I set him down like the dog-training video suggested and gave him the I'm-the-alpha-pack-leader stare that was supposed to magic him into submission or some shit.

He whined at me, and I rolled my eyes as we headed into the house.

Elton John sang about a yellow brick road from the kitchen, and my smile was instant. Persephone was home. I unclipped Cerberus's leash and urged him on. "Go find her."

He took off like a shot, skidding on the hardwood and nearly missing the turn into the kitchen. I cringed, but he made it. Barely.

"Hi, Cerberus! Did you have a good walk with Daddy? Mommy missed you all day!"

God, I loved the sound of her voice filling the house, the feeling I got just knowing she was here. I felt...complete, at peace, even.

I turned the corner into the kitchen and saw Persephone on her knees, holding Cerberus on her lap as he tried to lick her face to death. His tail wagged at a mile a minute. Hell, if I had a tail, it would wag every time I saw my wife.

Wife. Sure, we were married now, but in eleven days, we'd be saying I do all over again in front of our friends and family, and this time we'd remember it.

"How was work?" I asked, setting the leash on the counter.

"Hey, stranger." She smiled at me, and I swore the entire room lit up. She put Cerberus on the floor, and then rose.

"You looked good against Denver. That second period goal in game three was hot."

"You watched me?" I pulled her into my arms and felt the off-kilter pieces of me click back into place. We never talked about hockey when we called during road trips, and lately, Cerberus—and whatever he'd recently destroyed—had been the hot topic. It definitely warmed my chest to think she watched when I wasn't home.

"Of course." She wound her arms around my neck. "Now kiss me. I've missed you."

I lowered my mouth to hers and kissed her deep. Fuck, she tasted like the little lemon candies she kept on her desk at home. Her sheath dress was too form-fitted for her to wrap her legs around my waist, so I put one forearm under her ass and lifted straight up against me. Her feet dangled as she threw herself into the kiss.

My hand tunneled into her French twist, and I pulled the long, singular pin I'd often seen her secure the hairstyle with. Her hair tumbled free, cascading down my arm, and I groaned at the feel of it, her hair, her tongue, her mouth, her skin—all of it.

"I missed you, too," I finally said against her mouth when I found the willpower to stop kissing her.

Her thumbs stroked over my cheeks. "You're away next weekend, too?"

I nodded. "We can see if the hotel is dog-friendly, and you and Cerberus could come," I offered. Being away from her was pure shit. I was always distracted, wondering what she was doing, if she was okay, or just plain missing her.

She smiled, then kissed me softly. "That sounds like a plan." Cerberus whined, and we both looked down at him. "Jealous little thing."

I set her down reluctantly and then got to the business

that had become our ordinary life. She fed the puppy, and I started dinner for us while she got changed from work.

I'd just finished searing the steaks when she came back into the kitchen in a pair of tiny shorts and an off-the-shoulder sweatshirt. I loved her dresses, her suits, and her lingerie, but fuck, there was something about seeing her this casual—knowing I was the only one who did, that got me turned on faster than anything.

"What can I do to help?" she asked, just like she did every night.

"Want to set the table?" I suggested, just like I did every night.

Persephone might have been an amazing cookie-baker, but the woman was *not* a cook. Growing up with a team of chefs had left the woman clueless in most areas of the kitchen, but it didn't bother me. I liked cooking for her. There was something primal about feeding my wife that gave me an irrational sense of satisfaction.

"You got it." She smacked my ass as she walked by, and I grinned as I finished everything up.

After dinner, we tag-teamed the cleanup, which took a little longer with Cerberus underfoot. The guy always wanted to be in the middle of the action.

"You seem pretty relaxed," I remarked as she put the leftover steak into the fridge.

"Compared to?" she asked.

"Compared to most brides eleven days before their wedding." I leaned back against the counter. "Lillian was a fucking train-wreck at this point, yelling at vendors, sobbing when the bridesmaids' dresses came in all wrong. You name it, she was stressed."

Persephone shut the fridge and then came over to me. "Well, we have an excellent wedding planner who's doing all the screaming for me. Besides, we're already married, so I guess that takes a lot of the stress out, too." She shrugged, then hopped up on the counter across from me. "Plus, if that marriage only lasted six months, then she married the wrong man. Maybe it's supposed to feel like this when it's right."

I swallowed. More and more, she used words like *right* and *love*, like we weren't some accident that had happened in Vegas. Like we were going to be something when our timeline ran out, and the only thing that held us together was a piece of paper.

Cerberus yapped, indignant that he wasn't in Persephone's lap.

"You really are a big baby," she crooned at him.

I picked him up and held him in the crook of my arm. "Stop driving her crazy." Then I gave him rubs until he settled against my chest, sticking his very wet nose in my neck.

"You still like him?" she asked.

"I love him. He is exactly what I've always wanted, even if he is pretty much like having a baby. Nathan and I were joking about that earlier."

She grinned. "Scheduled, coddled, needy, yep. He's a baby."

"Do you want kids?" The question was out before I could examine why I'd even asked it. "Sorry if that's too personal. I've never had a relationship or been married, so feel free not to answer it."

Her smile faded slightly, but a hopeful light shined in those blue eyes. "Yeah, I want kids. A lot of kids. Growing up with Anne was a constant competition. Even if our parents didn't make it that way, we did, because who better to compare yourself to than your sister who's only eighteen months older than you are?" She shrugged. "I always thought that if I'd had another sibling, we wouldn't have gone at each other like it was a race. What about you?"

"I guess I never really thought about it." I shrugged. "Growing up was more about survival than succeeding, and Lillian and I did our best to get each other out alive. There's not a lot of competition in that."

"Right. I'm sorry. I didn't mean to make my childhood seem worse when I know—"

"Stop," I interrupted her. "What we find miserable in our childhoods is all relative. I'm incredibly thankful that you didn't go through what I did, but that doesn't mean you didn't have hard spots, too."

She gave me a wry smile. "Maybe the competition thing was less of a two-kid issue, and more of a growing up with Andromeda issue."

"I would agree with that."

"So you never pictured your life? Or what you wanted for a family?" She tilted her head, watching me carefully.

"No," I answered honestly. "I worked toward a singular goal—making the NHL. I knew if I did that, I could make enough money so Lillian and I, and now Owen, of course, wouldn't ever have to worry about where we'd sleep or what we had to eat. I didn't have the imagination or time to dream about anything else."

She swallowed, and I felt it again, that divide in our upbringing and priorities.

"Honestly," I continued just so she wouldn't feel awkward again, "I never thought much about a family until I woke up married to a certain blonde."

"And now?" Her lips tilted slightly at the corners.

I set Cerberus down, and he toddled off, no doubt looking for a cozy spot to take his post-dinner nap. "Now, I'm not sure what to think. I know that I love coming home to you. I love the feeling of having a home and not just a house." I walked forward and gently pushed her knees apart so I could step between them. "You've made me realize that maybe my life is missing something."

"Like puppies and kids?" she joked, winding her arms around my neck.

The vision of a dark-haired girl with Persephone's eyes and a blond boy with reckless nature filled my head, and a feeling filled my whole being that nearly brought me to my knees. *Yearning.* It was yearning. I gripped her hips and pulled her flush against me.

"Yeah, I could go for a few kids." But only in the world where she was their mother. Only in the world where I came home every day and found them here, safe and loved, and happy. Only in the world where we were married because we couldn't stand to live without each other, not because we'd signed a piece of paper while accidentally drugged and were making the best of it to keep her mom happy. I wanted a world that didn't exist, and that hurt like hell.

"Well, that's good, since we already have one," she teased.

I laughed, then kissed her gently. Fuck, I'd only been gone a few days, but my body roared for hers as if it had been years. "I know I already said this, but I missed you so damned much."

"What? No eager puck bunnies to fulfill your obsessive need for new positions?" she teased, but there was a question in her eyes.

Of course, she knew my reputation. She'd been a Reaper almost as long as I had, and since we'd gotten Cerberus, she hadn't been traveling with me as often.

I cupped the back of her head and looked into her eyes so she could see the truth in mine. "No puck bunnies. Even if we didn't have rule number six, I wouldn't touch another woman. I'd never hurt you like that."

She swallowed. "I know you wouldn't. But when that girl

from Detroit was looking at you like her next meal, I realized how…different I am from the girls you usually go for."

"*Used* to go for," I clarified, rubbing her hip gently. "And that woman was looking at me like her next meal *ticket*. There's a difference."

She rolled her eyes, and I bent slightly, running my lips down her jaw to get her attention back where it belonged. "Persephone, I'm not interested in any other women because I already have the perfect woman in my bed."

"I'm not perfect," she protested. "I'm also not five-ten, or covered in tattoos, and I apparently can't hold my liquor—"

"Fuck, I missed you." I kissed her, and she opened beneath me with a little moan that I felt in my dick.

"The bed is entirely too empty when you're not here," she whispered.

"Then allow me to fill it for you." I gripped her ass and lifted her in my arms. She locked her ankles behind my back, and I carried her to our room. That's what it was now, *ours*. The whole house was ours when I thought about it.

I laid her down in the middle of our bed, rid myself of my clothes, and then stripped her slowly, kissing each exposed inch of skin as it was bared to me. How the fuck could she not realize how perfect she was?

"I love the way my skin looks next to yours." I splayed my hand wide over her belly. "Like you're not tainted by the world, and I'm the only one who gets to touch you."

"You are the only one who gets to touch me." She arched her hips, and I dragged down her underwear, leaving her wholly, beautifully naked.

For now.

I lined my body up over hers, raising her knee so I rested between her thighs. "I love that you're tiny."

"Way to *not* say short," she giggled.

The laughter stopped when I stroked my thumb over her clit.

"Cannon," she cried, bucking her hips.

"Where were we?" I dragged my fingers through her slippery cleft and groaned at how wet she already was for me. "Fuck, I love how wet you get for me."

Her breaths came in little pants, but she kept her eyes on me.

"I love how you fit against me." My cock replaced my fingers at her entrance. "How I can curl my entire body around you until you're surrounded by me."

She rocked, trying to pull me into her, but I held back. "Cannon, please."

"Not until you get it." I ran my nose down her neck. "I love the way you always smell like apple blossoms, and I love the way you taste." My tongue danced over that sensitive spot on her neck, and she whimpered. "I love how I can never get enough of you. Even after I've just had you, I want you again."

"Same," she whispered, arching her neck to give me better access.

I slid down her body. "I love your breasts and how responsive your nipples are." I tongued them both, then continued the journey. "I love the way you gasp when I do this." My tongue found her clit and flicked at it.

She gasped, her hands sinking into my hair.

"I love every sound you make when I do this." I settled between her thighs and licked her in lazy, long strokes, like we had all the time in the world. Her cries came faster and higher as I worked her with my mouth, sucking gently on her clit to send her over the edge.

She screamed my name as the orgasm took her over, trembling around me as I licked her sensitive flesh through every aftershock.

Then I rose over her, bracing my weight on my elbows as my dick screamed at me to drive into her, to take her hard and fast, to brand her in a way that she'd never be free of me.

"I fucking love the way you scream my name when you come," I whispered in her ear, biting her lobe gently before kissing her so she could taste just how sweet she was.

"Cannon," she whined, shifting her thighs so the head of my cock lined up perfectly.

"I love the way you trust me and the way you share your body with me."

"It's yours," she promised, her thighs rubbing against my hips. "It's all yours."

But I wasn't done yet. I captured her gaze, then stroked the soft skin of her cheek. "I have never loved a woman's eyes the way I love yours. You brought me to my knees with one look. *One*, Persephone. Don't ever compare yourself to the women I used to settle for, because they were a series of faceless, nameless, placeholders, and you…" I shook my head, fumbling for the words. "You were everything I wanted and couldn't have."

"But you have me now." She grazed her hands down my rib cage, then squeezed my ass as she rocked forward with her hips.

I took the hint and eased myself inside her inch by delicious inch. "I fucking love the way you feel around me. Hot and tight and so very wet."

"Like I was made for you." She sucked in a breath, then moaned when I filled her completely.

"Like you were made for me," I agreed, wondering if she had been. If there was some other life where we would have been compatible for more than a few months. Some other life where we would have been together forever. My eyes closed at the pleasure that shot through me.

"I love the way you don't hold back when we're here." I

grasped her hands, threading our fingers together before I pinned them to the bed on either side of her head. "I love that I can take you slow and easy," I moved my hips in a slow, steady slide, and she groaned. "Or I can fuck you hard and long." I thrust deep and fast, reveling in the little cry she gave when I stopped. "But no matter how I take you, you beg for more. And the truth is that I might fill your body, but you fill my fucking soul."

"Cannon," she pled, her eyes soft on mine, but edged with need.

"I'll never want another woman," I swore, hating myself for the truth of it as I took her in slow, deep strokes. "I haven't wanted another woman since the moment I laid eyes on you. You'll always be it for me." No matter where this led, she'd ruined me for anyone else.

"I love you," she whispered, holding my face as she rocked with me.

Those words. I couldn't say those words. Couldn't make the promise they implied or even let myself believe that she truly meant them.

So I showed her with my body, loving her in the only way I could, locking my gaze with hers as I moved within her, building our pleasure with steady, mind-blowing strokes that felt better and better.

This time, when her orgasm took her, I could have sworn I saw stars in her eyes, and when she whispered, "I love you, Cannon," I saw the same stars behind mine as I came hard, spilling myself inside her. As we came down, I tucked her into my side and brushed a kiss across her forehead.

A tugging at the covers got our attention, and Persephone rolled slightly, then laughed. "Seriously? Right now?" She stumbled out of the bed, shaking her head as she headed for the closet.

I leaned over to see Cerberus playing tug of war with our covers. "Seriously, my man?"

Persephone emerged from the closet in her bathrobe. "I'll take him out."

"I'll get him," I insisted.

"Absolutely not." She pointed her finger at me. "You just blew my mind. This is the least I can do." She scooped up the puppy and headed toward the glass, double doors that led to the back yard. "You might act like a baby, but you're sure showing me I'm not ready for a real one, you needy little thing!" She giggled, holding him up to kiss his nose.

Once she was outside, I pulled on my boxer briefs and followed her as far as the door, watching her walk the yard in her bare feet with Cerberus at her heels.

You'll always be it for me. My words haunted me as I watched my wife in the moonlight.

The truth of it was damning. Even when this fell to shit, when she realized that I wasn't good enough for her, or she was unable to forgive my eventual fuck-up or slip of my temper, I would want her. My body…my soul would ache for her for the rest of my life.

Fuck, I was in this too deep.

We both were.

She might think she loved me, but it was really just infatuation. Love came with trials. With pain and acceptance. With sacrifice. She was high on endorphins from orgasms and the same rush of happiness I'd felt from us playing house the last few months.

When the chips were down, she'd realize it wasn't love.

Then we'd both be fucked.

I raked my hands over my hair and barely stopped myself from putting a hole in the fucking wall as the rage swept over me. I'd done everything I could to protect her mother's happiness and to give Persephone the same while we rode out this ruse.

But I hadn't protected her from her own heart.

I'd fucking failed her because when this all came crashing down, she was going to get hurt. And if agony tore through my chest at the thought of losing her—which it did, then I couldn't imagine the pain she'd suffer when this ended.

And I was twice the villain because I'd taken her heart without giving my own, and I couldn't bring myself to stop. I couldn't stop laughing with her, or touching her, or making love to her. I was the reason this had gone too far, and yet I knew as she headed back toward me, that I wouldn't spare us both and end it now.

I was too fucking desperate for her, too addicted.

As she reached the door, I swept her against me and shut it, ready for my next hit of Persephone.

16

PERSEPHONE

The weekend of wedding festivities had finally arrived. I surveyed the club I'd grown up in and the man standing next to me as we inspected the wedding rehearsal ballroom. My eyes took in the clean, crisp lines of whitewashed hardwood, the rich wooden tables draped in cream linens, and the elevated stage where Cannon and I would sit.

We'd officially be married at my parents' estate, but for the rehearsal? An elegant dinner and evening of dancing at the club is what we'd decided on.

I squeezed Cannon's hand in mine, glancing up at him. "Does it look okay to you?"

His eyes met mine. "It's beautiful," he said. "Your mother has amazing taste. Just like you."

I grinned up at him.

"What?" He furrowed his brow.

"You admit I have good taste."

He shrugged. "So?"

"That means I have amazing taste in *men*." I eyed him, and he rolled his.

Cannon opened his mouth, likely to argue, but my cell rang, cutting him off. "Speak of the devil," I said, showing him the screen alight with my mother's picture. I swiped to answer the call. "Hey, Mom, we're just checking out the club—"

"Sephie!" My mother's voice was tear-soaked.

"Are you okay?" I asked, dropping Cannon's hand as I instinctively headed toward the exit.

"I'm more than perfect!" she said, and I slowed my pace. Cannon rested his hand on the small of my back, a silent show of support. "Sephie," she said again, and a choked sob tore from her lips.

"Mama, what is it?" Tears filled my eyes, a building panic I couldn't understand.

"They found a donor! Someone with the same rare blood type as mine. They've scheduled me for two days after the wedding! Can you believe it? I get to see you get married, and then I get a kidney!"

"Truly?" The word was a gasp.

"Truly, sugar."

"Oh, Mama! That is wonderful news!"

Mom sucked in a breath, locking up her happy tears. "I know! Okay, that's enough fussing over me! Finish your appraisal of the club! We'll celebrate tomorrow!" She hung up before I could argue, before I could say more.

I turned around to face Cannon, who smiled down at me, clearly having heard everything.

"My mom gets a kidney," I said the words aloud, the truth in the statement stealing my breath. A crazed laugh left my lips as I launched myself into Cannon's arms. He scooped me off my feet, holding me against him as he spun me.

"That's fucking wonderful, Princess," he said, his cheek against mine.

Happy tears streamed down my face, but I pulled back

enough to crush my lips against his. "I didn't think it would happen," I said between kisses. "We never thought we'd find a match." I kissed him frantically and happily, and he took it all and gave everything in return. "Cannon, she gets it two days after the wedding!" I continued my happy rant between kisses.

His lips stilled against mine, something unreadable flashing across his eyes.

"Cannon?" I asked as he slowly set me on my feet and took a step *away* from me.

He slid his hands into the pockets of his slacks as easily as that wall slammed shut over his eyes. "You don't need me anymore."

I blinked, scraping my palms against my face to rid myself of the happy tears. "Wait, what?"

He shrugged, the movement so much colder than his demeanor moments before. "I'm truly beyond happy for your mother, Persephone," he said, and I could read that truth in his eyes. "You deserve to be happy. Deserve...everything."

I took a step toward him. "What are you saying?"

"You don't really want to go through with this, do you? Not now that you know your mother will be all right."

I gaped at him. "Of course, I want to go through with this." I reached for him, but he remained statue-still, like he was holding himself in place for fear he might fall apart. "Cannon, I *love* you."

His eyes held mine, but nothing was betrayed on his face.

Cold, freezing panic clawed at my insides. "But you don't...do you?" The question was a broken whisper.

"Persephone," he sighed my name, and I shook my head.

After all this time, after everything that led us to this moment...I was *sure* I'd felt it. Felt his love. Even if he couldn't say it, couldn't acknowledge it, I'd thought I *felt* it.

"Do you, Cannon?" I asked again. "Love me?"

He visibly swallowed.

"Do you?" I pressed. "Not love sleeping with me, or my ambition, or my ability to sass you into the next century, but do you love *me*, Cannon?"

"Persephone, I—"

A loud, shrill foghorn covered up whatever Cannon was about say, the sound so encompassing we both jolted.

"Bachelor party time!" a thick Scottish accent hollered from behind.

"Bachelorette party too!" a richer southern accent drawled.

We whirled to find a gaggle of our friends...our *family* rushing into the ballroom, outfitted in their finest suits and dresses.

Connell let the foghorn drop to his side and flashed me an apologetic grin. "I've never used one before. Had to try it out."

I mustered my best smile, allowing the happiness on our family's faces to erase the growing unease in my heart. Harper, Faith, and Echo rushed to my side as Annabelle, Delaney, and Langley followed them, each one donning a glittering party tiara. Annabelle placed the largest crown atop my head.

"You ready to kiss single life goodbye?" she teased me with a wink, linking her arm in mine.

I flashed Cannon a glance, making sure he was the only one I looked at when I answered. "I truly am."

Then the girls squealed and hauled me out of the room where a handful of Reapers dominated the space in the hallway, awaiting Connell to fetch the groom. Or would-be groom.

God, I didn't even know anymore.

The independent woman in me screamed at me to stop this party and go demand an answer.

The coward in me was too terrified to hear Cannon's truth.

So I let the girls pack me into a limo and whisk me away.

Let them lead me into some of Charleston's hottest bars and clubs.

Let each drink I had wash away the uncertainty, the pain, the fear until I could hardly remember what I'd been upset about before. Until I could do nothing but dance with my amazing friends, feed off their excited energy, siphon off that pure, unflinching love and let it replace every dark doubt in my mind.

"This is our last stop," Echo said directly into my ear so I could hear her over the live band that played.

"Good!" I said back, laughing. "I don't know if I can remain standing much longer!"

She laughed, too, nodding as we bounced to the beat of the music.

I lost myself in the sultry sounds of the singer's voice, the raspy tenor that pulsed and vibrated within the band's melodies, long after Echo had thrown in the towel and joined our friends at our booth in the private balcony above the stage.

And then red-hot reality jolted me right to the present when a man's hand found my hip.

"I'm a married woman!" I snapped, balling my fist. "Take your hand off me." When he didn't respond to my loud and clear command, I whirled. My father raised me with awareness, and I knew I was a tiny thing, knew I had one chance to get a good hit in, and buy me time to get to my girls.

My fist was stopped, gently and easily.

Cannon.

"Glad to see you know how to defend yourself against monsters like me," he said, relinquishing his hold on my fist, his dark eyes slightly glazed with drink, likely the mirror of mine.

"You're not a monster," I snapped. "And even if you think yourself one, you'd be *my* monster, so I have no need of defense against you."

"You sure about that, Princess?"

I nodded. "What are you doing here?"

He motioned over his shoulder, where Connell, Logan, Lukas, Nathan, and Axel all stood, sheepish looks on their faces. "Guess our friends think alike?"

I pursed my lips at him, the alcohol in my blood making me extra sassy. "Figured you'd be living it up at some strip club."

Cannon planted me with a look that screamed *you know better*.

I chewed on my bottom lip, all those emotions and doubts I'd spent the evening burying doing their best to claw their way to the surface. "What do we do now?" I asked, unable to hide the sadness in my tone.

Cannon stood there so long I wasn't sure he'd answer, or if he even had one.

"Dance with me?" he finally asked, hand offered between us.

I took it without hesitation. "Always," I said.

He positioned my hand on his chest, right in the center of it, and left it there to snake his hands around my waist. We swayed to the rhythm, the band switching to a slow, hauntingly beautiful song that seeped into my bones. I lost myself in Cannon's embrace, in his touch, in the way he controlled my body—spinning me in or out, drawing me closer only to push me away again. Back and forth, the dance mounted, as did my racing heart.

I felt like we'd been doing this dance since our night in Vegas, and now it was all coming to a head.

He tucked me against him again as the song wound down, his eyes fixated on mine.

Everything in me narrowed to that gaze, to the intensity behind it. To the unspoken words between us. The other dancers on the floor didn't exist, nor did our friends no doubt about to discover each other in the same location, nor the other bar patrons getting their fill of drink and food and fun.

Nothing but Cannon and me.

He leaned down, his cheek against mine, his lips at my ear—

"I lied!" Echo said, darting to my side, drawing both our attention. "One more stop," she giggled as she tugged on my arm. "There is no *way* you can end your single life in your husband's arms! I've got another place! Shoo!" She waved Cannon away, and I couldn't help but laugh as Logan came up behind him and grabbed him in a headlock.

Cannon *let* him pull him away.

So I let my friends.

And once again lost myself to the abyss and blissful ignorance, promising myself that—after many more drinks—everything would make sense tomorrow.

17

CANNON

My head fucking hurt. Sure, it was my fault, and I accepted that, but combining a huge hangover with a ridiculous amount of sun had my brain throbbing.

I yanked my sunglasses down and tried to listen to what Logan was saying next to me.

"So if we start our eighteen holes by eleven, we'll definitely make it back in time for the rehearsal."

I looked at him like he'd lost his mind. "I'm not playing golf."

He raised his eyebrows. "The set of clubs with that caddy over there seems to suggest otherwise."

I'd agreed to come out here and putt around on this stupid fucking green like I actually gave a shit if the ball found the hole, but I wasn't signing up for a full round of golf. No way in hell. I wasn't one of those douchebags over there with their neat little polos and green vests.

Like he'd heard my thoughts, head douchebag, Michael lifted his head from his perfect putt and high-fived his equally douchey friend. It was the practice green for God's sake, not the fucking Olympics.

"Seriously," Logan muttered, having seen the same thing.

"Right? It's not like anyone's even trying to take the ball from them. No goalie. No skates. Where's the goddamned challenge?"

"Hell if I know."

I looked over to the patio, where a private brunch had been set up by Persephone's parents, hoping to spot my wife. The VanDorens had some ridiculous rule about keeping us apart today, and I'd about had enough of their horseshit. I needed to talk to my wife.

Once the news had come in that her mother was going to get her kidney—that she'd be okay—I'd firmly expected Persephone to walk the hell away. Instead, we were in the midst of our wedding weekend, both trying to publicly act like we were fine, even though we just wanted a private moment to figure out what the fuck we were doing.

Do you love me, Cannon? Her words were on repeat in my head, and even drowning myself in alcohol last night hadn't washed them away.

Did I love her? It wasn't as simple as that. She acted like a four-letter word was the answer to every problem, and I knew it wasn't.

"Gentlemen," Persephone's dad clapped me on the back as he came to stand beside us. "Are you enjoying yourselves?" His eyes narrowed slightly, no doubt waiting to judge whatever would come out of my mouth.

"Absolutely. Thank you for setting this whole thing up." I gave him a smile, and he returned it, though his looked a little more like a threat than a gesture.

"Well, Sephie and her friends practically grew up here. Seemed fitting to host a little brunch before the women head to the spa, and the men get ready to battle the toughest course in South Carolina."

Holy shit, I wasn't going to make it through today, and if we really went through with this second wedding then this was what I had to look forward to. Mornings at the club with a man who actively hated my guts, playing the world's worst sport with other douchebags who hated my guts.

"It's a perfect day for it, sir," Logan responded when he caught on that I wasn't going to be able to.

"It is. Now, I had to pull a couple of strings for these—usually they're reserved only for members—but seeing as you're about to be family…" He presented both Logan and me with emerald green vests with the clubs logo embroidered over the left pocket.

"Thank you," I said automatically.

Logan echoed my sentiment.

"Good. I'm glad you like them. Now, if you'll excuse me, I need to check on my girls—"

"Oh, I'll come with you," I offered, already starting up that way.

"I wouldn't have it!" He laughed. "It's VanDoren tradition that you two only see each other at the rehearsal dinner and then the altar. That's why we have Sephie staying in the main house tonight." He clapped me on the shoulder again and headed for the patio.

My head pounded even harder. I couldn't even sleep next to my *wife*? We had shit to discuss, and it wasn't little, petty stuff, either. I'd been counting on the fact that we'd have all night in her old house to hash out our future…if we still had one.

"So we're supposed to wear this?" Logan asked, holding it up for appraisal.

"It's actually quite an honor," Michael noted as he sauntered over, his putter over his shoulder like it was stylish.

"Right," Logan muttered, but put it on and did up the buttons. "When in Rome, right?"

"I'm not wearing that vest," I muttered. I'd put on a button-down shirt and rolled the sleeves, and even agreed to khaki shorts, but a fucking vest was where I drew the line.

"What? Is it not quite cool enough for you?" Michael asked with a smirk. "Does it not meet your rebellious, stick-it-to-the-man standards?"

I shook my head at the guy. He was such a prick. Just the thought of Persephone ending up with him—or someone like him was enough to curdle what brunch I'd managed to stomach.

"Put the vest on." Her voice soothed my nauseated stomach as she appeared to my right.

"Hey," I said softly. She was wearing a simple, white sundress, and her hair was loose down her back. She looked clean and fresh, and so beautiful that my chest ached.

"Hey," she replied, stepping in front of me and nailing me with those blue eyes. "I know you hate it, but it would go a long way with my Dad if you wore it."

"You're using the eyes on me? That's not playing fair," I teased.

She smiled. "I'll use every weapon I have in my arsenal when it comes to you, Cannon Price."

"Whatever makes you happy, *Mrs*. Price."

Her eyes flared at the title, and I put the damned vest on. Surprisingly, it fit.

"Happy?" I asked in a low tone.

"Almost." She stepped closer and started fastening the four buttons that closed the garment. Our eyes locked and I couldn't help but grin. It was so like the moment she'd forced me to do up my buttons before the charity auction.

"You're always so concerned about my buttons."

Her cheeks flushed pink, but she pushed that last one home. "Someone has to be."

I cupped the nape of her neck and ran my thumb down her jaw, nearly sighing with relief when she leaned into my touch. How the fuck was I going to give her up?

Did I have to? I mean, we were already married, so the damage was really done. What would having a second ceremony hurt? What would happen if we decided to ride this out to whatever finish line we decided instead of one imposed on us? What if there was no finish line, and it was just us as we were right now, but for forever?

"You're incredibly beautiful today," I said softly.

She smiled, then rose up on her toes.

I leaned down and brushed my lips over hers. These were the lips I wanted to kiss for the rest of my life.

"Oh no, you don't! You know the tradition. You're supposed to be over there with Aunt Mildred!" Andromeda sang with a sugar-sweet smile, looping her arm through Persephone's and pulling her away. "You can make out with your husband once he's...you know, your husband again. Toodles!" She wiggled her fingers at us as she dragged my wife away.

"This family is weird," Logan said under his breath.

"Amen to that."

"You can dress like one of us all you want, but you'll never *be* one of us," Michael said, stepping forward now that Persephone was gone.

"Good. The last thing I want to be is one of you." I rubbed my temples and prayed to the hangover Gods that my misery would end soon. I'd taken pain relievers and drank half my weight in water already. When was it going to end?

Michael scoffed as he looked toward the patio, following Persephone's retreat. "God knows what she sees in you."

"I'll never quite figure that out, either, but I'm glad she sees whatever it is."

He turned a hate-filled sneer on me. "She won't see it for long. You know that, right? She'll never be happy married to someone like you. She was born and bred for better."

I ignored the direct hit to my worst fear. "Better like you?"

"Exactly," he hissed quietly. "So you can enjoy whatever it is you're doing with her, but just know that at the end of this —because it *will* end—she doesn't wind up with you."

I swallowed back the rising rage in my throat. The guy needed to be taught to keep his mouth shut, but I wasn't about to be the one teaching that lesson during my rehearsal brunch. "In case you missed it, that's my last name on her new driver's license, and my ring on her finger."

He snorted. "Well, enjoy that whole alpha *mine mine mine* thing for as long as it lasts. Just do me a favor and take it easy on her, would you?" His eyes took on a gleam that had my muscles tensing.

"Cannon," Logan warned, seeing the signs.

"I'll never hurt her, if that's what you're implying," I snapped at Michael.

"Oh! No. You wouldn't be stupid enough to end up behind bars like your old man," he guffawed, shaking his head.

"Cannon, don't," Logan muttered.

I saw red.

"I mean take it easy in the bedroom." He leaned in with a shit-eating grin like he was telling me a secret. "No doubt you've fucked her, but try not to stretch her out too much, would you? I've been waiting a long time to get in there, and—"

My fist connected with his face, and he flew backward.

"Oh shit," Logan sighed.

I stalked the motherfucker as he tried to scramble away, fear lighting his eyes.

"Hey!" his douchey friend called, running over from the edge of the green.

I grabbed Michael by the green vest he prized so much and lifted him off his feet. "I swear to fucking God, if you ever talk about my wife like that again, I'll do worse than punch you. I'll fucking end you."

"What is going on here?" Mr. VanDoren shouted, marching toward us.

"He attacked me!" Michael cried in outrage.

I dropped the sorry sack of shit on his ass. "Like hell I did. You don't even *want* to know what he just said about my wife."

Michael blinked in mock innocence. "What? That I warned you that you're not good enough for her?"

"That is not how that went down," Logan argued.

"I don't give a shit. Look around you!" Mr. VanDoren hissed.

I peeled my eyes from Michael's simpering little face to see that at least a dozen golf club members were staring at us, and two of them had their phones out.

Fuck, I was going to have to call my publicist.

"What happened?" Persephone asked as her gaze darted between Michael and me.

"He nearly killed me!" Michael stumbled to his feet. "I'll have a black eye!"

"Oh, God, Cannon, did you—"

"Come with me right now," Mr. VanDoren ordered. "Both of you."

Persephone went, so I did, too. We walked past the brunch crowd and into the club itself, passing through the full dining room, then the lobby, until we reached the ballroom where dinner would be held tonight.

Mr. VanDoren shut the door behind us and shook his head. "Honey, I tried. I really tried to give this man a chance, but it just won't suit."

"Daddy," Persephone whispered, coming to my side.

"No. This ends now."

I couldn't trust my mouth, so I kept it shut.

"We're already married. This isn't something you can decide to stop just because you don't like the man I love." She folded her arms under her breasts.

His attention focused on me, then Persephone, and back again until he pulled an envelope out of his vest. "Here's the thing. You're not." He held the envelope out to me.

"We're not what?" I snapped, taking the damn thing from him.

"You're not married."

Persephone's jaw dropped, and she looked to me for answers I didn't have. I opened the envelope and found a certified copy of our marriage license.

"That's just a copy," Persephone insisted, looking at the same time I did. "We have the original in the safe."

I read through the document, down to the very bottom—the signature lines.

Then I muttered a curse.

"What is it?" Her voice pitched high and worried.

"He's realizing that he didn't sign it with his legal name," her father explained softly.

"What?" She took the document from my hand and scanned it like I had. "You signed it right here!" She pointed to the line.

"Right." I cringed. "My legal name isn't Cannon. It's Sheldon. Cannon is my middle name, so I'm sure you can understand why I use that one instead." Holy shit, that morning in Vegas I'd been so focused on the way Persephone had taken *my* name that I hadn't bothered to look at my own. Fuck, why hadn't I thought to check the damned thing when the original had come in the mail?

Because you'd already agreed to stay married, so it hadn't mattered.

Persephone's eyes flew wide. "Your name is *Sheldon*?"

"My name is Cannon for every purpose except contracts."

"This is a contract!" she cried, shaking the paper.

"That I don't remember signing!"

Her face fell. "You're right. God, of course, you're right." She stood by my side and faced her father. "Okay, so what? We get married tomorrow, anyway, and at least we'll remember it this time."

Her father blanched. "No. God, no. Can't you see what a disaster it would be? He just beat the crap out of one of your oldest friends. You absolutely cannot marry him."

It was barely a punch, but whatever, my mind was *reeling*. All this time, we hadn't been married. We could have walked away from this at any time, but here we stood, and she was fighting for us. Fighting for us when I'd just done what she'd explicitly asked me not to.

"Daddy, I'm a full-grown woman, and—"

"You did this to make your mother happy. I admire you for it. I admire *both* of you for it. But what you don't see is that she's going to live now, and when you two crash and burn? *That* will kill her."

"You don't know that," Persephone whispered.

"He can't even make it through one morning at the club without humiliating this family! Without humiliating you! I am begging you, honey, don't go through with this. Think about it." He gave me a withering look and then left us alone in the ballroom.

I suddenly felt out of place, like an actual bull in a china shop.

"How could you!" Persephone shouted, turning on me.

"Whoa, what? Are you seriously pissed that I didn't sign my name right when we were both drugged out of our minds?"

"No! I'm seriously pissed that you punched out Michael on the damned putting green! Why couldn't you just hold your temper? Why?" Color rose in her cheeks.

"Because he said some really sick shit about you that doesn't even deserve repeating!" I backed away from her, putting more than a few feet of space between us.

"He said something? You punched him because he *said* something?" She shook her head. "Unbelievable! You broke rule number seven at our rehearsal brunch!"

I blinked. "Rule number seven. You're pissed that I broke rule number seven." *No fights.*

"Yes! You promised! God, why are you so incapable of expressing your emotions without using your hands?" She crumpled the copy of our marriage license in her fist as she shook.

"Un-fucking-believable," I said. "This is the rule you want to start shit over?"

She blinked in confusion. "I don't know what you mean."

"Sure you do, Princess." I stalked forward until I had her pinned against the wall, one of my hands on either side of her head. "You begged me to break rule number five. *Begged me.*"

"That's not the same," she said quietly, but there was no fear in her eyes, even though I had her trapped.

"Then you went and broke rule number four all on your own. I told you not to, and you did anyway. Did you see me throw a shit fit when you dropped that bomb on me?"

"Bomb?" Her eyes narrowed. "My love isn't a bomb, and if you knew how to use your words instead of your hands—"

"Princess, you like it when I use my hands. You fucking

love it when I use my body to show you how I feel about you." Fuck, I was on the verge of showing her right now.

"Do you want to marry me?" she asked, shocking me to my core.

I pushed off the wall, giving her an exit. "It has nothing to do with want. What I want isn't what's right, and it isn't what's good for you, that's for damned sure."

"Why? You give me one good reason why we shouldn't get married."

"One? You only need one?" I laughed. "Fuck, Persephone. I don't belong in your world. I hate the vests, and the parties, and the fake ass way people cut each other down with a smile. The only thing I remotely like about your world is *you*."

"That's enough," she insisted. "Liking me is enough!"

"It's not. You are good and pure and kind, and I have enough baggage to open my own luggage store. I'm dangerous. My temper isn't something I'm proud of. You're right, I'm shit at discussing emotion, and I know that's something you need."

"So we can work on it!" she cried.

"I'm not built like you! I can't just throw my heart around and watch and see what happens!"

"Throw my heart around? I love you, Cannon. I've only ever loved *you*." She moved toward me, and I stepped back.

"I know you think that."

She stilled. "Don't you dare belittle my emotions just because you can't express your own. I love you. That's real."

I shook my head. "Love...it isn't easy like this—" I gestured between us. "That's infatuation, and it was bound to happen. I'm the first man you've ever had sex with, and those chemicals are a bitch, but they're not real. Real love? It takes sacrifice. It means you're willing to lay your body down and take whatever pain you have to in order to keep it from the person you love."

Horror washed over her face. "Cannon…"

"Love means you make the best decision you can for that person with no thought for how it's going to destroy you. Love is brutal, and it's ugly at times. Love is what remains when all the fuzzy feelings disappear, and you're still ready to wage war to protect that person." I looked around the ballroom, at the expensive linens, the china, the crystal…the opulence. "Jesus, have you ever had to sacrifice for *anything*?"

She blinked, then perused the room the same way I had. "You're not being fair."

"Life isn't fair. It only looks that way when you're born into the type of privilege that makes you assume it is."

The door opened, and both our heads snapped to see who it was.

"We're busy!" Persephone called out.

"Well, that might be so," her mother said with a knowing smile as she glanced between us. "But we're going to miss our massage appointments if we don't get going."

Persephone's face fell as she looked at the crumpled piece of paper she held. "Mom…"

My own mother's face flashed in front of my eyes. The hectic way she'd packed the car, and the scared, but hopeful smile she'd given us as she made sure we were buckled in before she ran back inside to get her purse. She'd never gotten the chance to be happy.

"Go," I said softly to Persephone, cutting off her attempt at a confession.

"What?" Confusion wrinkled her brow.

I crossed the distance between us and took the license from her. Then I kissed her forehead, lingering a heartbeat longer than I should have to take in her scent. Fuck, this woman was my *everything*, but she wasn't my wife.

Of course, she wasn't. I wasn't the kind of man who was allowed to have good things in life, to include Persephone.

"Go with your mom. We'll talk tonight."

Her eyes searched mine, confused, apprehensive, and hopeful all at the same time.

"You heard what the man said! Let's go!" Mrs. VanDoren called out with a happy clap.

"Tonight," Persephone promised. She squeezed my hand lightly and walked out, leaving me alone in a ballroom where I didn't belong, holding a marriage license that never really existed, cursing an aching heart that felt as though it had been cracked in a billion little pieces.

What the fuck were we going to do?

18
PERSEPHONE

"*Real love? It takes sacrifice. It means you're willing to lay your body down and take whatever pain you have to in order to keep it from the person you love.*"

My mind hadn't stopped replaying Cannon's words from our earlier fight, and my heart had yet to stop breaking each time I heard his voice echo in my head.

"*Love is what remains when all the fuzzy feelings disappear, and you're still ready to wage war to protect that person...Jesus, have you ever had to sacrifice for anything?*"

"Are you all right, sugar?" Mom asked from her position in the massage chair. I glanced over at her, wondering how she could possibly tell I'd been chewing over the argument Cannon and I had had, but she'd always been good at reading me.

I smiled at the spa specialists who were currently giving us both pedicures. Something my mother and I had scheduled months ago. The day before the wedding prep. And now I wasn't even sure there would be a wedding. Rehearsal was tonight. Would that be the place we worked things out? Where the skies cleared and the clouds parted, and Cannon would finally realize my love was real and raw and one-hundred percent his?

"I'm fine," I finally answered.

"It's normal to get nervous before your wedding," Mom said.

"I'm not nervous," I said. "Besides, we're already married." Or, at least, I thought we'd been. My father's news had hit us both over the head, and now I truly didn't know what to believe. I'd pled my case, and then my mother had walked in, and Cannon had graciously told me to go so she wouldn't find out the truth. And I *couldn't* tell her. I couldn't *not* go through with our pre-wedding plans, not when they meant so much to her.

So I put on my bravest, happiest face, and talked about happy things.

Like the fact that she'd be getting the kidney she needed and deserved. The one that would lengthen her life. Allow her to possibly see her grandchildren, if that day ever came for me or Anne.

I smiled, my memory taking me back to when Cannon and I had compared Cerberus to a baby, and the discussion thereafter. My future didn't make sense without Cannon in it. It just didn't. But if he didn't love me...well, that was another matter altogether. One I feared I'd find out about sooner rather than later.

One spa treatment led to another, the rest of my bridal party having treatments done in succession until we were all sparking and ready for rehearsal dinner. I hadn't seen or heard from Cannon since our argument, and a small piece of me was terrified he'd used that incredible speed of his and bolted. Despite the news of my mother's fortune on the donor list, I didn't want to put her through the stress of a missing groom.

But I should've known better. Should've known Cannon would never do that because I found him waiting by the ballroom door, clad in a luscious all black suit—he'd even put on a tie—just for me.

"You look stunning," I said, the rawness from our fight evident in my voice.

He held his arm out for me after giving my mother a quick hug. "You're radiant," he said as I looped my arm in his. He led me through the ballroom, no mention of our argument, nothing but a firm smile—or as much of one as he'd offer a room full of people—planted on his lips as we were stopped by person after person. All congratulating us. All over the moon happy for us. And if I didn't think too hard on it, I almost believed them. Yes, their excitement was genuine, but deep down, I could almost make myself believe *this* was real. That in one day I'd marry the man of my dreams and we'd live happily ever after.

I'm not your happily ever after.

Cannon's words from months ago echoed through my mind, and I tried not to cringe.

He *had* warned me.

Told me not to fall for him. Told me in his list of rules, many of which we'd broken—together.

Maybe I had imagined it all—the love I thought I'd felt.

But he'd opened up to me, had given me pieces of himself he'd never given anyone else. That had to count for something. Maybe I should take those pieces and be grateful I'd received that much. Maybe I had yet to prove myself enough to him. Maybe—

"Persephone?" My name on his lips drew me out of my thoughts, and I found him reaching for me, somewhere in my battling we'd gotten separated. "It's time for dinner."

I nodded and took his hand, allowed him to lead me up to the table positioned on a stage off to the right of the tables situated around the ballroom floor. Took my seat and thanked my server as food and champagne was delivered all around.

I could barely eat from the twisting in my stomach, but I forced bites down, knowing my mother watched me with weighted eyes. My father too. They could tell, even if both of them didn't know the full truth of my anxiousness.

Cannon ate in silence, but touched me sweetly, an arm around my shoulder, a chaste kiss on my forehead. All for show. All so my mother's heart wouldn't be broken.

After the plates had been cleared, Logan tapped his knife against his champagne flute, rising from his seat as all eyes fell on him. "I believe it's my turn to make a toast," he said, the room quieting. My stomach clenched at the happiness in his eyes. "I was shocked and honored when Cannon asked me to be one of his best men." He grinned at the Reaper table behind him, packed with the men I'd come to think of as family. "As you know, he had many to choose from." A collective laugh from the crowd. "Those who come to know Cannon will understand his fierce loyalty to his friends and his teammates, his true family. And I can tell you that Persephone fit right into that family, from that very first day she came crashing into our world. And we're all so grateful that Cannon was quick enough to catch her."

A smaller group of laughter, for those close enough to know that I'd literally fallen into Cannon's arms the first time we'd met. He'd caught me on instinct as if he'd already been prepared to protect me before he'd met me.

"Cannon, you're one of my best friends, my brother on the ice, and one of the scariest yet most compassionate people I know." Logan raised his glass. "I wish you and your lovely bride the very best in the long, long years to come."

The crowd clapped and raised their glasses as well, and tears pooled into my eyes. Logan's genuine love for his friend stung every inch of my heart. I was a fool. A damned fool for letting it get this far. For thinking my love would be enough for both of us. For thinking he'd want to stay in this marriage with me after…after everything. Now it wouldn't only be me and mine who were hurt, but all of us. Our family. *His* family.

"Now it's time for the sister of the bride to say a few words," My father announced, and a new wave of panic hit me. I didn't think Anne had wanted to do a toast, let alone prepare one. I certainly hadn't asked her to.

"Thank you," she said as she stood to the claps of the people around her. She flipped her hair over her shoulder, the move as sharp as a razor. "My sweet, perfect sister," she said, and I swallowed hard. "You were the best in school, the best in all your extracurriculars, and well, just about the brightest star this town has ever seen." Some *awws* came from the crowd, but cold fear licked my spine. "It's safe to say that my perfect sister Persephone has never once made a real mistake in her entire life." She raised her glass toward me, and I couldn't help but feel like she aimed some sort of weapon at me with the way her eyes sharpened. "But let's be real for a second," she continued. "We're all human. Everyone makes mistakes. And Persephone has finally joined the human crowd and made one. Because we all know why we're *truly* here." She glanced around at the confused faces, a smirk of pure delight on her face, the glaze of a few too many drinks coating her eyes.

Cannon's hand found mine under the table, a steady comfort in an otherwise raging sea.

"A bottle of Ambien," she said, laughing loudly and showing a bit of shock when no one joined her. "I mean, come on," she pressed. "These two?" She shook her head. "Never ever *ever* would've happened if it weren't for that mistake in Vegas."

I squeezed Cannon's hand harder.

My father bolted from his seat, ushering Anne off the floor.

"Congrats!" she bellowed as he guided her from the room.

Lillian popped up from her seat, grabbing the abandoned microphone from my sister's table. "Well," she said. "*Sisters*. I'm pretty sure wanting to murder them and hug them in the span of a breath comes in the title description, am I right?" The crowd laughed, happy to have a different person to focus on. "I'm sure what she meant to say was that you two are amazing together, and we all wish you the absolute best." She glanced around the room. "Who wants to dance?" She waved her hand where the DJ had set up in the corner of the ballroom, and soon, music filtered through the speakers.

The dancefloor filled and drinks were poured and little desserts were offered on silver trays by waiters that flowed in and out of the room.

I let go of Cannon's hand, pushing away from the table. Needing to escape for a moment or a lifetime, I wasn't sure.

I hated that my sister had put a voice to one of Cannon's fears. Had breathed life into something I'd been trying desperately to quash. And I knew I was strong, knew I had to be to love a man like Cannon, but I didn't know how much fight I had left in me.

Because in the end, no amount of fight would prove my love.

And no amount of fight would make him love me back.

19

CANNON

Couples filled the floor, dancing to the live band that played hits from the forties. If this was just the rehearsal, I couldn't imagine what the decadence of the actual reception would look like.

Persephone left the dais and walked along the side of the ballroom, staying clear of the crowds before disappearing through a door that was constructed to blend into the wall. I quickly followed but wasn't as lucky dodging the well-wishers.

"What's going on?" Lillian asked, grabbing me gently by the elbow as I tried to sneak past her table.

"Well, Andromeda is a spiteful—"

"Not what I mean." She shook her head and handed Owen another French fry that we'd had the cooks whip up especially for him. "Your wife looks ready to puke, and that was long before her snotty ass sister said anything."

I rubbed the back of my neck, instead of the burning sensation in my chest. "It's been a hellishly long day."

Her gaze narrowed on me, reading through the bullshit

just like she always did. "Fix it, Cannon. Whatever is going on between you two, fix it."

I glanced around the ballroom, my gaze hopping from Mr. VanDoren to Michael and his black eye, to Axel and Langley on the dance floor. "What if I'm not supposed to fix it?"

"What?" she whispered.

"What if the best thing I can do for her is let her go?" I kept my voice low so no one else would hear.

"That's bullshit. That girl is the best thing that's ever happened to you." Her eyes spat fire at me.

"She is. But I'm not the best thing that's ever happened to *her*." My voice turned to gravel, and my jaw ticked as I struggled for control.

"Well, I call bullshit on that, too." She arched a dark brow at me. "You're one of the highest-paid players in the NHL, have a heart of gold, and though it's creepy to say this as your sister, but you're not that bad looking, either."

I scoffed. "I'm not sure I have a heart."

She tugged my sleeve, and I sat obediently in the vacant seat next to her. No doubt they were out on the dance floor. "You have the biggest heart of anyone I know, Cannon. You love me. You love Owen. The way you look out for us both speaks volumes about who you are."

I glanced at the ring on my left hand. "That's different. You and I kept each other alive. Persephone's idea of love is this fairytale romcom bullshit that's based on hormones and good times. She has no idea the kind of love it takes to—" I shook my head. "She deserves someone who thinks the same way, not someone who's always waiting for the other shoe to drop. She deserves someone who fits into this crowd." I nodded at the dancers.

Her hand covered mine, and her smile turned sad—so much like our mother's that my heart stuttered. "Then let her love you the way she already does, Cannon. What we survived...that's not how it's supposed to be. She shouldn't have to know the kind of love it takes to step in and take it when Dad's been drinking. She shouldn't have to go through something like that to prove her love to you."

I flinched. "I would *never* want her to experience that. I would never allow her to put herself in harm's way for me. Ever. God, just the thought of it turns my fucking stomach."

"She'll never have to experience it because you'll protect her." She shrugged. "Let her be naïve when it comes to that kind of pain. Let her be innocent to abuse and neglect. She doesn't have to live through the darkness we did in order to pull you out of it. If anything, let her be the light you follow. You deserve that, Cannon. More than anyone I know, you deserve to be happy and loved."

I swallowed. "And what happens when my temper snaps like it did this morning?" I nodded toward Michael.

"Well, if she's half the woman I think she is, she'll forgive you."

"I promised her it wouldn't happen, and it did." I twisted my wedding...make that *non*-wedding ring.

"You're human. You make mistakes."

"I can't make a mistake when it comes to her. Do you realize how small she is? How fragile?" My voice dropped to a whisper.

Lillian's entire posture softened, and she squeezed my hand. "Big brother, you are *not* our father."

"I have the same rage in me. He was right about that." And I hated the fucker for it.

"Have you ever put your hand on a woman in anger?" she questioned, tilting her head.

"Fuck! Of course not."

Some guy—I think it was the VanDoren's attorney,

turned my way, and I gave him a polite smile and nod, before lowering my voice again.

"Never."

"Right." She handed Owen another fry. "And I know the honeymoon stage is all sex and fun, but have you gotten into a fight with her? An honest-to-God, frustrated, want to shake-some-sense-into-you fight?"

I grimaced. "We're kind of in one right now."

"And you didn't hurt her, did you?"

"Physically? No. Of course not. I'd rather die. But emotionally...that's another story." I snuck a fry and reached across Lillian to hand it to my nephew. So help me God, that kid would never go through what we did.

"That's just...love." She shrugged. "Whether or not you admit it, Cannon, love isn't always forged in the hell we grew up in. Sometimes it grows tall in the sunlight. That doesn't mean it's not just as strong."

"I'm not good enough for her." The words choked my throat.

"Why don't you let her decide that for herself?" When I was silent, she let out a sigh that moved the flame on the tea light in front of us. "Tell me this. Are you really prepared to live the rest of your life without her? Because it sounds like you're on the brink of doing something incredibly stupid."

"I just want what's best for her." I leaned over and smacked a kiss on her cheek. "I love you, Lillian."

"Don't fuck something up because you think it's too good to be true," she lectured as I stood. "Sometimes, good things are just...good."

Apparently, my sister had been drinking the Kool-Aid around here. I nodded and headed after my wife. Shit, she wasn't even my wife anymore. What the hell was she? My lover? My friend? Whatever label I put on us, was I honestly ready to live the rest of my life without her if it was for her own good? If it kept her safe? Made her happy in the long run?

My head spun as I opened the door wide enough to slip through and closed it behind me. It was another ballroom, but this one was smaller. The room was dark, but Persephone was illuminated in the moonlight that shone through the picture window at the end of the room.

Fuck, she was beautiful. Her white, lace dress had a modest neckline but hugged every one of her delectable curves until it ended above her knee. The woman was pure fucking class.

She turned when she heard me approaching and leaned against one of the large banquet tables that lined the edges of the room.

Our eyes locked, and my heart fucking *hurt* with everything that was stuffed inside it. It felt like the stupid organ was ripping at the seams. God, how could I ever walk away from her? How could I find the strength to do what was right for her, when all I wanted to do was fall at her feet and beg her to love me? To keep shining her light in the places I felt the darkest?

"Cannon," she whispered as I came closer.

I didn't slow my approach or lower my eyes.

Hers widened, and her tongue darted out to lick her lower lip.

I took her face in my hands and kissed her hard and deep. She moaned as our tongues twined and rubbed, the sound filling the dark room. This was my heaven. Not the ice, or between the pages of a book, but right here with Persephone in my arms.

I lifted her onto the table without breaking the kiss, and her fingers found my hair as she tilted her mouth beneath mine. I slid my hand to the back of her head, careful not to fuck with her hair—we'd eventually have to go back out there—and she melted against me, surrendering to the power of the unquenchable desire between us.

I kissed her in every way I'd come to love—deep and wet, soft and slow, hard and needy, until we were both panting, straining to get closer to the other.

She unbuttoned my suit coat and slid her hands inside, skimming the edges of the area that still burned—and would for a couple of days—before reaching around my back and scoring me lightly with her nails. I hissed in pleasure and moved my mouth to her neck. I fucking loved her neck. Loved how responsive she was. Loved how she gave everything over to me without reservation. I just fucking loved h—

"Stop!" she said suddenly, pushing me away with both of her palms on my abs.

I stilled, frozen in the moment.

"Cannon, please," she pled.

I raised my head and managed to find the willpower to step away from her. My hands slid from her hair, and a chill washed over me from the loss of her warmth.

"Don't do that," she insisted, smoothing out the lines of her dress.

"Don't do what?" I asked, barely recognizing my own voice.

"Kiss me like it's the last time," she whispered. Her lip trembled.

We stood at the proverbial fork in the road.

"Persephone, what are we doing?" I asked her softly.

"I hope we're getting married." She forced a smile.

I sat on the table next to her, aware of the inches between us, of the warmth of her skin and the scent of apple blossoms in her hair. "I need to ask you a question."

"Anything," she responded instantly, her pinky nearly grazing mine as we both grasped the edge of the table.

"If we hadn't gotten accidentally fucked up in Vegas, would we be here?" I turned to study her face.

Her lips parted, and her brow crinkled. "I don't understand."

"Yes, you do." I kept my tone gentle. "If we hadn't woken up married…or not married, whatever, would you ever have given me a shot? Given me a first date?"

Her mouth twisted into a wry grin. "Would you ever have asked?"

"No," I responded as honestly as I could.

Her face fell, and the pain I saw there ripped another seam in my heart.

"I never would have asked because I knew I wasn't good enough for you. I knew I could never make you happy or give you the things you were accustomed to. I'm not talking about money. I'm talking about social acceptance and an easy relationship."

"I don't need any of that," she countered, her voice breaking at the end. "I just need you."

I sucked in a breath.

"You see, I would have given you the first date," she continued with a little laugh. "I did. Remember? I wanted you so desperately that I bought you at that charity auction. I couldn't stand the thought of another woman touching you." She shook her head. "Did you lie to me when you told me that you would have bought me, too?"

"Lie? I've never lied to you. I meant every word of it. Fuck, even the thought of someone putting their hands on you…kissing you…" My jaw clenched. "But I was prepared to watch you date someone else—hell, marry someone else because I knew that I could only bring you pain, and that's all I've done since this thing started."

She startled. "You've been tender, and kind, and protective, and everything I could ever want. You haven't hurt me."

"I punched out one of your oldest friends this morning and embarrassed your entire family—including you," I reminded her.

"Oh. Right. *That.*" She huffed a laugh. "Well, Michael is an ass."

"You've seen the online gossip since this morning. I know you have." The shit with Michael had gone public fast, and the worst part is that every article dragged Persephone into it.

Was she saddling herself with a violent man?

Was Charleston's belle of the ball married to a man who would eventually find himself behind bars?

Was I a domestic violence case waiting to happen?

Every headline had been worse than the last.

"I've seen them, and I don't care." She shrugged.

"You don't care?"

She shook her head. "I've been tabloid gossip since I can remember, and though I've tried my best not to give them much fodder, Andromeda's antics have taught our family to roll our eyes and move on."

"Right, but marrying me—for real this time—would give them that fodder you tried so hard not to."

"Okay."

My stomach sank. I was going to drag her very good name through the mud. The name that got her the job as the head of the charitable foundation and opened doors into a society that I had thought only existed in movies.

"Cannon, those reporters don't know you. They don't know what you've suffered for your family. Or how much of your salary you give to the women's shelter downtown. Or that your favorite book is *Wuthering Heights.*"

I balked. "My favorite book is *not Wuthering Heights.*"

She grinned. "I know. Because you'd never stand by and

watch the woman you loved marry someone else. I remember. I was just checking to see if you were listening."

"That stuff isn't anything the world needs to know about me. I don't want people talking shit about *you* because I can't contain my temper."

"I've never cared much what strangers think about me," she said with a whisper. "I know the truth. I know the man you really are."

Did she? Had I shown her the best and the worst of me while we'd been married. *Married.* The ring on my finger mocked me. It was a fucking tease.

The silence stretched between us to the soundtrack of the band in our ballroom next door.

"We're not really married." The words tasted like sand.

"I know. I still can't believe it, but I know."

"We can call this whole thing off," I offered slowly. "We were only doing it to make your mom happy."

"But we ended up making ourselves happy, didn't we?" She brushed her finger along mine.

I couldn't lie to her. "We did. But I don't think it's the kind of happiness that lasts."

The door opened, and a crack of light filled the room as Mrs. VanDoren walked in. "You two! I swear, you can't stay away from each other!"

"We just needed a minute, Mama," Persephone replied.

"Well, you have exactly one minute, and then I'll be back in here. Cannon, your job is to stay and entertain this rowdy lot as long as they'd like to dance."

"Yes, ma'am." I nodded.

"Persephone, your job is to come home with me and get some beauty sleep…and maybe give Anne a piece of your mind for that little stunt she pulled."

"Yes, Mama."

"One more minute. You understand?" She pointed her finger at us, but she was smiling.

"I'll send her right out," I promised.

"Good. And that suit looks mighty handsome on you, Cannon. You should wear ties more often." She winked.

Fat chance in hell, but if either of these women wanted me to, I would.

"I'll keep that in mind."

Mrs. VanDoren gave us a little wave and closed the door behind her as she returned to the party.

Persephone sighed, then lowered herself from the table and faced me.

"Okay, I'm going to talk now, and you're going to listen."

I arched an eyebrow.

"I want to marry you."

My lips parted, but her fingers covered them before I could speak. I barely kept myself from darting my tongue between her fingers out of sheer habit. Fuck, touching her, kissing her had become so common to me I couldn't imagine *not* doing it.

"Nope. I'm talking," she reminded me. "I want to marry you, and I'm not afraid to say it, to put my heart out there on the line. I know you think I'm weak—"

My eyes flared, and a growl worked its way up my throat.

"But I'm not. I'm strong enough to stand here and tell you that I love you, even though you..." She shook her head. "I want to marry you, Cannon. I've never been happier in my life than I have been as your wife. I want to sleep next to you, make love to you, walk Cerberus with you, cheer you on at games, have babies with you—all of it. I want everything with *you*." Her face fell, and so did her fingers from my lips. "But you just keep listing all the reasons we shouldn't be together instead of everything we have going for us."

"Persephone," I pled. For her to stop? For her to continue?

Fuck, I didn't know. The only thing I was certain of was the ache in my chest, ripping my soul from my body when I thought about the rest of my life without her. But how many painful moments like this morning would I bring her if I selfishly stayed?

Would I be stealing away her real chance at happiness with someone who was a better fit for her just because I couldn't bear to let her go?

"So here it is, Cannon." Her shoulders straightened, and her chin rose. "I love you. *That's* my reason for wanting to marry you. I *love* you, whether you believe me or not. I'm sorry that I haven't had to make the sacrifices you have. I'm sorry that my life has been so much easier than yours, but that doesn't mean that I don't love you, because I do. If that's not enough of a reason for you..." She sucked in a breath that stilled my heart. "Then maybe you're right, and we shouldn't be married because I'm realizing that the more I love you, the surer I am that I can't walk down the aisle toward someone who doesn't love *me*."

She didn't wait for me to reply or give me time to process. She just turned and walked out of the room with her head held high, and shut the door, leaving me alone in the darkness.

Where I'd been before I'd fallen for her.

Telling her the truth in my heart wouldn't solve our problems. It wouldn't make this easier. It would be the tether that bound her to me. The fuse on a lit bomb that would eventually destroy her.

My phone buzzed for the millionth time that day, and I finally slipped it from my pocket. A text message alert from my personal publicist—one of at least a dozen lit up the screen. Eventually, I was going to have to call her back. Eventually, I was going to have to deal with the shitstorm I'd created because Michael had been successful in pushing my buttons. He'd gotten exactly what he wanted when I lost my shit.

Eventually wouldn't cut it for the timeline on my biggest problem.

I had less than twenty-four hours to figure out if I was strong enough to walk away from the only woman I'd ever truly wanted.

My hand rested over that burning patch of skin on my chest.

I meant what I'd told her—that love meant sacrifice. It meant being willing to lay your own body down to protect the person you loved from pain.

That's what I was doing for her—protecting her even though it was fucking killing me.

I had to protect her because I loved her.

Fuck. I was in love with Persephone.

But my heart felt like it always did, like it always had since that moment.

Chills shot down my spine with the realization.

I'd been in love with her since—

The woman fell into the hallway, and I opened my arms, letting both my stick and helmet crash to the floor as I caught her.

She was a tiny thing—ridiculously light as I carefully set her back on her feet. Feet that were clad in equally tiny, sexy heels. They matched her light blue sundress and sweater that buttoned modestly over her breasts and had a little bow at the back. Red soles.

This woman reeked not just of money—but of class. The kind you couldn't buy. The kind that got passed down through generations of the same.

"Are you alright, lass?" Connell asked from a few feet away.

She untangled herself from a waterfall of long blonde hair. It was pale as moonlight, the strands soft as silk as it grazed a bare strip of skin between my glove and jersey, and long enough to imply that she lived in a tower. A tower I had no business climbing because she was clearly so out of my league that we weren't even playing the same sport.

"I'm just a bit embarrassed, but I'm okay." Her voice was sweeter than honey, lilting with a southern drawl that slid over me like velvet and stirred my cock to life. Holy shit, this woman had just turned me on, and I hadn't even seen her face.

Then I did. She turned to look up at me, and her eyes punched me in the damned stomach. Crystal-fucking-blue and rimmed with thick lashes that did nothing to hide the emotion in them. Fuck, I bet this woman wore her heart on her four-thousand-dollar sleeve. Innocence, embarrassment, honesty—it was all right there for anyone to see, for anyone to take advantage of. An inexplicable, almost primal urge to protect her slammed into me with the force of an avalanche.

She was the most beautiful woman I'd ever seen in my life. So perfect that she couldn't be real. No one was that flawless outside the pages of a book...and yet she was. Her nose was pert and a perfect fit for her heart-shaped face and her plump, bow-shaped lips were a kissable shade of pink.

"Thank you so much for catching me—" She started to say, but then those eyes widened in surprise and recognition. She probably knew who I was, which meant she probably knew I was the last man whose arms she should have tumbled into.

Then her pupils dilated slightly, and her lips parted. Apparently, she liked what she saw, too.

Not for you. Not for you. Not for you. My brain tried to get the thought through to the rest of my body, but couldn't seem to break past the swelling in my chest that screamed its own chant.

Mine. Mine. Mine.

Holy shit, I was losing it. Right there in the hallway of my own rink, surrounded by my teammates, I was sinking into insanity, driven mad by a woman who had such little disregard for her own safety that she was running in heels on a rubberized hallway slick from the melted ice dripping from our skates. I scrambled for the first words I could think of.

"Next time, don't run down the hallway in heels," I growled, narrowing my eyes in hopes I'd scare her off. Big bad wolves like me ate innocent little girls like her for breakfast.

If she wasn't careful, I'd eat her all night long.

My teammates groaned at my lack of manners. Fuck them. I was who I was, and it was for her own safety that she learned it fast.

"Jesus, Cannon, can't you just say you're welcome?" Connell chided.

Instead of running like she should have, the woman arched a delicate brow at my tone, making it clear that neither my size, my reputation, nor my tattoos intimidated her.

She wasn't scared of me.

My heart fucking stilled, and when it began pounding again, the beats felt like they didn't belong to me. Like I no longer belonged to myself in general.

"I'll be more careful in the future," she drawled softly, her eyes dropping from mine to where my hand cupped her elbow, keeping her steady. No wedding ring.

Shit. Had I been touching her this whole time? I cursed my glove, wishing I could feel my bare skin against hers just once. Once, and I'd be content.

That was a lie. Something told me that if I ever got this woman under my hands, I'd never be content, or capable of letting her go. She looked like ambrosia, food for the ancient Gods, and just like ambrosia, all it would take would be one bite to ruin a mortal, flawed man like me.

It felt like slow-motion, but in reality, my grip snapped open as I found the strength to let her go. That protective instinct swirled in my gut, pairing with that heavy, sweet ache in my chest to turn me inside out.

Protecting her meant keeping my damned hands off her, which I vowed right there and then to do. Besides, she was everything I hated, right? Obviously wealthy, educated, and a member of the upper class who had always sneered at those more unfortunate than they were.

Right. I should have hated her.

I should hate her designer shoes, her diamond stud earrings that were bigger than most engagement rings, and the refined way she held herself.

There was only one problem with hating her.

One fucking look and I'd been a goner.

My hands clenched at the memory, at the effort it had taken to let go of something so innocent as her elbow. Now I knew her—I knew her heart, her soul, and her mind. I'd found solace in her arms, and mind-bending pleasure in her body.

I knew the taste of her kiss, and the depth of her pure, unscarred heart—a heart that had tricked her mind into thinking that she was in love with me.

My cell phone dinged with yet another text—no doubt another article publicizing my evil temper and her naiveté for marrying a man like me. Another article shaming her.

This wasn't her elbow anymore—it was her future, and I wasn't sure I was strong enough to let her go this time.

I loved her. My soul belonged to her.

I had to protect her…even if she'd hate me for it.

20

PERSEPHONE

Raised voices tumbled through the half-open window of my old room in my parents' house, so I set my coffee down in a hurry. When I heard Owen—Cannon's nephew—start wailing, I rushed outside, not even bothering to shut the door.

Early morning light illuminated the dark scene—Cannon's father, somehow on my property and yelling at Lillian, who tucked a crying Owen behind her back.

"You get your no-good piece of shit brother out here right now!" Cannon's father yelled, jabbing a finger toward Lillian. "Or I swear to God I'll—"

"Excuse me," I cut him off, stepping between him and Lillian, so close I had to push his hand away so it didn't touch my face. "I'm not sure how you got on my property, but you'll be leaving now." I typed a fast text to Gerald, knowing he'd make it around to the back of the estate in minutes.

He sneered. "I had an invitation," he said, waving a familiar piece of cardstock between us. "Some *Ms. Conroy* sent it to me. Security didn't think twice. Dumbasses."

My heart clenched—Ms. Conroy was my mother's

personal assistant. She must've overlooked the fact that this man was definitely not family. Fire boiled in my blood as his eyes fell back to Lillian, who stood trembling behind me, her eyes drenched in panic, fear.

"Fetch him," he said to her. "Now."

I glared at him before turning to Lillian. "Take Owen inside," I said, motioning to the main house where a proper security detail would be waiting. Not to mention the handful of Reapers who'd gathered to scarf down the brunch spread we'd served in the formal dining room. Not Cannon, though, but I assumed—or *hoped*—it was because he was on his morning run.

She hesitated, her eyes darting between us. "I'm fine," I assured her. "Please, Lillian. Get Owen a second breakfast or some chocolate milk." The little boy stopped crying for a moment upon hearing that, and Lillian nodded as she scooped him up and hurried toward the main house.

Cannon's father moved to follow her, and I stepped in his path, putting my back to the main house but effectively stopping him. He glared down at me, surmising my tiny frame which he easily towered over.

"I'm not afraid of you," I said, though adrenaline rushed through my veins. All I had to do was keep him occupied long enough for Gerald to get my message, or for Lillian to alert the house—where half the Carolina Reapers had slept last night. "And I don't know how you came by that invitation, but it clearly wasn't issued to you. Only family was invited."

"I *am* that boy's family." He scoffed. "Blood." He shook his head. "I should be ashamed to admit that too. He's the laziest, most arrogant piece of shit there is. Won't even take care of his kin. Problematic. Always has been. That's why his poor sister never got adopted when I lost my rights. Every bad thing in her life and mine is because of him. Because his stupid mother spoiled him rotten. I tried to make him a man, but he never did listen. And that temper of his?" His eyes trailed the length of my body, and suddenly I wanted a second shower. "You're hiding bruises under that pretty little sundress, aren't you?"

Rage, unfiltered and undiluted rushed through my blood, my *soul*.

"Shut your ignorant mouth," I snapped. "Cannon is a *hundred* times the man you'll ever be, and thank God for that. He's your opposite in every way. Brilliant where you are dim." I stepped toward him, my anger radiating off of me in waves. So much the man *retreated* a step. "Compassionate where you are cold." Another step, another retreat. "Perceptive where you are oblivious." I stopped, glaring up at him, my fists shaking at my sides. "*Worthy* where you are not."

He clenched his jaw, his face turning ten shades of red.

"You are nothing. And he is *everything*, and I swear to the Lord above if you don't get the fuck off my property, I will use all my considerable power and connections to ensure you never live another easy day the rest of your pathetic life." My heart galloped so fast the words came out a little breathless, but no tears pricked my eyes. I stood my ground, held my spine straight.

His eyes lifted up and behind me, but I didn't dare turn around in case it was a trick to cause me harm. "I promised you this reckoning would come!" he snapped, still looking over my head. "This is what you get for turning your back on your family." He pointed down to me. "Marrying a heartless little upper-class piece of ass? I at least thought you were better than that." He moved to step around me, and I finally turned to see Cannon standing there, fists clenched at his sides, but his eyes? They were on me…shock and awe and disbelief and pain churning in their dark depths.

I spun back around to face Cannon's biological father,

and I moved on instinct, on the sheer will of my soul that screamed to protect him.

"Don't speak to him," I said, stepping between him and Cannon. The man reached for me, and I tilted my head. "I *dare* you to put a hand on me. Go ahead," I urged, my entire body shaking with adrenaline. "*See* what happens."

He paused. In my peripheral vision, not one or two but *four* Reapers rushed toward the scene.

"Axel," I said without having to look at the giant to know he'd made it to my side first. "Would you and Lukas please help remove this man from my property?"

"With pleasure," Axel said, and Lukas nodded as they rounded on Cannon's father.

"Don't you put your damned hands on me!" he yelled, but I eyed him.

"Resist, and I'll phone the police."

He stopped his struggle, and Axel and Lukas herded him toward the front of the property where I could see Gerald and two of his security detail rushing for us.

Logan and Connell flanked Cannon's side, but it wasn't until I watched Axel and Lukas hand off his father to our team that I could truly look at Cannon.

Frozen—the man hadn't moved, save for the tremble in his fists and the tick in his clenched jaw. I sighed, flashing a grateful look toward Logan and Connell, who were clearly there to help him if he couldn't hold himself back from the violence I knew surged through his veins. I nodded to them both, and they understood the silent plea, turning around to meet up with Axel and Lukas closer to the house.

I breached the distance between us, slowly, as if approaching a feral jungle cat. Close enough to touch, but I didn't…couldn't. "Cannon," I said, sighing. He'd shown incredible restraint, locking himself down from going after his father…especially after his stream of foul words.

I waited—not reaching for him, not pushing him—simply waited in silence with him as he collected himself. As his breathing evened out. The rise and fall of his chest relaxing as the seconds ticked by. My own heartbeat had yet to calm, and I wrung my hands in an effort to stop their shaking.

Cannon moved then, some leash on himself dropped. Gently, he held my hands palm up, tracing the lines with his thumbs, massaging them until the trembling had soothed. Something heated and electric pulsed between us, between those innocent touches, and I looked up at him, my eyes pleading. Words, there were so many *words* I needed to say, wanted to say, but my emotions clogged my throat until I could barely breathe.

He took a step back, letting my hands fall to my sides. And that step back felt like an ocean between us, a raging sea I needed to cross but had little strength to do so.

"You haven't called off the wedding," he said, glancing around the property like the band might start playing *Here Comes the Bride* at any moment.

"Neither have you," I answered, my voice cracking. Our eyes locked, and the charged emotion churning in his sparked something right down to my soul. Some inner piece of himself I had never seen before and couldn't decipher. The wall gone, I stared at him and begged for understanding. For that common ground we had not so long ago.

"Cannon," Anne's voice was soft, apologetic as we both turned at the sound of her approach. "Lillian is asking for you. She's really upset."

Cannon turned back to me, a battle raging on his features.

"Go," I said, nodding toward the house. "She needs you."

Not that I didn't need him, but I'd never keep him from his sister. Especially after what just happened, Lord knows what she was going through right now.

He nodded, and jogged up to the house, leaving me alone with my sister.

I turned my back on her, prepared to return to my room, and simply focus on breathing for the next few hours.

"Sephie," she said, stopping me. "Wait."

I paused, turning toward her. "What is it, Anne?" I sighed. "Want to get a few more jabs in before I put on my dress?"

She stumbled toward me, her navy pumps sticking in the lush grass. "No," she said, chewing her bottom lip. "I wanted to apologize. About the toast, about the fitting…about everything, really. I'm sorry. At first, I was happy to hear you'd gotten hitched in Vegas, it meant you were human. Like me. But then with everyone so excited and amped up and throwing this big wedding for you, I was jealous. No one has ever made that fuss over me and my marriages."

I arched a brow at the plural use of that word, therein lied the reasoning for no one getting excited.

"I know," she pressed on. "None of mine have been serious. All on a whim like everything else in my life. I thought this thing between you and him was the same thing. I didn't realize…" She sighed. "I didn't realize how much you truly love that man."

I swallowed hard, nodding at the truth I couldn't possibly deny.

"He's the best person I've ever met," I said.

"And he brings out the best in you." She smiled. "Not that you could get much better than you already are."

I rolled my eyes.

"Seriously, though, Sephie," she continued. "I've never seen the fire in you like I have since he's been around. It suits you."

"Thank you."

"And," she continued, swallowing hard as her eyes filled with tears. "I know you still hate me for not getting tested—"

"I don't hate you," I cut her off. Severely disappointed? Exhausted from trying to help her and getting my hand slapped away? Sure, but never hate.

"It's okay. I...I'm trying to do this thing where I tell the people I trust the truth." She laughed darkly. "Only thing is, I don't trust many people anymore." Something distant churned in her eyes, and I reached for her hand. She let me take it, brushing away some tears with her free one. "I *did* go to the doctor," she said. "But it was...well, it was for something else. And he told me that some of my nightlife activities —and my dependency upon them—made me an unfit match for Mama. Not only that, he said if I kept up with my ways, I'd be dead in a year. Something about my liver levels—"

"Anne," I gasped, throwing my arms around her. "We'll get you help. You could've come to me. Why didn't you—"

"Because I didn't want you to see me like this," she said, squeezing me harder. "I'm a fucking mess," she admitted. "More than you'll ever know."

"Let me help you," I pleaded, breaking our embrace to meet her eyes.

"I hate myself because what if I could've been a match? What if I could've been the one to save her, and I couldn't because of what I've done to myself."

"You can't think like that," I said, my voice soothing. "She's getting what she needs now. So, we'll have to focus on you." I raised my brows, a desperate, silent question.

She nodded. "I'm ready. To get help. If you're willing."

"Always," I said, already thinking of the best rehab and therapy clinics I could enroll her in. And, selfishly, I hoped she'd let *me* in on what fueled this decade of madness in the first place.

Anne opened her arms. "Sisters?"

I wrapped her in a hug. "Sisters."

She blew out a breath and wiped under her eyes. "Good,

now that *that* is done with," she said. "All I have to do is get back in Father's good graces. I suppose not drinking at your wedding will be the first step."

"Sounds like a good one to me."

"You ready?" she asked. "For today?"

I took in a slow breath, checking my heart. I hated that I didn't know if Cannon would decide to leave me to walk toward an empty altar, but I *knew* in the depths of my soul that I loved this man—for better and for worse. And when you love something that deeply, you show up for them. Every day. Even if you don't know if they'll show up for you.

So, I'd show up.

And I'd keep loving him, keep showing him he was worthy of love until the day he told me to stop. Until the day he told me he didn't reciprocate.

Which he hadn't.

Despite all the drama we'd gone through, he'd never, not *once* said he didn't love me.

And for now, that was all I needed.

"I'm ready," I said and turned toward the house where I had a wedding dress waiting for me.

21

CANNON

I was convinced that the VanDoren women were really undercover secret operatives. That was the only logical explanation to the way they'd intercepted me each of the seven times I'd tried to see Persephone since that shit had gone down in the front yard. If this place actually *had* a designated front yard.

"You sure you want to do this?" Logan asked as we flattened ourselves against the wall in the upstairs hallway.

"Do you think I'd ask you to come up here and play Mission Impossible if I didn't?" I challenged.

He tilted his head. "Okay, that's reasonable. But you really don't think this can wait forty-five minutes until you see her?"

I narrowed my eyes at my best friend. "You honestly think that standing at the altar in front of all our friends and family is a good time to have a heart to heart?"

He mulled it over and nodded. "Again, reasonable."

"Can you please just open that fucking door so I can talk to my wife?"

"On it." He stood tall, adjusted the tie of his tuxedo, and knocked on the door between us.

There was a faint sound of rustling before it opened.

"Oh! Logan! How can I help you?" Mrs. VanDoren asked.

Logan turned on the charm with a regretful smile. "I know these minutes are sacred, but Cannon just sent me up. There's apparently an issue with the flowers at the altar—"

"The peonies?" she gasped.

I held my breath and prayed that she didn't look through the crack in the door that would show me doing a shit job of hiding.

"Right, the peonies," Logan continued. "It turns out he thought you said posies?"

"Are you kidding me?"

"Mama, is everything okay?" I heard Persephone ask, and my heart jumped.

"It's fine, darling. Don't you worry about a single thing."

"Right, so the florist said that Cannon is wrong, and they're supposed to be posies, and they're still down there arguing—"

"They are most certainly supposed to be peonies. Of all the silly things to go wrong today. Honey, I'll be right back. You just stay right here, and we'll get your dress on in a few minutes, okay?"

"No problem." Her voice was the only thing I'd wanted to hear all day.

Logan stepped back and held his arm out to Mrs. VanDoren, facing the opposite way from where I was hiding. She took his arm and headed down the hall. The minute they turned the corner, I yanked open the door and stepped inside.

Persephone's childhood bedroom was pink...and not just a little pink. Really fucking pink. And frilly. The door to the ensuite bathroom was open, and as I headed that way, Andromeda stepped into the doorway.

"Oh hell no! You don't get to see her before the wedding! Get out!" she snapped.

"What? Who is that?" Persephone asked.

"I've been trying all day to talk to my wife, and you know it." I folded my arms across my chest. "You've stolen her cell phone, posted a guard at the bottom of the staircase, another guard at the tree that grows just outside her window, refused the flowers I sent up to her—"

She grimaced. "We gave her the flowers...we just kept the card from her."

"The card was *all* I cared about!"

"Well, I'd certainly read more romantic notes. *Call me so we can talk*, certainly didn't make the top ten in my life—or hers, I might add." She cocked her head at me.

"You did what? Andromeda get out of my way right this minute!" Persephone demanded.

I cocked an eyebrow at my fake sister-in-law.

She grumbled but stepped aside so Persephone could come through the doorway.

Her hair and makeup had already been done, the first in an elaborate updo that had my palms itching with the knowledge that I'd pull every pin loose later, and the second a more formal version of the minimalist style Persephone favored. She looked beautiful.

She tucked the edges of the white, silk bathrobe closer around her and looked up at me with wonder, her gaze skimming over the details of my tux before coming back to my face. "Cannon."

"We need to talk."

Some of the light shuttered in her eyes, but she nodded. "Anne, get out, and don't you dare come back until you see Cannon leave."

"Are you serious? You know that seeing the bride on the wedding day is horrible luck! I might buck tradition, but even I made sure not to violate that one." She tapped her foot under a lavender bridesmaid dress—the same one I'd just seen Lillian in as she dressed Owen.

"And look how that turned out for you," Persephone offered with a smile. "Now do me a favor and stand guard for Mama. I'm not kidding. We need a moment."

Anne rolled her eyes but walked out the door, muttering something about tradition.

Persephone and I stood staring at each other for at least a minute after the door closed.

"I've been trying to get you alone all day." I rubbed the back of my neck to keep from fidgeting with my tie. At least it wasn't one of those pansy-assed bow ties. "If I'd known that taking care of Lillian meant I'd lose my only opportunity to talk to you, I would have stayed outside with you." She'd been gone by the time I got my sister calmed down and reassured that our father had been hauled off the property.

"You needed to be with her. I understood that," she said softly, taking a few steps so she could sit on the pink-cushioned window seat. "I was really proud of you."

I startled. "You what?"

"I was proud of you," she insisted, gripping the edge of the cushion so hard that her knuckles turned white. "I can't imagine the effort it took for you to stand there silent and not let your temper loose on your father. You were practically shaking with it."

"It was one of the hardest things I've done in my life." I'd wanted to rip him limb from limb for daring to come, for scaring Lillian and raising his voice at Persephone. But I'd known that if I'd moved one inch or even opened my mouth, I would have given Persephone's father yet another reason to call me out. "Hell, it was probably the hardest moment of my life before this one."

Her shoulders sagged in defeat, and her gaze fell from mine.

"No. Persephone, no." I fell to my knees in front of her. "God, I fuck everything up, don't I? I can't even do this right."

"Do what?" She slowly brought her head up just enough to meet my eyes. Never again, I promised myself. Never again would she wear the look of apprehension that paled her face right now.

"Tell you that I'm in love with you."

Her eyes flared, and her lips parted. Shit. She was speechless, and I was out here hanging on a limb.

"You put yourself in front of me today. You literally stepped between my dad and me." That moment had almost brought me to my knees.

Her expression changed from shock to confusion. "Wait, what?"

"Today, when my dad was here, you put yourself between us—"

"I remember. I was there. But what does that have to do with you being in love with me?" She shook her head.

"You don't get it." I braced my hands on either side of hers. "In my entire life, no one has ever put themselves between us. Mom was already too bloody by the time he'd start on me, and Lillian was always smaller, so I was usually the one stepping in. No one's ever put themselves in the line of fire for me. And as much as I wanted to haul you over my shoulder and carry you back into the house—and away from him..." My eyes squeezed shut. "I was in such awe of you in that moment."

I opened my eyes to find her staring at me in slack-jawed disbelief.

"Cannon Price, are you telling me that you fell in love

with me on our wedding day because I yelled at your father?" Her voice rose to an almost scary level as she progressed.

I cocked my head to the side. "No, but I hadn't seen you since that happened, so I needed to tell you."

"Tell me that you loved me? Or tell me that you're in awe of me?"

"Yes." Fuck, this was not going any of the four million ways I'd planned in my head. "This isn't going well, is it?"

"Well, it's not going great." Now both her eyebrows were sky-high. "You have me so confused that I don't know what to do with myself."

"Welcome to my world," I muttered.

Her eyes narrowed, and then her expression shifted, crumpling a little and taking my heart with it. "Cannon, you just have to tell me if you're calling off this wedding or not because I'm dying inside. My soul has shriveled a little with every hour that's gone by, not knowing what's going on in your head. So tell me right now—are we getting married today?"

"That's up to you."

I might as well have told her that Neil Armstrong was outside and prepared to walk her down the aisle for the look she shot me.

"Okay." I gathered up all the courage I had. "Maybe this will go better if I can just get it all out. Because I'm fucking this up left and right. So, let's make a deal."

"A deal?" she repeated.

"Yep. I'm going to talk, and then I'm going to leave. And you will agree not to say anything until I'm gone." I nodded, quite pleased with my little plan.

"So I don't get to respond?"

"Of course you do," I assured her. "But it's an actions-speak-louder-than-words kind of thing. I'm just worried that if you interrupt me, I'll never get this out, and we're kind of down to the wire on this will-we won't-we thing."

"Right." She sat up straight and folded her hands in her lap as she crossed her legs. The silk split with the motion, revealing a smooth, creamy thigh that reminded me it had been *days* since I'd made love to her.

If this didn't go well, it would be an eternity.

"Okay. You talk. I'll listen, and then I won't say a single word until you're gone, I promise on my Mama's life." She swallowed, her eyes laced with fear, but she nodded anyway. *My brave girl.*

I took a deep breath, steadied my nerves the best I could, then yanked my tie loose.

Her eyes flared wide as she watched me pull the knot apart, and unbutton the top few buttons on my shirt, but she was true to her word and didn't speak. I was careful to leave the edges of the shirt closed, but if all else failed, I had a visual aid.

"I love you, Persephone," I began.

She pressed her lips in a firm line as her eyes searched mine.

"I'm never going to be the man you deserve. I'm not the man who sits quietly, sipping mimosas on a Sunday morning at the country club, listening to all the douchebags prattle on about their 401K's. I'm not the man who spills his guts when something is bothering him. I'm not the man your dad wants or your friends want, and I'm pretty sure I'll never be allowed into a PTA meeting. I'll never be the man in a bowtie or the man in the green vest. And to be honest, that kind of guy isn't the one you fell in love with."

She sucked in her breath but stayed silent.

"If you say you love me, and you really do, then you have to accept who I am, not who you think I can be. I will always struggle with my temper. Chances are I'll get your name dragged through every tabloid at least once a month for something stupid I do, or they'll just make shit up like they usually do, anyway. I can't promise that I won't beat the shit out of Michael—out of anyone who has the nerve to say shit about you in front of me."

Her brow furrowed.

"When I can't find the words to talk about how I feel, I read them. I'm not saying that I won't work on communication, but I am saying that you have to accept the fact that I'm not the poetry and hearts guy. I travel too much. I swear too much. I'm covered in scars from shit I would rather die than have you experience, and most of those scars aren't physical. I'm not big on tradition—I'd rather find a newer, better way to do something. My job isn't stable—I can be traded to any team when the terms are right. I really hate jello, and it's even worse when people stick fruit in it."

She cracked a smile.

"Persephone, I love you. I'm *in* love with you, and I have been since the moment you had the nerve to throw sass at me in that hallway two years ago. I just didn't recognize the emotion until I was staring down the barrel of losing you. And if this is really what you want, then I'm changing our rules. Four is out—because I love you and you love me. Five is out because I plan on making love to you for the rest of our lives. I can't guarantee seven, because I tend to get into fights on the ice in at least eighty percent of the games I play in."

I shifted forward on my knees, and my shirt fell open.

Her eyes shined, and her lip trembled as she reached for the white, crisp fabric and held it apart just far enough to see my new ink, still swollen and lightly scabbed in places.

In a sea of black on my chest, the once-empty heart now had her name scrawled across it in crimson red, against a backdrop of pomegranate seeds that filled the heart to the brim.

"I got it done instead of playing golf," I admitted. "Even though your dad had just told us that we weren't married, and I knew I was going to have to walk away for your own good—"

Her eyes flew to mine in a panic.

"—I realized that *you* own me, and that fact won't change if you decide not to marry me today. You will always own me." My brows knit. "And I guess that's another con for the list—I'm never going to willingly play golf. Ever. It fucking sucks."

She took in a breath, her lips parting, and I gently lifted her chin with my fingers.

"You promised," I reminded her.

She swallowed as tears filled her eyes.

"I love you. I want to marry you, but I'm giving you this one last out because my biggest fear is becoming your biggest regret." My self-control hung in tatters, but I made it to my feet. "If you can accept me for who I am, then I'll see you out there, and if you can't, if you need more than I can give you, I'll understand. I just want you to be happy."

I left the room quickly for fear that I'd fall at her feet and beg her to lower her standards for me.

"You guys all done?" Andromeda asked as she leaned against the wall in the hallway.

"I guess that's really up to her," I answered, leaving her bewildered as I made my exit.

Thirty-five minutes later, I stood at the altar, Logan at my side, and a few Reapers backing him up.

The October breeze was mild, rustling the flowers that laced the massive arbor we stood under as we faced the two hundred guests that made up what Mrs. VanDoren had called *an intimate affair*.

If this was intimate, I would have hated to see what she considered friendly.

"You have got to relax," Logan muttered in my direction. "And for fuck's sake, don't lock your knees. You're too heavy to catch if you go down, and Axel is three guys away."

I grunted my response and tried to slow my heartbeat as I stared down the very long, very empty aisle. My left hand felt bare, and I wondered if Persephone would leave it that way.

My thoughts raced. Had my words been enough to convince her? Or just enough to make her realize that I really wasn't the guy she wanted? Now that I'd given her my heart, was she going to break it? To be fair, I'd left the woman on pins and needles since we realized her mom was going to be okay, so me sweating it out for a little over half an hour as she made up her mind was getting off easy.

The string quartet just off to my left switched songs.

"Here we go." Logan gave me a little nudge with his elbow.

My jaw locked as Lillian came down the aisle, holding a bouquet. That was a good sign, right? Next came Andromeda. When they both stood across from me, Sterling appeared. He had not worn a leisure suit, thank God. He walked slowly, but somehow still managed to swagger as he pulled a wagon up the aisle containing both Owen and Cerberus.

Okay, I wasn't one for gooey shit, but that was fucking cute.

Lillian lifted Owen into her arms, and Sterling did the same with Cerberus, tugging the wagon out of the way. He must have hooked it up to some kind of spreader because it trailed flower petals in its wake.

The music shifted again, and everyone stood.

My heart galloped. I remembered what Logan said and bent my knees just slightly.

Please, God. Please. I take back everything I said in her bedroom. I'll be whatever she needs. I'll wear the fucking vest and make friends with the douchebags. Just please let her love me.

She appeared at the end of the aisle with her father by her side.

My breath abandoned me—she was that radiant. She'd shown up. She was going to marry me. Emotion clogged my throat and stung my eyes as she walked closer. Her dress was long and white, clinging to her every curve and shimmering in the dying light of the sunset with every step she took. Her veil trailed behind her but didn't cover her beautiful face.

Our eyes locked and held as joy filled every molecule in my body.

My smile echoed hers as I stepped forward to take her hand. Her father kissed her cheek, then transferred her hand to mine and leaned forward.

"There's a new, correct, legal license waiting for you both to sign in my study."

My eyebrows shot up. "For someone who doesn't want this to happen, that was a step out of your way."

He scoffed. "I'm man enough to know when I've been overruled by my daughter's heart. Treat her well."

"I will," I swore.

He stepped away, leaving me to stare at Persephone as the preacher started the ceremony. We didn't look away for much, both content to take in every last detail of each other in those moments. God, she was beautiful and smart, and generous, and loyal, and so fucking mine that I wanted to pull a Princess Bride and demand the preacher just skip to the *Man and Wife* part.

I found a ring in my hand, and saw she had the same, and just about fist-pumped that we were moving right along.

"Oh, we're going to do our own vows. Cannon's not one for tradition," Persephone said, tossing a wink my way.

We're doing what? I stared at the love of my life in complete and utter shock.

She had the nerve to grin but went first.

"I, Persephone Julia VanDoren, swear to love you, Cannon Price, for the rest of my life. I will be your shelter in every storm, even when you swear it's not raining. I will bake you peanut butter cookies and walk Cerberus by your side every night, but the early mornings are on you."

A chuckle went through the crowd, and my heart soared.

"I promise to abide by rules one, three, six, and eight, knowing that rules four and five are off the table, and hoping that you might wiggle a bit on rule number two."

I huffed a laugh. I was never touching her money. Ever.

"I promise to be your biggest fan, consume two-thirds of your closet, never make you eat jello, and always keep you up to date on the latest magazine articles." Her eyes took on a wicked gleam, and I nearly kissed her right then. "I will love you the rest of my life, Cannon, just the way you are because you're already perfect for me." She slid the ring onto my finger, and my soul clicked back into place.

"It's your turn," the preacher reminded me when I stood there staring at Persephone.

Shit. Right. Okay.

I took her wedding band between my thumb and forefinger and poised it just at the tip at the end of her finger.

"I, Sheldon Cannon Price—"

You could have heard a pin drop when Sterling muttered, "Whaaaaat?"

"—swear that I will love you, Persephone Julia VanDoren, for the rest of my life, and every second of forever that follows. I promise that while I don't have gentle manners, I'll always be gentle with you. When I travel too much, I'll carry you with me in my heart. When I can't find the words, I'll read them to you. When I lose my way, I'll follow you, knowing that your light is all I need."

A single tear slid down her face, but her smile was brighter than ever.

"I swear I'll bring color to your life in every way, and to always have your back. I will build you a bigger closet for your tiny clothes, and get whatever you want, whenever you want it, from the highest shelves. I will always catch you when you fall, and I will never forget what a gift your love is. I will protect you, cherish you, adore you, and worship you every moment for the rest of our lives."

I slid the ring onto her finger and heard more than a few sniffles from our audience.

"By the power invested in me by the state of South Carolina, I now pronounce you husband and wife. You may kiss your bride."

I was already on it, cupping the back of her neck as I brought my mouth to hers. She tasted like love and home, and happiness. She tasted like Persephone.

She was mine.

"Not a poet, huh?" she whispered against my lips as the crowd clapped behind us.

"I guess you bring out the romantic in me."

She grinned, throwing her arms around my neck. I swept her into my arms and kissed her thoroughly, uncaring if the audience thought it was too much. Then I mentally did the math and cursed the hours we'd have to wait before I could take this exquisite dress off her body.

I felt a tap at my shoulder and broke the kiss, ready to get the PDA lecture, but instead, I found Logan and the rest of the Reapers gawking at me.

"Your name is *Sheldon?*" Logan blurted the question with huge eyes.

"His name is *mine*," Persephone corrected him, then pulled my face back to hers for another kiss.

I carried my wife back down the aisle to the cheers of our friends and family, letting the happiness soak in as we took our first steps into forever.

And this time, we remembered every single second of it.

EPILOGUE

EIGHTEEN MONTHS LATER

Persephone

I rubbed my palms against my eyes, pushing off from the couch where I'd accidentally fallen asleep —an *hour* ago? What in the world? I thought I'd just closed my eyes for a second, but I hadn't been getting regular sleep for a few months now.

I cinched my soft cotton robe around myself, having not bothered to throw a shirt on underneath it—not when I had to whip the girls out every five minutes it seemed these days. My legs bare, I padded down the hallway in search of my husband.

I turned not into our room, but the room directly across from it, softly opening the door to spy inside.

My heart skipped a beat as I held my breath.

Cannon sat in the rocking chair in the corner, shirtless, our three-month-old baby girl cradled against his chest. Her white blanket practically glowed against the midnight ink decorating his skin, but she slept soundly tucked against his chest. His eyes were on Melony, gazing down at her like she was an answer to a question he'd been asking his entire life. A soft hum radiated from his throat, a slower version of a rock ballad that had quickly become her personal lullaby.

Tears pricked my eyes, pure happiness and unbelievable bliss soaring through me in waves. How did I get so lucky?

I didn't bother moving, didn't make a sound, yet Cannon's eyes slowly trailed to mine, as if he'd known the minute I'd opened the door. He flashed me a wicked smile, slowly rising from the rocking chair and gently laying Melony in her crib. The girl didn't even make a peep—she was already Daddy's girl, sleeping for him much easier than she ever slept for me.

I backed out of the doorway, allowing Cannon to softly close it behind him.

"I thought you were sleeping," he whispered as he followed me into our room.

"I didn't mean to," I said, pushing back my long blonde hair. "You could've woken me."

He wrapped his arms around me, pulling me against him. "Never," he said. "Plus, I like it when I get to put her down. Gives us some bonding time between feedings."

The mere mention of feeding had my breasts aching, and I groaned.

Cannon massaged my upper back, kneading his fingers into my tense muscles without me having to tell him where I ached.

"Mmm," I sighed against his chest. "That feels amazing."

"Careful," he warned. "Talk like that, and I definitely won't let you sleep."

Instantly, I melted for the man.

"I'm very much awake now," I said, glancing up at him.

He cocked a brow at me, then flicked his tongue over my lips. "How awake?"

"Fully," I teased and backed out of his touch until I'd found the bed. I untied my robe and let it fall to the floor. I had nothing underneath except my soft cotton panties.

Cannon hissed, his eyes taking their fill of my post-baby body. "You're incredible," he said, spanning the distance between us. "Gorgeous." He dropped to his knees on the bed and kissed the planes of my tummy. "Mine," he growled as he nipped at my inner thigh.

"Impatient," I growled back as he teased me over my panties.

He laughed, dipping his head between my thighs, and sliding the fabric to the side. He slid one finger between my heat, then two, and I arched against his hand.

"So wet," he said. "I love how responsive you are for me."

A moan was my only response as he worked me with those fingers and that mouth until finally, I lifted my hips high off the bed, silently demanding he take my underwear off.

He obliged, as well as striping bare for me, and the sight of him, even after all this time, made my mouth water.

Cannon settled between my thighs, our bodies aligned as he teased my center with the tip of his hard cock. His eyes burned into mine before he kissed me, a claiming of lips and tongue until I was a writhing, needy mess beneath him.

"I love you," he said and punctuated those sweet words by sliding into the hilt.

I moaned, breathless as I nipped at his bottom lip. "I love you," I breathed against his lips. I rolled my hips, adjusting to the sheer size of him, my entire body trembling with coiled heat.

Cannon pulled all the way out only to slam home again, sending waves of electricity crackling along my skin. Again and again, the man claimed me, body and soul until both our breaths were ragged, and sweat slicked our bodies.

More, I always wanted more when it came to Cannon Price.

And he constantly delivered.

Driving into me faster, harder, he took us to that sweet edge until my body crashed and shattered, trembled, and sparked beneath him. Until he found his own release inside me, and I was wrung with pleasure and sheer, delicious exhaustion.

Cannon gently cleaned us up before tucking me into his side, our faces nose to nose as we lay in bed, simply breathing in each other's presence. My lids heavy, my muscles loose, I practically melted into his arms.

"Thank you," he whispered as I nearly drifted into sleep.

"For what?" I asked.

"For loving me for *me*. For giving me the world. For making me a better man." He kissed my forehead, holding me close.

"It's not hard," I said. "Loving you is as easy as breathing, Cannon Price."

He smiled down at me. "Only for you," he argued.

"Tell that to your daughter."

Water coated those dark eyes, the smile on his lips free and genuine and raw. I reached up and kissed him, soft, easy, loving. Silently showing him just how damn easy he was to love, and hoping one day he'd accept it.

Until then, I certainly didn't mind proving it to him every single day for the rest of our forever.

CONNECT WITH ME!

Text SAMANTHA to 77222 to be the first to know about new releases, giveaways, & more!

Sign up here for my newsletter for exclusive content and giveaways!

Follow me on Amazon here or BookBub here to stay up to date on all upcoming releases! You can also find me at my website here!

GRINDER SNEAK PEEK!

If you love the Reapers, you'll love Gage! Turn the page for a peek at the first chapter of Grinder and learn how the hottest player in the NHL became the Reapers' coach!

GRINDER

GAGE

Getting a three-year-old to sleep should be an Olympic event.

"Is that better?" I asked Lettie, smoothing back her thick brown hair from those summer blue eyes as she drained the small glass of water. She nodded, her smile full of tiny, gapped teeth as she settled back against her pillow.

If hockey was my world, where I made my living breathing the game, the ice, the needs of my team, then Lettie was my sun—the only thing in this universe that thawed my heart.

She was also the only thing I'd ever be caught waxing poetic about, but I couldn't help it, I was owned by a tiny three-year-old.

"Thank you, Daddy," she said, but the way she plucked at her covers and wiggled her tiny feet told me there was something else on my daughter's mind.

"What's up, sunshine?" I asked.

She looked up with excited eyes. "I like that Bailey is here."

"Me too," I said, unable to stop the smile that spread across my face at her happiness.

"I like Bailey."

A small chuckle rumbled through my chest. "Well, me too," I said, ruffling her hair.

"And now she's here all the time? Mornings and everything?"

"Yep," I answered, reaching for her bedside table. Bringing Bailey to live with us as Lettie's full-time nanny was a no-brainer. As often as I'd need her to travel with me for away games, and with the unpredictability of my schedule, it was really the only way for her to have a life...for either of us to. She'd been doing the job for six months already, but with the season starting up, it was the right time.

"So when I get up she'll be here?"

I paused before turning out the light and took a deep breath. "Yes, but Lettie, let's wait until the clock has a seven on it, okay? Not everyone likes to party at five a.m."

She bounced slightly, her eyes lighting with mischief. "I just can't wait to see her."

"You just saw her, remember? She tucked you in," I said, bringing her covers back up to her chin and urging her to lay down.

"I know, wasn't it amazing?"

I leaned forward, kissing her forehead. "Yes, it was amazing. And it will be amazing again tomorrow night."

"She's the best," she said, her eyes as wide as her smile. "Maybe she wants to see me before the sun is up!"

I pursed my lips, fighting the laughter that came so easily around my daughter, but only her. "Scarlett McPherson, you leave Bailey alone until morning. Do you understand me?"

Her lower lip extended in the cutest damn pout. "Yes, Daddy."

"Okay. I'm going to run for a little bit, so if you need me I'll be in the gym, okay?"

She nodded and flung herself forward, hugging me tight.

I held her close, savoring the smell of her strawberry shampoo, and the simple joy she emanated. Everything was simple in her world—her daddy loved her and Bailey adored her.

For the first time since she was born, there was a sense of stability in this house, and by God, I was going to keep it that way.

"I love you more than the stars," she said with a hard squeeze.

"I love you more than the moon."

"The stars are prettier," she argued.

"Well, the Earth needs the moon, so I love you more."

Her face scrunched momentarily before she shrugged. "Okay. But only because you need a win."

I hugged her again and put her to bed, silently cursing Rory for saying that yesterday when he was here, arguing to let Bailey move in.

I turned off Lettie's light and shut her door softly behind me.

My watch read 8:15 p.m. I could get in a couple miles and then meet the guys for drinks. Or I could get a couple miles in and maybe chill for the night.

Yeah, the second was probably the more responsible of the choices.

The refrigerator shut as I passed the kitchen, and I turned to see Bailey unloading a bag full of groceries. Her top was perfectly respectable, but the slight dip in her neckline gave me a mouth-watering glimpse of her cleavage.

Don't look at her like that, you asshat.

"Hey," I said, instead, as smooth as a fucking seventh-grader.

"Hey," she answered with a bright smile as I leaned across the island. "So I picked up some more of that Greek yogurt you like, and some stuff for cupcakes tomorrow. I figured I'd bake with Lettie to kind of celebrate our little..." she gestured around her, "arrangement?"

A corner of my mouth lifted in a smile. "Bailey, you're living with us. There's nothing illicit going on."

Pink stained her cheeks and damn if it didn't make her even more beautiful. Not that Bailey needed the help. She was petite but packed a powerhouse body that had found itself under mine in a few of my more drunken fantasies. And that face? Damn, she was perfection—huge hazel eyes, thick lashes, and olive skin with the most kissable mouth I'd ever laid eyes on.

But that was all I was ever going to lay on her.

"Well, yeah," she said, pulling her long, dark brown hair into some kind of knot on the top of her head. "It's just a transition."

"Hopefully a good one." It had to be. Lettie adored Bailey, and we'd been friends since we were kids, so it wasn't like I could afford to piss off Bailey...or our mothers.

"It will be," she promised. "Besides, I was practically living here anyway. Now I don't have to drive back to my place in the traffic."

"Agreed." Seattle traffic could be a nightmare.

She paused, leaning back against the opposite counter, inadvertently putting those lush curves on display.

Fuck my life. If I didn't get out of here I was going to sport wood harder than the fucking floor.

"I'm going to go get a couple miles in," I told her, pushing back from the island.

She reached over and into the fridge, then tossed a bottle of water my direction. "Have a good run. Oh, and I heard Rory and Warren talking today while we were moving in. If you want to grab a couple beers with the guys, I'm totally okay here with Lettie."

"Thanks. I'll think about it, but I'm pretty sure I'm just going to turn in." *And get the hell away from you before I lose my nanny to sexual harassment.*

"Okay, well the offer always stands. I don't mind." She crossed her arms under those perfect breasts. "It's not like I have a boyfriend or much of a social life outside Jeannine and Paige."

I opened the water bottle and took a few quick chugs. "Yeah, and your friends are always welcome here. Seriously. This is your house now, too."

Her smile was small but genuine. "That means a lot."

I nodded awkwardly. "I'll catch you later."

"Later."

I ran out of there so fast the room may as well have been on fire and headed down to the lowest level of the house until I got to my gym. The floor-to-ceiling windows opened up to a view of Lake Washington, where the sun was in that last moment of setting.

I powered on the treadmill, slipped my earbuds in, turned up the Eminem and hit it. My heartbeat was steady as my feet pounded at the machine beneath me, my breathing even. Maybe I wasn't that badly out of shape after all.

After taking most of the last season off when I tore the fuck out of my shoulder, I wasn't sure I'd ever get back to the Sharks, but the coach kept me on the roster, and I was still leading for my position if that baby of a rookie didn't beat me out for it.

Fuck that, it's mine.

Yeah, six months ago I couldn't have run at this speed without screaming in agony. Six months ago I'd still been in a sling, still broken as fuck from the way Helen left us.

And then Bailey had walked back into my life, fresh out of

her graduate degree at Cornell. It wasn't fate, I wasn't fucking stupid. It was our mothers pushing us together, not romantically—they weren't stupid either—but I needed help, and Bailey needed a job until she figured out what the hell she was going to do with her life...and her double degree in Art and Philosophy.

It had been perfect until I'd seen her again. The girl she'd been while we grew up, while I went to college at U-Dub and she went Ivy...well, she was long gone. It wasn't like she'd had one of those chick-flick makeovers, no, she'd always been pretty, doe-eyed, and just as beautiful inside than out. But now...

Fuck, now she was a knockout and seemed unaware of it somehow.

And worse, it was like my body had fucking Bailey-radar. She came into a room, I got hard—even when I reminded my body that she was a no-go.

It wasn't that I didn't like sex.

Fuck, I loved sex.

I adored women.

I fucked a lot of women.

Then they left.

The first woman I'd ever loved had left while I begged her to stay...

Now they left because I told them to...Let's be fair, it's not like they didn't know that was part of the package while I was dropping their panties.

I said I fucked women...I didn't fuck *over* women.

There was a difference.

Of course, they were all blonde lately. Anyone blonde or red-haired, but never brunettes. Never anyone I could accidentally mistake for Bailey.

I was never going *there,* and it didn't matter how badly my dick begged otherwise.

If she wasn't off limits because we'd grown up together—our mothers were best friends—she was definitely unfuckable because at the heart of everything, she belonged to Lettie.

And I didn't steal anything from my daughter.

Hell no, she deserved the world, and that was exactly what I was going to give her.

At mile number three, I ripped off my shirt, wiping the sweat off my forehead before tossing it and hitting two more miles. Nothing like a little run to get out some sexual frustration.

It would pass. I'd get used to having Bailey here. She'd become like a sister, and all these sexual urges would fade. It wasn't like she had them. Fuck, then we'd both be in trouble.

But it was just horny-as-hell me, lusting after the girl I'd never had, and I wasn't a little boy anymore. I was a full-grown man, a forward for the Seattle Sharks NHL team, and the best damned grinder in the league. More importantly, I was Lettie's dad, and since her mother had about as much maternal instinct as a fucking rock, I was all Scarlett had.

I had to be enough.

Better than enough.

I had to be everything.

Mile six sounded, and I lowered the speed of the treadmill, rolling my shoulders and stretching out my muscles before I headed up to the shower.

That was exactly what I needed. I congratulated myself for running out my baser needs instead of jumping my nanny as I walked up the stairs. Look at me, all civilized and shit.

I was so focused on my feet that I didn't realize Bailey was on the steps to the third floor until I nearly ran into her.

"Shit, I'm sorry," I said, catching her very smooth, very bare shoulders.

"Oh, my fault! Lettie asked for more water, so I took her up a glass," she said, but I barely heard her.

Fuck my life. Is that what she slept in? The light purple silk shorts barely covered her thighs and the spaghetti straps on the matching top looked flimsy enough to break. With my teeth.

One. Good. Bite.

"Gage?"

My eyes slid shut. Why did my name sound so damn good coming from her mouth?

I felt her fingers softly graze my sweat-dampened skin.

"Hey, are you okay? Is it your shoulder?"

I swallowed and opened my eyes, shaking my head with a forced smile. "Nawh, I'm okay."

Her eyes were wide, flecks of gold among the swirls of green as she examined my chest, tugging her on lower lip with her teeth. "Are you sure? I mean...I could ice it for you, or rub it down?"

Her forehead puckered at the same moment my dick hardened at the thought of her gorgeous, talented hands on me—hands that created masterpieces of abstract art. God, the last thing I needed was having those hands on my skin.

Apparently the run hadn't worked as well as I'd thought.

I needed to fuck her out of my head before I screwed up the one good thing I had going.

"You know, I think I will head out for a little bit. You okay with Lettie?" I asked, looking anywhere but the braless breasts that rose and fell in my face with her breaths.

"Yeah, of course. No rush. Try to relax, okay?"

I nodded, then nearly cursed as a thought came to me. "Shit, sometimes I bring women home..."

She laughed slightly. "I'm well aware of your nocturnal activities. This is your home, Gage. Feel free to..."—she flung her hands out— "do whatever it is you do. Seriously, no judgment."

I nodded again—like an idiot—and retreated up the stairs before I could further make an ass out of myself, or tell her why I really needed to get out.

A shower and a fresh change of clothes later, I was speeding away from my house in the Aston Martin toward my best friends and women who wanted the one thing I was capable of giving: my body.

No judgment, she'd said.

Hell if I wasn't judging myself for this one, though.

ABOUT THE AUTHOR

Samantha Whiskey is a wife, mom, lover of her dogs and romance novels. No stranger to hockey, hot alpha males, and a high dose of awkwardness, she tucks herself away to write books her PTA will never know about.

ACKNOWLEDGMENTS

Thank you to my incredible husband and my awesome kids without which I would live a super boring life!

Huge thanks must be paid to all the amazing authors who have always offered epic advice and constant support! Not to mention creating insanely hot reads to pass the time with!

Big shout out to A.H. for making this shine. And thank you to each and every single one of you AMAZING readers who love the these books as much as I do!

Printed in Great Britain
by Amazon